PRAISE
GO YOUR
SERIES

"4.5 Stars… This is a character driven novel that beautifully shows us the journey of two young men, bad boy Lennox McAvoy and the innocent Will Osborne. It was a pleasure to go along with these two fantastic characters through their first true love experience while they take their first baby steps towards romance."

—M/M Good Book Reviews on *Go Your Own Way*

"Against all YA novel formulae, it is Lennox's beauty that is Will Osborne's window into his better self. Will's intense physical attraction, his own desperate need for love (or, possibly, just hormones) makes him study Lennox so closely that he begins to see light through the darkness; begins to see the sad little boy behind the abrasive exterior. Only Will has the key to Lennox's prison cell."

—Prism Book Alliance on *Go Your Own Way*

"I was shocked to learn this was the author's debut novel. It was well written and held such realism that one felt as if they were transported back to the halls of their high school. The good, the bad, and the ugly of being a high school student are there for everyone to see."

—Joyfully Jay Book Reviews on *Go Your Own Way*

"Five Stars—I adored watching [Lennox] come into himself and learning that maybe he did deserve love and happiness. I also loved watching Will grow and become more confident, and stand up for what he believes in."

—Bayou Book Junkie on *With or Without You*

WHEN IT'S TIME

ZANE RILEY

interlude ✦ press • new york

ISBN 13: 978-1-945053-50-4 (trade)
ISBN 13: 978-1-945053-51-1 (ebook)
Published by Interlude Press
http://interludepress.com
BOOK DESIGN by Lex Huffman with CB Messer
COVER ILLUSTRATION by Colleen M. Good
10 9 8 7 6 5 4 3 2 1

interlude press • new york

..ıll one

LUSH GREEN TREES WHIPPED PAST the car windows. Lennox McAvoy pressed his forehead against the glass and watched the hills rolling taller and wider. Early June had burned into a blazing July, only dampened by the storms that thundered on their side of the mountains. This summer hadn't been very humid. The air wasn't heavy and dry enough to crack his throat; the sunlight darkened his brown skin but didn't burn until he peeled. The natural green that filled the world out here seemed to absorb the heat in a way cities and suburbs couldn't.

Everyone else in the jeep had their windows down. Oyster had raised himself high enough to stick his head through the sunroof, but Lennox kept his window shut. Beside him, his boyfriend, Will Osborne gestured wildly as he spoke about his new college friends.

"We met during an Ice Breakers game. They wanted to meet up once we're all on campus."

"That's great, honey," Karen said. She tucked a strand of brown hair into her baseball cap.

Eastern High Varsity Baseball. The logo from their old high school flashed in the sunlight. He and Will had graduated almost two months ago now.

"Did you get to sit down with your advisor?"

"Yeah, my schedule's set. Did you get yours done?" Will elbowed him.

Lennox glanced first at Will's freckled face and neck, then at Will's parents, Karen and Ben, in the front seat. Ben was driving, but their eyes met in the rearview mirror. He looked away. Overhead, Oyster barked into the jeep's slipstream.

"Should have made you drive with that new license. Get some practice in."

Lennox grunted.

"Come on, spill. How was it, kid?"

"Fine," Lennox said, but one word never cut it with Will or Karen. "A lot of sitting around listening."

"And your classes?"

"We pick them after we move in."

Karen frowned. "That seems really late."

Lennox slumped. "I don't make the rules. They give us placement tests first."

Will kissed his cheek for the seventh time since Lennox had hopped off the bus in New York City. "I'm sure it's fine, Karen. Music majors are different, that's all."

"I guess that's true. Did you play?"

Lennox shook his head. He hadn't done anything musical during the day and a half he'd been at Berklee College of Music in Boston. The visit hadn't been worth it. All day had been filled with lectures, smaller class discussions about life on campus, an exhausting campus tour, and then a brief social event to end the day. He'd hovered in the corner for five minutes before leaving.

"It was just a lot of talking," Lennox said.

Will caught his eye. It wasn't much, but it was enough for Lennox to realize this conversation wasn't finished, not between them.

Will directed the conversation back to his long weekend in New York City for his New York University visit. The rest of the ride was filled with talk of Will's life: his new friends, the towering city landscape, and the great atmosphere he'd found in only a few days. Lennox was glad. Will deserved to have a wonderful experience after all the hard work he'd done to get into NYU. He couldn't be the only radiance in Will's life, after all.

Lennox turned back to the green world zipping past outside. Oyster howled overhead—a clear, high note only a husky could manage. The sun slipped downward in the periwinkle sky.

Last summer, Lennox had made this same trek with his grandfather. So much uncertainty had awaited him then, and yet so much hope and wonder too. Cameron McAvoy had left his grandson to live at a dank, dangerous motel while he finished his final year of high school. No other school system in Virginia would accept him with his record and the ankle monitor he'd been sporting. Last July, Will and his family hadn't existed for Lennox. He'd been as alone as he'd ever been, forced to hit the ground running and hope he kept up.

Then Lennox's senior year had started. He'd met Will and earned himself a harsh slap across the face for his crude remarks. Lennox had certainly made no secret of his intentions, but Will had always been different. Thoughts of him had lingered and caught Lennox as delicately as fog brushing his hand. Will had been interested in him, too, but demanding of something more than physical intimacy. They'd grown together and grown up some as they discovered a deep bond. Lennox had let Will in, and, a year later, after Ben's heart attack and a vicious attack on Lennox that had driven him from his motel home, they were living together in Will's basement bedroom, best friends and boyfriends.

Now Lennox was a high school graduate about to embark on a college education he'd never dreamed of. Berklee had been a strange world this past weekend: academia and musical expertise. None of it was anything he'd ever challenged himself to strive for. College was for Will. If Lennox was lucky, he just might keep up once more.

Oyster led the way into the house. Lennox offered to take their bags downstairs. He shut the door on his way down to Will's basement bedroom. He lingered beside the bed, unzipping their bags and then zipping them back up.

Will's steps hurried downstairs. "Hey, we're ordering pizza. You want pineapple again?" Will moved to kiss his cheek and Lennox pulled away. "What?"

"Nothing. Just tired."

"No, you're giddy and have no filter when you're tired, like last week when we spent all day out back fucking."

Lennox made a face. "I thought you hated that word."

"At one point I did. Things change," Will said. He tugged on Lennox's sleeve until they were both sitting on Will's bed. "What happened?"

"Nothing."

Will only looked at him, patient and gentle and always way too eager to rescue him from the uncertainties of this world he'd walked into: Will's world. College was Will's world.

"I don't know. They gave out a fuckton of information, and I guess I thought we'd be playing music? It was like a big school assembly."

Will nodded. "So was mine. It'll get better once classes start and we've got real things to do—when you start meeting people."

Lennox didn't say anything as Will opened the duffel bag he'd used for his Boston trip. Will's bag. Almost everything he had these days was borrowed. Will pulled out the thick folder they'd given Lennox and flipped through the first few pages.

"Looks simple."

"Well, duh, shithead. I mean *these*."

Lennox dug through it to the pages on picking courses and how many credits different classes were worth. None of it made any sense. Will flipped through them once and shrugged.

"It's similar to NYU. See, they've listed the options."

Lennox stared at the wrinkled piece of paper and finally blurted out the question he'd been too embarrassed to ask at Berklee.

"Do I have to take *all* of these?"

Will laughed so hard he snorted. Lennox flicked the end of his nose and gave him a sour look.

"That's *not* a stupid question, okay? Because I can't do half of these—what do you call them?" Lennox yanked the list out of Will's hands. "Majors? Where did they even get that word?"

"No, you don't." Will chuckled. "These are all the areas of study they offer. You get to pick one you'd like to pursue."

"Just one?"

"Some people do two."

Lennox stared at the list. Somehow having to slash out a dozen options to focus on only one suddenly seemed impossible. What if he messed up? If he picked the wrong one and realized it later, would they kick him out?

"Stop." Will's fingers brushed his cheek. "Some people go through a *dozen* majors. It's okay to—"

"It's not. I'm going to school *for* music. I should already know what I'm studying."

"What you want to study is music, and I think you, of all people, know just how many directions that can go," Will said. He settled on his stomach on the bed beside Lennox and gave him an encouraging look. Lennox mirrored his position. "Read through them and cross out ones that aren't you, okay? I'll see what's on their website."

Lennox skimmed the list as Will dug his laptop out of his bag.

Music management? Production and Engineering?

He crossed those off. What did that have to do with playing?

Film Scoring? Was that a major for rating films? Why would you go to college for *that*?

Electronic Production and Design? What did that even mean?

He crossed those off, too.

Music Education and *Music Therapy* went next. He wasn't a teacher. He wasn't some happy-go-lucky, soothing voice therapist either.

Will rejoined him on the bed with his laptop. He glanced at Lennox's vicious pen marks and nodded.

"See? You're already down to six. It's not hard once you read them."

"*Professional Music*?" Lennox muttered as Will brought up the website. "Instead of what? Amateur Music?"

"Here. You can read more about them if you want. I'm going to let Oyster in before he bakes into the deck."

Will tramped upstairs, feet stomping and limbs knocking into things. Sometimes it amazed Lennox that such an uncoordinated walker could be an athlete and a wonderful lover. Lennox turned to Will's laptop and started clicking. Every major gave him lists, and then lists of lists, and pages and paragraphs explaining so many things he didn't understand.

What were credits? How did he get them? Did every department really need its own website? And every major kept mentioning entrance tests he needed to take, but knew nothing about.

By the time Will returned with Oyster, Lennox had narrowed his list to five after counting the word "professional" thirty-one times in two paragraphs for the Professional Music major. It sounded boring.

"Performing or some type of composition." Will rested his chin on Lennox's shoulder to read what was still legible. "That sounds more like you. Didn't they mention composing during your audition?"

"I think so."

"Try that then."

Lennox nodded. "I'll talk to that dude I'm supposed to meet with when I go back, I guess. What do you call them? Advisors? College has so many weird nouns."

Will tensed. "What day do you move in again?"

"Um, the twenty-third? It's the Sunday before your classes start."

"I'll take the bus to Boston with you," Will said. "Help you move in."

"Don't you have your honor-pledge ceremony that day?"

"I can skip it."

"I'll be fine," Lennox said, but a knot of uncertainty wedged itself between his ribs. "I'll ask Lucy to meet me."

"Are you sure?" Will's teeth tugged at his lower lip.

"Don't worry about me. I promise I won't self-destruct and cover the bus seats in bloody bits of Lennox."

Will continued to worry his lip, but his expression changed. He raised both eyebrows, lowered one, and then tried to wink. "Maybe you could, um, cover me in, um—"

"Semen serum, the Lennox variety?" Lennox snorted as Will flushed.

"I'm trying to be sexy!"

"You don't have to try, you goofball."

Lennox grinned as Will's face went from pink to splotchy red. "I'm just teasing. But, if you'd like, I could help you take some of the heat out of your face and relocate it."

Will dodged his kiss and toppled off the bed. He snarled as he reappeared. "*See*? That's what I'm going for and instead I just sound creepy."

Lennox gave him a blank look. "What?"

"You," Will said, flapping his arms at Lennox. "I tried to turn your words into something sexy and I sucked at it."

"I could find something else for you to suck at."

"*Lennox!*"

Lennox laughed as he was tackled to the bed. They wrestled playfully, Lennox's infectious laughter soon joined by Will's. It took Will's elbow knocking his laptop off the bed for them to stop.

"You're so uncoordinated," Lennox said as Will glanced at the floor where his laptop had fallen. "It okay?"

Will nodded as he dropped his weight onto Lennox's body. Despite the summer heat, they were comfortable like this for a while. Will's basement bedroom was like the Artic compared to upstairs.

"I'm going to miss having you around all the time." Will nuzzled his nose against Lennox's cheek.

"Is that why you keep waking me up by kicking me?"

"Then stop putting your boney chin in my liver."

"You don't even know where your liver *is*."

Will swiped his tongue over Lennox's chin until Lennox squirmed. "Ugh, no dog kisses."

As Will settled against his chest again, Lennox gazed at the ceiling. Every day it got harder to say anything about Boston and New York. Leaving Will seemed insane. Yet not going to Berklee was impossible. He had to see this through, no matter what the outcome. The haze of Berklee on the horizon was warmer and steadier every day. That sun was rising, and soon it would be his turn to rise with it.

"You'll be fine," Will said. "It's okay to be scared of being on your own."

Lennox sat up abruptly, knocking Will off him. "I *have* been on my own before. I made it this far without any help."

"No, I meant as an—"

"What? An adult? Done that too," Lennox said and he could feel his defenses going up like cement hardening in his veins. "I might have been eight, but I took care of myself and my baby sister while you were sitting around crying over Legos."

Will's hand squeezed his shoulder. "I know."

Lennox gritted his teeth. "Sorry. I'll be fine at Berklee. You don't need to worry about me; I've been on my own before and I figured it out. Worry about yourself."

Will shook his head. Lennox almost said something, but Will would figure it out, too. He had after all. It wasn't hard.

"New York's been my plan for a long time," Will said. "I'm set. I want to make sure you are, too."

"I am."

It was a lie—a small one, but a lie nonetheless. Lennox was far from set. He'd seen the lists: supplies to bring for his dorm room, the basic textbooks he needed, the laptop he'd have to figure out once he got to campus. That didn't cover his future roommates or how he got his dining money or if he needed a key or a card to enter his room.

Lennox didn't mention any of this as Will went to the bathroom for a shower. Somehow, despite how uncomfortable all of the lists were, it seemed insignificant. This was Will's dream. College was the future he'd designed for years, and, while Lennox was hopeful about studying music, he wanted these last days to be for Will. Will's life was evolving as he'd always planned. These next days and months were his, and Lennox would stand aside if it meant Will found his spotlight.

..ıl two

It took Will three days to find out everything about Lennox's time in Boston. A couple lectures about campus life, another about the dorms, and a fourth event that sounded like a welcome party—a party that Lennox had hurried out of instead of socializing. Will did his best to talk to Lennox about his fears, but it did no good.

Ben and Karen stayed out of it. They'd been giving them a surprising amount of space since graduation, and, while Will was suspicious of it, he was glad too. Ben and Karen spent their free evenings going to dinner or movies. They went for hikes in the mountains on cool days and even spent a long weekend at Lake Louisa, leaving Will and Lennox with the house to themselves.

The first week in August, Karen and Ben made plans to go away again. Will almost wished he was going with them for this one since it was to Kitty Hawk, North Carolina, but the prospect of having the house and Lennox all to himself was too good to pass up. He woke early Friday morning to help Karen pack the jeep.

"Do you really need all of these shoes?" Will heaved the last duffel bag into the jeep with a grunt.

"That's your dad's."

"Dad doesn't own enough shoes to fill a duffel bag."

Karen only smiled as she helped him shut the back door.

"Wait, what *is* in the bag?"

"Nothing that would interest you."

His immediate thought went to the sex toys website Lennox had browsed last night. "What? Like *toys*?" Will made a face and went inside. Karen chuckled as she followed him into the hall.

"It isn't *that*. God, you have nothing but sex on your mind these days. If anyone in this house has an exotic box of sex toys, it's *you*."

"I do not!"

"Then what's in that box under your bed that I always hit when I vacuum?"

Will flushed. That box wasn't full of sex toys, but he wasn't going to tell Karen that.

"Will's got a secret box of sex toys? How come I haven't seen them?" Lennox came down the hall. Half his face was covered in shaving cream, but he was grinning.

"Lennox, get back in here!"

"I don't need you teaching me how to shave," Lennox said as Ben appeared, razor in hand. "Teach him. He's your kid."

"Yeah, and Will's face is as smooth as a baby's bottom." Ben grabbed Lennox's upper arm to drag him back to the bathroom.

"So is his butt."

"Shut it, or all the cuts on your face are going to be from me." Ben pulled Lennox back into the bedroom and shut the door.

Karen shook her head. "It's a wonder Ben hasn't stitched his mouth shut."

Will chuckled and helped Karen put together a cooler of drinks and sandwiches for the road. Then they packed some of Oyster's treats, food, and his dog bed.

"Are you sure you want to take Oyster? We're fine with him. He *is* my dog."

"He also loves the beach. Who knows when he'll get the chance to go again?"

Will glanced at Oyster snoozing under the kitchen table. He was closing in on eleven, and, while he'd never acted his age, Will doubted the husky would leap around the backyard forever.

Ten minutes later, Ben, Karen, and Oyster backed out of the driveway and sped off. Lennox wrapped his arms around Will's waist and nuzzled his neck.

"I hear you've got a box of sex toys hidden under your bed. Been shopping for all the ones I drool over?"

"I can barely buy condoms and lube without blushing hard enough to burst a blood vessel. Do you really think I have sex toys?"

"A guy can dream," Lennox said as he deflated. "So what *is* in this mystery box? It's not, like, full of Barbie-doll heads or something a Games of Thorns person would do, is it?"

"Thrones. *Game of Thrones*."

"Right. Well, the North remembers, but the *South* is horny," Lennox said with a pointed thrust of his hips against Will's ass. "So—stop laughing!"

"You are *such* a nerd. Like, the most ridiculous nerd I have ever met."

Will dodged Lennox's next kiss and raced into the house; Lennox chased him.

"If I'd known that the boy I first met, who never stopped talking about his dick, was the biggest dork in the world—" Will ducked one arm, but got snagged by the other. They toppled onto the couch; Will still choked on his own laughter as Lennox pinned Will's hands over his head and growled at him.

"I *still* talk about my dick—and yours—all the time."

"Yeah, but in the dorkiest way known to humans."

"Do not."

"You just used *Game of Thrones* to entice me into having sex with you. Nerd."

Will raised his head to nip Lennox on the chin and then gasped when Lennox began to tickle him. They spent half the morning having a tickle fight, from one end of the house to the other, and ending up in the pool, swimming in their underwear since they'd shoved each other in while they were still in their pajamas.

"I kind of miss Oyster right now," Lennox said as he drifted under the diving board out of reach. "He'd rescue me from your treacherous embrace—*ah!*"

Will dunked Lennox's head, and Lennox's hand tugged him down. He choked and went under, too. Coughing, they broke the surface. He shoved Lennox and received a harder shove.

"Stop dunking me! I want to drown in sex-sweat, not chlorine."

"We aren't having sex in the pool," Will said even as Lennox pressed him back against the pool wall under the diving board. He sighed at the relief the small wedge of shade provided. "Okay, maybe if it means we stay in this spot."

Lennox sucked at his neck and gagged. "Ugh, now *you* taste like pool water."

"I do not! You do!"

Their argument led them up the pool steps and onto the backyard grass. Lennox wrapped his towel around himself like a cocoon. Will followed him to the shade under a weeping willow and took a seat beside him.

"I wonder if they have pools in New York," Will said, as he wiped water off his face.

"Probably only for the elite. Bet they're all indoors too." Lennox yawned. "Doesn't seem like much of an outdoor place besides that big park. No mountains or stars or anything you've got here."

Will frowned, but nodded. New York City would definitely be a big change, but he was ready. "I'll find new things to do. Those kids I met were really nice. Tyra and Jake."

"You're going to do great."

"So are you. You'll meet people. In classes and clubs."

Lennox nodded, as he did so much these days. He was going to Berklee, to Boston and an entire new life and world, but Will couldn't help but worry. In so many ways Lennox wasn't ready. He shied away from interacting with people, tried to hide in his music, and still threw up a wall of crude remarks and cuss words. Would anyone else be willing to push through Lennox's rough exterior to know the wonderful boy beneath? Would Lennox ever let them?

"Come on, let's go shower so we don't taste like pool. What do you think about camping out here tonight?"

THEY BROUGHT THE OLD AIR mattress out that evening and took turns trying to blow it up on the back deck. Crickets chirped as the musky twilight settled around them. Summer evenings were an eloquent peace for Will, a long-held solace that reminded him of himself as he was: the summer heat as warm as his breath, the flickering of lightning bugs spotting the dark air, hot grass between his toes after a day of playing baseball or swimming with his friends. This year, this final summer, was different—one last season at home in Leon as a kid. In a few weeks, he'd leave this behind forever.

As the first stars flickered beyond the treetops, Lennox decided to try the old bicycle tire pump.

"Maybe we should just drag your mattress up." Lennox huffed and puffed through a few more pushes on the tire pump before giving up.

Will rolled his eyes. "Give it here."

"Get busy, muscle man. I'm too weak for all this physical labor."

Will stuck his tongue out at Lennox, but went to work. After ten minutes, the air mattress was pumped up, and they were fighting for sides.

"You *always* get the left side."

"Yeah, cause it's my bed, and I get to pick first."

"This isn't your bed. It's an air mattress that's been collecting spiders in the garage."

Will finally caved and gave Lennox the left side. They shifted their pillows and blankets around until they were comfortable. Together, they looked up at the stars, which were growing more intense as the minutes passed.

"It's so nice out here at night," Lennox said.

"This sky's my favorite. Dad's always said it's why he stayed."

"You won't see this in New York, that's for sure." Lennox whistled a tune and pointed skyward. "That's Neptune, I think."

"You can't see Neptune without a telescope. Same with Uranus."

"Only because Uranus is full of my d—"

"Do *not* make a Uranus joke."

Lennox pouted but accepted Will's soft kiss. Will rolled toward him, one finger twisting around a curl of hair. Before his Berklee audition, Lennox had shaved his long, unruly curls and left short, dark bristles. His hair was still short five months later, but it had begun to turn into springy curls again.

"I've missed your curls."

Lennox hummed and snuggled into him. "I might shave them off again. Or at least the sides and neck. It's too hot. Way too much maintenance."

"I'm going to miss you, too. I can't believe we only have a few more weeks."

"You won't. You're going to be so busy in New York with all your classes and new people." Lennox shrugged and turned back to the stars. "You won't have time to miss me."

"I will. Even if I'm having fun and meeting new people. You won't have a lot of time either once you're in Boston."

"I guess."

Will watched Lennox's outline in the dark. The nightlight they'd left on in the kitchen window cast a shadow on his face. He didn't look scared, but Lennox rarely looked how he felt.

"Are you nervous?"

Lennox shook his head.

"College is a lot of changes at once."

"You sound like a guidance counselor."

"I just want to make sure you're okay, that's all."

"I am. I'm with you."

And when you're not? Will couldn't bring himself to say it out loud. Every time he tried to bring the subject up, Lennox turned him in another direction. Yet, in every false reassurance, Will saw a nugget of truth. Lennox was terrified, and he refused to say anything about it.

"Lennox, please—"

"I'm fine, Will. I'll figure it out. Just worry about yourself, okay? You're going to one of the biggest cities in the world and you get lost just driving to Fredericksburg."

"And I'll figure that out, too. I'm ready. I've been planning this since I was a kid. It's you I'm worried about. I want you to talk to me when you're anxious or worried. Or a friend. It's important to have friends to talk to about things."

Lennox glanced at him, then turned onto his side away from Will. "I've got Otto. And Lucy."

"I know, but Otto's going into the military. Lucy'll be nearby, but she won't be around much. I just want you to go to Berklee and make friends, to not hide from people."

Will rolled over and curled up behind Lennox with one arm around his chest. "It's okay to let people in. Every friend you make doesn't have to be some deep emotional connection. They don't have to know the stuff you don't like to talk about."

Lennox tapped his fingers on Will's hand where it rested against him. Eighth notes, then a brush of sixteenths. He slowed to quarter notes, as Will tightened his hold and kissed his neck.

"I don't know how to do that."

Will was quiet. Lennox had made friends this past year—not easily, but he'd done it. Yet as Lennox twisted a little in his arms, Will thought of all he now knew about Lennox's life.

Lennox had opened up a lot with him. He'd told Will about his mother's death when he was eight, about his father's drunken stupor afterward. He spoke in detail about raising his infant sister almost entirely on his own, except for a few short months when their paternal grandparents had intervened. His entire childhood had been as unlike Will's own as possible. No parental support, a younger sister relying on him, and intense homophobia and bullying at school. It was no surprise Lennox had ended up hospitalized after the bullying turned to brutality, or that he'd retaliated and been locked up in a juvenile detention center because he'd had nobody to defend him. Never once had he mentioned friends, not as a boy or a teenager.

"You can learn," Will said.

"You mean learn to not run off at the mouth."

"Yeah, that's part of it." Will smiled. "Don't jump at people so much when you talk to them. Don't be so defensive after a few words. They're not asking about your life story; most of the time it's just small talk, like the weather or what you're learning in class."

"It's a reflex for me, honestly."

"Why?"

As Lennox grew quiet, Will looked at the stars. Soon he'd never see this sight. Certainly not in New York City. They wouldn't be visible when he visited Lennox in Boston either. The quiet would be filled with car horns and sirens and the clunking of garbage trucks in the middle of the night. A shuddering subway track would be his life—one that might derail or get him lost.

"For my sister."

"What?"

"I started doing that to turn people away. For her," Lennox said. His brow was furrowed as he squinted at the sky. "I didn't want people getting close to us and asking questions. I thought they'd separate us if they realized Dad was a shitty parent and I was all she had. I guess I don't have to worry about that anymore."

"She's doing okay with your grandparents. When your grandfather brought her to our graduation, she was so happy."

"Yeah, she is. I guess I did it for me too. I didn't know how to talk about anything that had happened. I still don't."

"And you don't have to. Not with everyone. It can just be me or Karen or Lucy for now. That's okay, too. You can let people get closer at your own pace. Just let them know that instead of being mean and pushing them away, okay?"

Lennox only nodded and blew out a deep breath, but Will relaxed. He was going to figure it out and be fine. After all, Lennox had done that his whole life. He'd been down paths like this before, only in a darker direction. Lennox was heading upward now. As long as Will was around, he could make sure Lennox kept going.

..ıll three

THE BOYS SPENT THE FIRST weekend without parental supervision camping out under the stars; cooking green onions, pineapple, and chicken on the grill; and having sex in the large blanket fort they built in the living room. Will's friends came over, too. Aaron, Will, and the rest of the baseball team tore up the backyard knocking baseballs around. Roxanne and Natasha stopped by to sunbathe and play volleyball in the pool.

Lennox tried his best to participate. Will's advice from that first night without Karen and Ben hung around his ears. Be nicer. Don't get defensive. Try to have conversations that don't end with offending half the country. For a few days, it worked. He managed to swallow the sexual innuendos and the cruel remarks. His small talk, however, was a bunch of nodding and being awkward.

Aaron tried to talk baseball and college with him and smiled too much. Natasha only offered him bubblegum and goofy stares. Roxanne was probably his favorite of Will's friends, if for no other reason than she was happiest having conversations with herself.

By week's end, Lennox was ready to drop back into snarls and nastiness, but Will's encouraging smile kept him from doing just that.

"See? It's not so bad."

They were waving Aaron and the baseball team off as the sun set over the tree tops. It had been another long afternoon for Lennox, but he had managed a nice conversation with one guy, Todd. But that had mostly been sex jokes, so Lennox wasn't sure if it counted.

"I suck at this," Lennox said, as they returned to their blanket fort in the living room. "None of them have anything in common with me. Like, I'm glad you've got friends and stuff, Will, but..."

They aren't my friends. How much would he hurt Will by saying that?

"They're my friends, not yours. I get it."

"Really?"

Will chuckled. "Look, I never expected you to become besties with my friends. I just want you to try to get along with them. It's good practice for next week."

Lennox swallowed. Seven more days. They would be on a train bound for New York City to drop Will off, and then... then he'd be on his own for a bus from New York to Boston and whatever tumultuous world awaited him there. "I mean, they're nice. They're just too nice? I don't know."

"You don't know baseball or nineteen flavors of bubblegum or Roxanne's entire course catalog. They're not your kind of people. It's okay."

Will's laugh was genuine and put Lennox at ease.

"I guess it's the same for you and Otto, huh?"

Will nodded. "He's better than he used to be, but I doubt we'll ever be good friends. How's he doing anyway?"

Lennox tugged out the phone Karen had bought him a few weeks ago. He still wasn't sure how to use all its features, but he had figured out how to text Otto, who'd left at the end of June. "He's okay. I think he's probably murdered his brother, but he's having fun visiting his grandparents."

"Montana, right?"

"Minnesota," Lennox said as he scrolled through the stream of messages they'd exchanged over the last few weeks. Otto's mother, Malia, had insisted both her sons go visit her parents for the summer. Only then would she let Otto join the army. "They live on a reservation. He's having fun, even if he keeps saying he's not. Look, here's some pictures."

Lennox passed Will his phone and watched his magnificent smile bloom. He was going to miss seeing that sight every day.

"Wow, it's beautiful there. Looks like they're having fun. Is that a dreamcatcher?"

"Yeah, his grandmother was teaching them how to make them. Gabe loves it, but Otto's not as big on his heritage."

Will passed the phone back, and Lennox pocketed it. "So what do you want to watch tonight? I'm starving. Let's order pizza again."

"Can we watch cartoons?" Lennox kissed Will's neck and nuzzled his sun-warmed, freckled skin. "You smell like sunblock again."

"For someone who wants to watch cartoons," Will said as Lennox kissed up his neck, "you're doing an awful lot of neck sucking."

"Well, I want to fuck while cartoons play in the background. I thought that was obvious."

"Mmm, pizza first."

Lennox groaned and fell back into their pile of pillows as Will went to call for delivery. He flipped on the television and found a channel playing a cartoon he didn't recognize. Will returned, frowning.

"So it'll be at least an hour and a half."

"Well, it is Saturday. Sex while we wait?"

Will's reluctance lasted only as long as it took Lennox to get their shirts off. They spread out as they had all week, on their heaps of pillows, cushions, and blankets. It was clumsy fumbling on the pillows, but the goofiness brought a smile to Lennox's face as he pressed Will's body down with the weight of his thrusts.

"There?"

"No. Angle yourself more."

They fumbled a little more, and Lennox's hand slipped on the pillows. Will laughed as Lennox dropped on top him.

"Not that I don't love being inside you," Lennox said, as he raised himself again, "but I think I prefer bottoming. Tell me when I find your prostate, okay?"

Will only giggled at his next thrust, which meant he'd found it. For whatever reason, it didn't make his entire body shudder the way Lennox's did. Lennox glowered at him and thrust harder. Will snorted.

"What?"

"Sorry. It sort of tickles?" Will rubbed his hands over Lennox's taut biceps and smiled at him. "Like I can feel you against it, but maybe we should try something else. I mean, I know this works for you, but it's not for me."

"Doesn't take much for me," Lennox huffed and dropped to his elbows. Only yesterday, Will had coaxed two orgasms out of him. He nipped Will on the nose. "Switch?"

"Please."

As Lennox dug the lube bottle out of their pillow pile, the doorbell rang. Will flushed and grabbed his shorts. Even as he tried to pull them on, it was clear he wouldn't be able to hide his erection.

"Use your waistband," Lennox said as he stood and helped Will dress. "Here, put your shirt on to cover your dick poking over the top."

Someone knocked on the front door. "Pizza delivery!"

"Coming!"

"I wish you would." Lennox grinned.

Will smacked his arm and left to accept their delivery. They each ate their own pizza in comfortable silence as cartoons played on the television. Lennox plucked several pieces of pineapple off his pizza and popped them into his mouth.

"What's it feel like?" Will accepted a piece of pineapple, too. "Prostate orgasms. They look pretty wonderful from my view."

Lennox shrugged. He wasn't embarrassed to share, but, after months of having them frequently and not managing to coax one out of Will's body, it seemed too much like bragging to talk about in detail.

"I don't know. It's kind of like the orgasm stops inside you and builds up instead of going to your dick."

Will crinkled his nose. "Sounds weird."

"It's nice. We'll find a way to give you one. One of those prostate wands maybe."

They finished eating and then put the leftover slices in the refrigerator. Lennox hugged him from behind and ran his hands under Will's shirt until he was rubbing his nipples.

"So, back to having sex?"

"Well, you are still—*oh*, keep doing that."

"Yeah? Maybe if I fuck you *and* suck on your nipples you'll have a prostate orgasm."

"Only one way to find out."

* * *

LENNOX POUTED FOR THE REST of the weekend when his plan didn't work. No matter what route he took, Will's body refused to have a prostate orgasm. He glowered at Ben and Karen when they returned Sunday afternoon, and then frowned at Oyster's unbridled enthusiasm for the kiddy pool Will filled with ice that evening. As Will showered Oyster in ice, Lennox sat on the back steps and watched.

"Get the stick, Oyster!"

Will raced around the yard with Oyster, waving a long stick at his side.

"That dog missed the hell out of you two," Ben said from behind him. "I don't know how he's going to survive come next week."

"Buy him a treadmill and an igloo."

Lennox heard the sliding glass door shut, and then Ben sat beside him, chortling.

"It's going to be too quiet around here," Ben said. He sighed as Will and Oyster jogged around near the tree line. "You need another shave."

Lennox groaned. "I'm growing a beard for the rest of my life. Shaving is ridiculous."

"Come on, one more go, and then you can go away to college and go for the longest-beard world record."

Ben dragged Lennox inside to the master bathroom. He made Lennox sit on the side of the tub and pulled out a canister of shaving cream and a razor from the medicine cabinet.

"You're doing it this time. What's the first rule?"

"Be born with a face that doesn't grow hair?"

Ben turned the hot water on. "First rule."

"Warm my face with hot water, yeah, yeah, I know."

Lennox followed the steps Ben had been outlining for the last three weeks. Hell, it was five if he counted the two weeks when he'd refused to let Ben show him anything. It was weird to have Will's dad teaching him to shave. Nobody had taught him anything about growing up. As he dragged the razor over his left cheek, Lennox glanced at Ben behind him in the mirror.

"Nice and smooth," Ben said as Lennox rinsed off the razor. "You shouldn't feel a lot of snagging."

Lennox made an indistinct noise in his throat and focused on his reflection. Would his own father have done this? Maybe his sister would have been sitting on the tub's edge like Ben, giggling and begging for their father to let her try too. His mother might have stood in the doorway with a smart joke on her lips while she placed bets on who would cut his face first.

He swallowed and glanced at the curls of hair and plump clumps of shaving cream spinning in the water.

"You cut yourself again?"

"No." Lennox shook his head and then flinched when Ben's hand gripped his shoulder.

"What? You going to run out on me again? You're doing really good with this. Took me years to figure it out, even with my dad teaching me since I was a kid. Used to shave with him in front of his mirror. He had one of those fancy razors like the barbers use."

"Like in *Sweeney Todd*?"

"In what?"

"Movie Will made me watch." Lennox picked up the razor and ran it over his jawline. "Did Will shave with you as a kid?"

"Nah, he just wanted to play with the shaving cream," Ben said. Chuckling, he shut the toilet lid and took a seat. "He used to hop in the bath with his mom and 'help' shave her legs. He thought it was hilarious."

"He's a weirdo for sure."

"Well, he likes you."

"Hey!" Lennox splashed water at Ben, who surprised Lennox with another laugh.

"Guess I'm no longer needed. Time to round up that crazy dog and his kid."

Lennox followed him with his eyes in the mirror. "Ben?"

"Hmm?"

"Thanks. For... you know. This. All of it."

Ben nodded. "Glad to help. Guess I'll be teaching you about tying ties next, huh?"

"When am I *ever* going to use that?"

"You're a college musician now, Lennox. You really think you won't be wearing ties for concerts and performances?"

"Ugh."

* * *

THE WEDNESDAY BEFORE WILL AND Lennox left for college, Karen took them to Fredericksburg to shop. Will bounced from one store to the next, buying notebooks and pens, towels and bedding. Lennox refused to buy anything. He didn't stop either of them from tossing little things on the register at checkout, but he grimaced and snarled when they tried to get him to pick out bedding and pillows.

"What about this one?" Will held up another bedding package, this one covered in vibrant turquoise splotches.

"I don't need it."

"Are you just going to sleep on a bare mattress?"

Karen put the item back, calm as could be, but Will was starting to lose his temper.

"You need blankets and stuff, Lennox. What we've got at home doesn't fit on the college beds."

"I'll figure it out once I get there." Lennox gave a pointed nod toward the shopping cart bloated with everything Will was getting for himself. "We're going to have a hard enough time lugging all of your stuff around New York. Let's not add more for me, okay?"

Lennox agreed to let them buy him pens and notebooks, but he left the rest of his lengthy list unchecked.

Back at Will's house, they heaved all of Will's purchases inside and downstairs to his bedroom. Will was happy to throw them on his bed and worry later, but Lennox began unpacking them.

"You don't have to do that."

"I want to help. I've seen how you packed your suitcase," Lennox said, tugging price tags from towels and a cute rug shaped like a baseball.

"You *could* be packing your own stuff." Will sat at the head of his bed and watched Lennox's fingers work. They both glanced to the corner, at Lennox's backpack, recently reupholstered with stripes of white and purple duct tape. Just a few clothing articles, comics, and a lot of sheet music from their band teacher, Mr. Robinette. "I got too much."

"You got the whole list."

"Yeah, but…"

Will's eyes drifted back to Lennox's single bag.

"Look, I'll get my stuff once I'm there. Stop worrying. I've still got money saved from what my grandfather was giving me. It should cover the basics."

They set Will's bags in the corner and returned to the bed. Will's hand gripped his hard as they sat together, and for all his smart-mouthed wit Lennox couldn't think of anything to say. In three days, they would be on a train to New York City, and then Lennox would be on his own once again. He hoped he'd fare better this time around.

"I'll come visit for a weekend once we're settled," Will said. He kept ahold of Lennox's hand as he lay back on the bed. "We can rotate trips every few weeks. Skype every day once we figure out our schedules."

"I'll let you know what my class schedule looks like."

Will's hand tugged on his, and Lennox fell backward on the bed with him. His legs swayed where they dangled off the edge. The heel of his sneaker knocked into something under the bed. Will didn't seem to notice when he kissed Lennox, but, after several more thumps, he pulled away and glared at Lennox.

"It is *not* a sex-toy box."

"Says *you*." Lennox swung his foot and tapped the box under the bed. "A lot of things can be sex toys if you have enough imagination."

"Well, nothing in that box is, even with your perverted imagination."

Lennox pecked him on the nose tip and rolled onto his stomach; his hands pulled up the hems of the blankets. Panic in his eyes, Will dove after him and grabbed his wrists.

"What? Have you been collecting human bones or something that I should be worried about?"

"No, it's private."

"Will, I've had my tongue in your ass."

Will flushed.

Lennox kissed his cheek and then his lips. "Well?"

"It's just old dreams. Treasures."

"From when you were a kid?"

Will nodded and let go of Lennox's hands. "You promise you won't laugh?"

Lennox watched the hesitation in the way his teeth tugged at his lower lip. How could he laugh at Will for his dreams—even the silliest ones his younger self had invented? "Never. Now come on, what's in this dreams box?"

Will crawled onto the floor and pulled a large cardboard box from under the bed. The edges were beginning to cave in; the top flaps crisscrossed but were dusty. He cradled it in his lap before he opened it. The outside was covered in stickers. Lennox recognized a few—Power Rangers, Lisa Frank, and Digimon—as he slid off the bed to join Will on the floor.

"So, these were my Power Rangers. Do you know what—"

"Yeah, Power Rangers were around before my childhood went to shit. The yellow one was my favorite."

Lennox grinned as Will handed him the yellow action figure. It was a little worn, but the switch on the back still made its arm swing forward. They played with the karate chop actions, slapping the arms together until Will was overcome with giggles.

"So why'd you keep these? You could buy this just about anywhere."

Will laid the figurines on the floor between them. At first, he didn't move or speak, but when he finally did his voice was strained. "These were my last gifts from my mom. I don't remember it, but I've watched the old video from that Christmas a dozen times."

Lennox nodded. The guitar he'd kept with him despite all the moving around he'd done had been a gift as well. Maybe not the final gift from his mother, but certainly the one he cherished most. Last year, when the men harassing him at the motel had broken in, that guitar had disappeared. Even now he wasn't sure what had happened to it. Most likely it had been destroyed.

"So what else do you have in here? Ninja Turtles?"

Will shook his head; his fingers traced the face of the Red Ranger. "No, um, let's see… Oh! I'd forgotten about this!"

From the depths of the box, Will pulled a flattened dinosaur mask.

"You wanted to be a T-rex?"

"Duh, didn't you?" Will shook the mask out and coughed at the cloud of dust it released. "Should probably wash that before I try it on, anyway…"

Lennox slid closer and peered into the box too. Two yo-yos were on the bottom, along with a tiny dog collar, a number of small jerseys, half a dozen trophies, and a pile of medals. Lennox picked up the nearest medal and wiped the dust from both sides.

"Little League World Series?"

Will stopped digging. His body went stiff. Lennox flipped the heavy bronze medal over. It didn't seem special to him, just an old baseball medal Will had won in middle school.

"I was *really* into baseball when I was a kid."

"You still are."

"Not like I was." Will pulled out another medal, silver and shaped like a baseball diamond. His face was solemn as he pulled a jersey from the box too. "I used to be as bad as Aaron. Baseball was *everything* when I was a kid."

Will held up the small orange jersey for Lennox to see. Southeast Region.

"Sounds like a big deal," Lennox said as he ran his fingers over the fancy golden letters. "Did you guys win?"

"No. I did it for two years. There's an age limit since it's Little League. My first year we didn't make it into the tournament, but the second year we got the regional title and third overall. Went up to Pennsylvania to play. It was televised and everything."

"That's really cool." Lennox examined a few of the trophies: all baseball, years and years of Little League, travel teams, and photographs from school and local teams and a state tournament. An entire life existed in this box. "Why'd you stop?"

"I didn't," Will said, puzzled.

"I don't mean playing; I mean all of this. You love baseball," Lennox said. "We drove all the way to Pittsburgh to see your team in June. Otto's said you're really good, and those scouts were interested in, like, recruiting you. Why'd you never go for it like Aaron is?"

Will squinted at him as if nobody had ever asked him such a question. "I don't know. I mean, it was practical to find something else. Eventually you have to grow up. Get a real job."

"Says the boy who pushed me to go to college for music."

"You're incredible. Besides, you can't study baseball in college."

Lennox rolled his eyes. "Duh, baseball's got professional leagues. You could probably play. Make a fuckton of money too."

"Baseball isn't about the money." Will's voice dropped, but Lennox caught each word.

"Neither is music, not to me at least."

Will shook his head and folded the jersey. "It's an old dream. I put it away a long time ago. I could never make a career of it."

"Why?"

"Like I said, it's not practical."

"But *why*?"

"Forget it." Will went back to sifting through what remained in the box. Something more was involved in that deflection, but Lennox left it. He wouldn't force Will to explain right now. Will never had forced him.

"What's up with the yo-yos?"

Will pulled the tangled pair of yo-yos from the box. "Did I ever mention I wanted to be a dual-wielding yo-yoer?"

They spent the rest of the evening on the floor, while Will attempted to untangle his yo-yos and laughed at the notes and scraps of paper that littered the bottom of the box. Lennox watched him: the freckled starscape of his skin shifting under the lamplight, the quirky little upturns of his lips, and the flashes of amusement in his eyes. Every glance seemed to hold some secret nostalgia that Will was sharing with him—some different, more hopeful, version of himself. It seemed impossible to imagine Will more hopeful than he was now. Yet, as they pieced the box's insides back together, Lennox noticed slips: the ache as the Power Rangers were laid inside, the fondness for the yo-yos, and the regret that flickered in his eyes as each trophy, medal, and jersey was nestled carefully on top.

Will fell asleep fast, but Lennox lay awake. Less than three days and this would be over. The short-lived normalcy he'd allowed himself to sink into would fade into something larger than himself once again. He shifted as Will curled into his side and pressed his nose to the strawberry scent of Will's hair.

Did he know enough of Will to keep this? Did either of them know each other well enough to kindle this brief year of happiness into what Will kept dreaming for them?

..ıll four

WILL WOKE THE FRIDAY BEFORE college with what felt like a watermelon in his stomach. Tomorrow he would move into his dorm in New York City. Tomorrow he'd say goodbye to his parents and Oyster and spend one last childhood day with his boyfriend. He rolled out of bed and went to the shower. Lennox was already gone, but that wasn't unusual these days. Lennox spent half his mornings in the pool.

When Will finished his shower, Lennox was in his room wearing an old pair of Will's swim trunks and a towel around his shoulders.

"Morning."

"It's noon," Lennox said. He tugged Will in for a warm kiss that smelled of chlorine and sunblock. "Happy birthday, butthead."

"Birthday?"

"Your birthday's the nineteenth, right? Don't tell me I got it wrong, because your dad's making a cake upstairs, and I can't imagine he's wrong, too."

"Oh, yeah, it's today. I forgot."

Lennox frowned and kissed him again. "I got you something."

Will pulled on his boxers and shorts. "Is it a dildo?"

"No. Maybe Christmas on that. Here."

Lennox handed him a flimsy, thin package wrapped in newspaper. Will bit his tongue to keep from remarking on the wrapping paper. They had an entire box of wrapping paper and gift bags in the garage, but Lennox never took their offers for help. Will ripped the paper off and smiled at the comic books.

"Spider-Man? I thought all of your comics were destroyed at the motel."

"Most of them were," Lennox said. "This was one of my favorites, though. Miles Morales as Spider-Man. I never know what to get anyone, so it's kind of stupid, I guess. Just something I really like that I thought you might like too."

"No, it's great. I'll read it." Will smiled and kissed Lennox on the cheek. "Reminds me of Aaron actually. He got sick of people giving him baseballs, so he started telling everyone to give him a copy of their favorite book."

Lennox went back upstairs, but Will lingered, taking longer than necessary to get dressed. How could he have forgotten his own birthday? Sure, college began tomorrow, and he'd been overwhelmed with worry for Lennox and about being able to carry everything around New York City until they got to his dorm, but to forget his own birthday…

"Will, do you want these presents or not?"

"Coming, Dad!"

WILL'S LAST DAY WAS DIFFERENT than he'd imagined. He'd planned to spend the day with his dad and Karen and the evening and midnight hours wrapped up with Lennox downstairs. Instead, his friends who were still in town came over, both to say goodbye and to wish him a happy birthday. Aaron had already gone to the University of Virginia for baseball camp. Natasha came and went quickly. She left that afternoon for her new school in Virginia Beach. Roxanne, however, stayed longer than he wanted.

"Did you get the shower caddy that was on the list? Because I thought it was really dumb. I've got a bathroom attached to my room."

"Mine's somewhere down the hall."

"Lennox, did you—"

"Didn't buy a damn thing, so leave me out of this."

She went on for several hours, but she'd also given him three movies as a birthday present, so Will let her take her anxieties out on them. It was easier than voicing his own. After Roxanne left, he spent the evening with his dad and Karen while Lennox took a final swim in the pool. Ben and Karen's presents were the most expensive, and it gave Will pause as he held up the Andrew McCutchen baseball jersey and the new catcher's mask.

"This is great, really, but I don't think I'll ever use the mask, Dad."

"I thought you were going to play in college." Karen said.

"Maybe. Isn't it time to focus on school and a career?"

Ben hummed, but he didn't nod or shake his head. "Well, it's yours either way. Who's ready for some ice cream and cake?"

He left Will and Karen on the couch to take the cake out. "You nervous?"

Will swallowed. "More for him."

"Lennox'll be fine," Karen said. "He's navigated places a lot more hostile than college. I think he'll surprise you with how well he does."

"I hope you're right."

Karen hugged him tight. "It's going to be amazing, Will. You'll both have a great time in college. You won't believe how much there is to do in the city."

"I hope my roommate's nice."

Karen chuckled. "Well, if there's one piece of roommate advice I have, it's to not become best friends too quickly, if at all. Be roommates first."

Will nodded, but didn't say anything. He could only imagine how Lennox would be with strangers in his living space: like a piranha with legs rampaging around a small city.

"And you'll let me call you in the middle of the night when I get lost?"

"Will, I downloaded the subway app onto your phone. But yes, if you still need directions, you can call. As your parent I'd rather you get home safe than get mugged."

Will glanced at her after those words. *As your parent.* And she was, but she also didn't seem to want to take on the title he'd accidentally given her months ago. She was his mother in every way that mattered to him, and yet broaching the subject again wouldn't change anything. Karen would still shy away from that title, even if she embodied it.

"Right. Does that happen a lot?"

"It's New York City, honey. It's not uncommon, but don't go out late by yourself and you should be fine."

Ben corralled all of them into the kitchen for birthday cake. The whole evening was surreal: one minute listening to Roxanne prattle on, the next watching Lennox splash around the pool with Oyster, and then the dim kitchen lit by nineteen candles melting a square cake.

Will curled up on the back deck with Oyster afterward. Crickets chirped around them; sparks of light glowed around the backyard. Will caught a lightning bug and put it on Oyster's nose. He had a good laugh when Oyster yelped.

"Will? Don't stay up too late! We leave early tomorrow."

"Okay, Dad."

Just a few more hours. His arms shivered. Every pore seemed to tingle, each clogged with one of the many thoughts he'd worried over since their acceptance letters had arrived. The wait had been unbearable, but now that he was so close he wanted to restart this whole summer, just to do it one more time, to have more time getting to know Lennox, to chase Oyster around the yard, to figure out how to tell his dad and Karen goodbye without actually saying it.

"Arrooo!"

"Shh," Will murmured. He rubbed Oyster's furry white belly and kissed his forehead. "I'll be back at Thanksgiving, buddy, okay? I'll make sure Dad plays with you every day. He needs the exercise too."

Oyster whined and pressed his face into Will's chin. Lennox found him like that twenty minutes later, curled around Oyster's warmth with white fur all over his shirt.

"I see *someone* has claimed my favorite spot." Lennox sat beside them and wrapped them up with a blanket. Oyster whined at him. "Fine, but only because you won't see him for a while."

Oyster's tail thumped on the deck like the crack of a wooden bat. Will looked at Lennox, at the springy curls limp on his forehead and the nervous tick of his lips trying and failing to smile.

"You okay?"

Lennox nodded once and rubbed Oyster's belly. "You?"

"I'd be better if Oyster learned how to brush his teeth."

Oyster chattered at them and wiggled around.

"Oh, hush, seafood dog." Lennox scratched Oyster's head to calm him. "How are you really?"

Will met Lennox's eyes and glimpsed the same black hole that devoured his own insides. He smiled at Lennox and nodded the same lie too.

* * *

SATURDAY MORNING WAS A RUSH of packing their belongings into the jeep, eating a quick meal, and hugging Oyster goodbye. Oyster whined as they nudged the front door closed. Lennox rested his head against the window, but Will swiveled to watch the house, the rocky driveway, the faded shutters and the well-kept porch, the bushes scorched yellow from a long summer of blazing sunlight. Oyster pawed at the living room window as they turned onto the road and the trees blocked the house from view.

"You two sure you have everything?"

Lennox tugged at the strap on his backpack to say yes, and Will nodded. This was it. How long until he was back home? Or until New York City felt enough like home that he wouldn't miss this place? A thrill ran through him.

"Yeah, I double-checked everything last night."

"Good. That's..." Ben swallowed and fiddled with the radio as Karen drove. He didn't say anything else until they were at the train station. Will dreaded his words. Until this morning, he hadn't stopped to think about what New York meant for his dad.

They unloaded the car and pulled everything onto the platform. It was empty except for a group of teens at the far end. Karen examined all their bags as Ben looked around.

"Nice day for it. I hope it's not raining in New York, or your stuff is going to get soaked."

"The subway is underground at the train station. Stop's only a few blocks from Will's building," Lennox said.

He seemed unfazed by the bustle of the morning, but Will recognized his façade of confidence. Right now, however, his focus was on his dad and Karen. Ben continued to stare around, trying his best to look calm. Karen wasn't crying, but she kept giving him watery smiles that made his stomach knot.

"Dad?"

Ben squeezed Will's shoulder and didn't speak for several minutes.

"I'm proud of you, you know that, right? Whatever you end up studying or doing, or if you end up at another school or going on to get a PhD or whatever, I am so damn proud of you." Ben tugged Will into his arms, and Will gasped, both at the abruptness and at the swelling in his chest. "You're going to do great. You need anything, you call, okay? And you keep that boy close," Ben added, his mouth close to Will's ear. "You're good for each other."

Will nodded into his dad's shoulder, hugged him tight, and inhaled the scent of pine trees and the steaming gush of a hot iron. Too soon, Ben pulled away and held him at arm's length.

"When did you grow taller than me, huh?" Ben chuckled, a choked sound like a plug being pulled from a drain. "I love you, Will. Your mom would be so proud if she could see you right now."

Will nodded even as his eyes drifted to Karen. She and Lennox were saying their goodbyes as the rumble of a train approached and a whistle sounded. They traded places as the train slowed into the station. Ben and Lennox had a brief word and handshake, but Will lingered with Karen as Lennox climbed aboard.

"You stay out of trouble," she said as they hugged. "Call us at least once a week; let us know how you're doing. If you need *anything*, call. I've got plenty of vacation time to come visit you and a few friends in the city you can go to as well. You still have their numbers and addresses?"

"Yeah, I put them in my phone. Thanks for everything. You're— I love you a lot." Will started to pull out of their hug, but Karen squeezed him close and kissed his cheek.

"I love you, too, Will." She stepped back and fixed his hair. "I know it's been a little strained with us ever since… ever since you called me Mom, but I do love you. You're my son as much as Ben's. I hope you know that."

"I do."

LENNOX ENJOYED THE TRAIN RIDE so much Will got annoyed. Four hours of sitting next to someone mumbling "chugga-chugga" every five seconds was grating, but every time he looked over at Lennox, Will couldn't bring himself to tell him to quit. Tomorrow morning, Lennox would stop being a constant in his life. Will tried to not let himself dwell on that thought.

Penn Station was a stifling wall of people. As he had in the spring, Lennox melted right into the shifting and bustling crowd. Will kept a tight hold on his luggage and a firmer grip on Lennox's hand.

"I'm not sure where the subway is here," Will said, glancing around. "Maybe we should head to the street and go from there."

"Nah, it's somewhere. Gotta figure it out eventually."

But as Lennox led him through the crowd, Will took several deep breaths. His high school's entire population had been smaller than this crowd.

"Over there! I see the sign."

The subway was no better than the train station. Everyone from the station seemed to have decided to cram themselves into the same subway car. Lennox shrugged his bag to give himself some space, but Will shut his eyes and rested his head on Lennox's shoulder.

"You okay?"

"Just tired."

Will swayed with the people pressing into him on all sides. If it hadn't been for them he'd have fallen, since the nearest pole was several feet away. He stared at the dull shine of the floor as the stops passed. Four, five, six, then Lennox tugged his sleeve.

"Next one's you."

Will was the first one out. His duffel bag caught on several people, who glowered at his haste. He walked to the first staircase he saw without looking at the signs and wound his way up two more flights and then through an exit turnstile.

"Will! *Will*, slow down!"

Lennox raced up to him and shoved through the turnstile.

"You have to be there at a set time or something? Damn, Will, I almost lost you in the crowd. We should have gone out a different way."

"There's more than one exit?"

Lennox rolled his eyes. "I am going to get so many late-night calls from you getting lost, aren't I?"

"Shut up."

Will stared up for most of the walk; a smile formed on his face at all the towering buildings and the smells from the restaurants. Then he spotted his first sign of his new home: an NYU flag outside of a building on the next block. A buzz of excitement started in Will's head. Kids their age passed by. Some were hanging out on the sidewalk, chatting and laughing.

His dorm had more kids his age outside of it and a small welcome banner over the entrance. Will took the lead into the hall to the registration table. Another person his age was there. She smiled and took his information, then gave him his room key and a thin folder.

"Top floor," Lennox said, eyeing the room number on his keycard. "Hope you have an elevator, or you're going to *hate* this."

Will didn't get a chance to disagree as they found the door for the staircase. He'd hunt for an elevator tomorrow, or later if Lennox didn't feel like running around the city. Halfway up the stairs, however, Will began to have regrets.

"Why do these people insist on having so many stairs?"

"Cause it's a major city on an island. Like Japan. You build up or you move the whole damn city."

"Well, they should replace every staircase with an elevator. Every. Single. One. *Ugh.*"

"One more floor. Come on, you big baby."

Will huffed and puffed up the final two flights and into a narrow hallway with several doors with no signs or labels. He glanced at his room number and then at the doors. "Am I just supposed to guess?"

Lennox poked his head through one, a second, and then the third on Will's left. "This way. That's 1144."

Will followed him into another hallway, this one carpeted and slightly wider. He found his room three doors down on the right. The room was smaller than his at home and smelled strongly of furniture polish and tangerines. Lennox threw everything he was carrying onto a bed and sat down.

"At least your roommate isn't here yet. Is the loft bed yours?"

"No, must be his."

Lennox climbed up onto it as Will unpacked his duffel bag. His hair brushed the ceiling.

"Glad you didn't get this. We'd never have sex again."

Will threw his pillow at Lennox. "Come on, help me unpack."

They spent the afternoon putting all of his belongings away, getting his laptop connected to the campus wifi, and decorating with the few posters Will had brought. It wasn't much, but the room felt more welcoming when they were finished. Talk of dinner turned into a long debate over the merits of pizza or a sit-down restaurant that Lennox wanted to try.

"Meatballs, Will. They serve a fuckton kinds of meatballs. Pleeease?"

In the end, Will agreed because it was close. It wasn't bad either. His meatballs were served on top of a salad that had apples and all sorts of vegetables and fruits hidden between the spinach leaves. As the music thumped loudly through the narrow restaurant, Will watched the cooks behind the counter and the other customers, who were talking and laughing. His ears throbbed. It wasn't home, not by a long shot, but it was comfortable for an evening out with Lennox.

He'd get used to the noise and the crowds and the blistering shrieks of life that filled New York City, even without Lennox being his goofball self across the table from him.

"Do you think I could fit the whole meatball in my mouth?"

"If you spew your food all over me, I'll gut you."

They spent the following five minutes wiping up Lennox's mess, then decided to walk back instead of taking the subway.

Will startled at the screeches of the subway through the vents in the sidewalk and the gushes of steam that rushed through the grates into the semi-darkness of the city. He glanced at the sky and found no comfort in the missing stars, but no sign of any clouds either. A rim of orange hovered along what he could see of the skyline. The same orange painted splotches of light on the sidewalk.

"What's your wildest dream?" Lennox asked, catching his hand as they crossed another street.

"What?"

"Your wildest dream. Like, if there was one thing you could do, no restrictions or limits, what would it be?"

"I have no idea." Will laughed as Lennox tugged him close and danced them down half the block. "It's kind of silly to think about it, since it can't happen."

"I don't think so. I mean, dreaming's like everything else, isn't it? If you don't practice it, then you lose it."

Will pulled away from their dance as they continued to walk down the block then turned the corner at his new home.

"Dreams aren't, like, a sport or instrument though. They're just dreams."

"Yeah, but I forgot how to as a kid. I think of Berklee sometimes and... I don't know. I think that's a dream I can't imagine, but it's happening tomorrow. I wasn't even sure I could want it until you convinced me to go after it."

"You deserve it," Will said. "What brought this on?"

"Too much thinking. Just figuring out what optimism is like again." Lennox stopped them outside the entrance to Will's dorm. "You gave me that."

"No, I helped remind you of it. It's all you. I can't give you something like that, just nudge you in the right direction."

"Thanks." Lennox tangled his fingers into Will's hair and rubbed his scalp. "You never answered."

Will frowned as they walked inside and up the stairs. "I'm not sure I have one."

"Mine's to start zero-gravity, pro-skateboarding competitions in space."

Lennox launched himself onto Will's bed when they reached his room, but Will took his time shutting and locking the door. He couldn't think of a single answer beyond what he was doing now. The practical life: studying journalism and writing and most likely becoming a sports writer with a focus on baseball. That was the dream he'd created after the rest had faded or been cut short.

"So what other dreams do you have?"

Half an hour later, Will still couldn't put any coherent answer together. Lennox had invented three more, each more ridiculous than the last, which involved creating the world's most orgasmic sex toy that ruined modern society. Nothing came to mind that he hadn't already passed on or was aiming for, and hardly any of them were absurd. Well, the dual-wielding yo-yoer was a little out there; all he'd ever managed to do with those yo-yos was break several windows.

"What time do you leave in the morning?"

"Ten."

As they lay in Will's new bed, Lennox played with Will's hair, mussed his blond locks, and then smoothed them. He didn't ruffle any answer out of Will's head, and, as he shut his eyes, Will doubted he had an answer at all.

WILL SLEPT IN CHUNKS. HE woke first around midnight to sirens echoing on the street below, and then a few hours later to the slam of a door in the hall and shouts of laughter. He climbed out of bed at daybreak and watched what he could see of the sunrise through the skyscrapers. The colors and layers of light weren't anything close to the sunrise back home.

After a quick breakfast at a bakery down the street, Will and Lennox walked to where Lennox's bus to Boston would pick him up. Once they found the right queue, they sat against the fence behind an older couple who were speaking German. Lennox pulled up a map on his phone and zoomed in on their location. A bunch of lines popped up in every shade of the rainbow. Will frowned at the squiggles, but paid attention. He needed all the help he could get if he was taking the subway back alone.

"That's the seven, the one we just got off. Take that to Times Square here, get on the N or R to downtown—the yellow ones—and then get off at the NYU stop."

Lennox traced the path on the map.

"Seems a lot simpler when you explain it." Still, Will wrote it all on his hand, just in case.

All too soon, the bus pulled up, and the first call to board echoed down the street. The rest of the line crowded down the block to get seats, but Lennox lingered with him, his hand clutching Will's.

"Are you sure you don't want me to go with you?"

"You sound like a mom."

"That's not an answer."

Lennox squeezed his hand and attempted to smile. "I'll be fine. Lucy's meeting me at the bus, remember? Besides, *you* have your honor ceremony in, like, six hours."

Will didn't argue. Attendance was mandatory. Still, he traced the lines of Lennox's face with his eyes, tried to note every dip and curve of his cheeks and jaw, every tiny curl of facial hair. Lennox seemed both older and younger. His eyes held steady with resolve, but also shifted with a trace of fear that took Will right back to that damp motel room from last year.

"I really can go with you. I'll make some excuse."

"No. I've got to do this on my own." Lennox turned to him and nodded. "I'll text you once I get to Boston, okay?"

Will nodded, too, before diving at Lennox and almost knocking them both to the ground. He gripped Lennox tight, almost ripping his ratty old jacket with how hard his fingers dug into Lennox's back.

"I don't want to say goodbye."

"We aren't," Lennox said as he kissed Will's neck. "I know goodbyes, okay? This isn't like that. I'll see you in two weeks."

"Yeah. I love you."

"Love you too."

Will kissed him with force then. Even as the line moved past them and the calls for boarding continued, he kept his mouth against Lennox's and captured every piece of him he could: the buttery-toast taste of his lips, the warm brush of Lennox's cheek against his, the tickle of those long eyelashes against his skin.

"Last call for Boston, ten o'clock! Last call! Anyone else for Boston?"

"Gotta go. Text me if you get lost getting back."

Lennox pulled away with a hand raised in farewell. Perhaps it wasn't a goodbye like those Lennox was used to enduring, but it was one too many for Will. He watched the bus pull out ten minutes later, then turned back toward the heart of Manhattan.

..ıll five

A BOSTON STREET GREETED LENNOX when he woke up several hours later. Lennox sat until everyone else had climbed off the bus, then grabbed his bag and Will's old pillow and stepped out onto the street. A warm breeze blew his jacket open. Everyone else was already heading to their destinations, but Lennox took his time grounding himself.

Several shops lined the street, along with narrow houses and what counted for yards in the city. He pulled out his phone and checked the map as he walked. Lucy wasn't meeting him, no matter what he'd told Will. This first day in Boston was going to be his alone.

As at NYU, the street and buildings began to change as he passed the edge of campus. More and more people his age appeared, many unpacking cars to move into houses and apartments, others skateboarding past him. Giant flags blew around the next few buildings and another hung like a banner from one down the street. He remembered that building. The tour he and Will hadn't finished in the spring had started there.

He turned down the side street where his dorm was supposed to be and found the building at once. It blocked all of the houses beyond and had the name carved right into the front. His dorm wasn't as tall as Will's, but it made up for that in width. The building was made of gray stone and had huge windows that sparkled in the sunlight. The green space and the street around it were full of parked cars and people unpacking. Lennox went inside.

Chaos greeted him. People went crashing past with luggage; a basketball sailed over his head and was caught by someone rolling past on a skateboard. Lennox found the front desk and stared around.

"Hi! Are you here to check-in?"

The man at the desk beamed, and Lennox tried to smile too. Instead he grimaced and tried not to say anything stupid.

"Great, I'll just need your name."

"Lennox McAvoy."

As the man pulled up his information, Lennox turned to look at the entrance hall again. Across from the desk a notice board displayed a bunch of colorful flyers. More people were stumbling inside, their arms full of clothes, bags, instruments. A girl went past with a saxophone hanging around her neck.

"Ok, looks like you're in room 236, second floor."

The man handed him a folder and then ushered him around the open doorway and into a little office to take a picture for his I.D. card. Lennox did his best not to make a face, then hurried back to the entrance hall to wait. Five minutes later, he had his new I.D. card in hand.

"Ok, that'll get you into your room and meals. Just park out front. It's fine to block the road; it's closed off for the day while everyone moves in. Your R.A. is," the man consulted a list at the desk, "Benson. Let me know if you need anything!"

Lennox nodded and went upstairs with his backpack and pillow. He took the stairs and pushed through the only door on the second floor. The hallway beyond was wider than Will's. The walls were lined with more flyers and a bulletin board with a title announcing, "What's your favorite song?" with a blank blue expanse waiting for answers.

He counted the room numbers outside the doors. Room 202, 203... on and on, past some doors decorated with whiteboards and posters and others flung wide open to reveal people laughing and the cacophonous echo of musicians learning to play together. Finally, he reached 236 at the end of the hall. The door was shut and, so far, not decorated. Lennox swiped his new card on the reader and pushed the door open.

"Oh, where'd you get that one? I love the lace trim— Looks like our last roommate's finally here!"

The door swung open and the two women inside the room stared at him while their smiles faded.

"Um, I think you've got the wrong room."

Lennox eyed them and then the black numbers etched into the wall outside the door.

"This is 236, right? My card worked on the door."

They continued to stare. They were both in sweatpants, one wearing a football team hoodie and the other apparently in the middle of showing off her bra. Lennox kept his eyes on their kneecaps.

"Let me see that." The girl in the hoodie took his card, stepped outside into the hall, shut the door, and then opened it with his card.

"Huh, that's weird. But you're a *guy*. I mean, I know this dorm is co-ed, but I figured the rooms would still be by gender."

Lennox had assumed the same.

The second girl hurried to put a shirt on, then stood awkwardly beside one of the three beds. She gestured to the only one without blankets.

"I guess that's yours, then."

Lennox eyed it, too. This couldn't be right. Will's roommate was a guy, so surely he should also be rooming with a guy. He took a seat on the edge of the bed and sat his backpack and pillow beside him. Already the two girls had decorated part of the room. A strand of lights was hung above the desks between their beds. Several posters from *Star Trek* and something called *Full-Metal Alchemist* covered the rest of the wall.

"Do you need help carrying stuff in? I'm Ava, by the way."

Lennox looked at the one who had spoken. She had a flat nose, wide, brown eyes, and a lift to her chin that made him sure she could beat his ass. Ava tugged at the hem of her hoodie and looked from him to the other girl, who still stood as far away from him as she could.

"I'm Lennox."

Someone knocked on the door. Ava opened it and greeted a short, muscular guy who seemed to be a few years older. He had bright green hair.

"How's it going, ladies? Hall meeting tonight at eight, okay? And— oh, hi. You on my hall, too?"

"I think they might have mixed up his room, Benson," his unnamed roommate said. "He's been assigned to ours."

Benson frowned and asked Lennox for his card and the information packet they'd given him.

"Let me go have a look at the list downstairs. They probably read the wrong line."

Benson left, but Ava continued to watch Lennox. He bit his lip and tried his best not to snarl something offensive. But, after several minutes of uncomfortable silence, he had to say something.

"Can you two relax? I'm not going to jump your bones. I'm not into girls."

Every ounce of tension seeped out of Ava. She gave him a real smile then, and the second girl introduced herself as Danielle. While she still seemed a little leery, Danielle pulled her desk chair closer to him and sat on it facing backward.

"You have a boyfriend, then?"

Lennox dug his phone out and pulled up a picture of him and Will from earlier that summer. His throat ached at the sight Will's arms circling around Lennox's chest as they both tried to squeeze into the small picture.

"Oh, he's so cute."

Ava leaned in to see. "I guess. I'm not big into jocks."

"Or guys."

"Yeah, well, I'd rather be watching Netflix than dealing with boys."

Danielle offered him a picture of her own boyfriend before the girls turned the conversation away from boyfriends. They talked at length about a sci-fi show on Netflix, and Lennox was just deciding he'd be better off as a fly on the wall when Benson returned.

"Okay, Lennox, someone messed up somewhere. I've got the hall director looking into it. All the guys' rooms in our building are already tripled up, so you're probably going to end up at the dorm down the street once they figure all of this out."

"And tonight?"

"You can stay here if all three of you are okay with that, or you can crash in my room."

Ava and Danielle made the decision for him. Benson was all but tossed out after they gave their consent, and Lennox never got a word in. He sat on the edge of his bed, not talking or making eye contact. If they'd turned the conversation to something he had a clue about, he might have tried, but he had no idea what *Gallavant* or *Jessica Jones* were about, only that they were on Netflix.

He fiddled with his phone and tried time and again to open his mouth to say something. Nothing but dick jokes came to mind. Somehow, he didn't think Ava and Danielle would appreciate those.

Lennox didn't bother unpacking. He let Ava and Danielle drag him along to the dining hall for dinner and then ducked away from them into a line. Why did something have to go wrong as soon as he got here?

Ava found him in the crowd. She steered him toward the drink fountains and offered him an empty cup. "Are you always this quiet? You seem like you're scared to death of us."

"No."

"Is it because you saw boobs as soon as you walked in? Do gay guys really get that squeamish about tits?"

Lennox bit his tongue and repeated everything Will had encouraged him to try when he got here.

*Don't make a sex joke. Or a dick joke. Or a tit joke. Who the fuck
am I if I can't do any of that?*

"Tits don't hang from the right place to make my dick hard."

Ava's cup overflowed all over her hand. Lennox cringed. He started
to turn away and then—Ava laughed. At least, Lennox assumed the
noise she was making was laughter. It sounded like a cross between
a high F, the wail of a siren, and the harsh, screeching buzz of the
Osbornes' dryer.

"*Finally.* Just means more for me." Ava shook the splattered soda
from her hand and slid down for him to fill his own cup. "You and I
are going to get along like an epic movie friendship."

LENNOX SNUCK HIMSELF AND HIS pillow out of their room after
dinner. Ava and Danielle had insisted on a dance party to celebrate
their first night in college, but Lennox hadn't wanted anything to do
with it. He'd snarled and fought and eventually insisted he needed
to call Will to get away from them.

He wandered the dorm searching for a quiet room. The halls
of bedrooms were packed with noise, but the entire basement was
empty. The rooms were devoted to practice and study. Some were
single-instrument rooms with a chair or bench. Others could fit
six people and their instruments, and still others already had some
of the bigger instruments set up and waiting for a group to play
them.

After a few laps, Lennox settled in a small room that seemed to
be a study lounge. It was the only one with a couch that he'd seen,
yet even here he found several music stands covered in sheet music.
He got comfortable with his pillow and curled up before dialing Will.

"Hey, butthead. Hold on."

Something shuffled around on Will's end, then a door slammed
shut.

"Still there?"

"Yup. All cozy on this couch."

Will made a noise of disbelief. "Your room does *not* have a couch."

"And if it does?"

"Then I might be a little jealous and willing to trade my roommate for it," Will said. Lennox heard the squeak of hinges and another door shut. "He literally brought a crate of Cheetos with him and spent all day on his computer playing some shoot-'em-up war game. Didn't even unpack."

"Sounds charming." Lennox rolled onto his back as the lights flickered out. They blinked back on after a few waves of his arm. "So how was your honor thing?"

"Pretty boring. I got my last few books, got lost on the subway again. Ended up at the stop for Central Park. Oh! I saw this street musician earlier too. You would have *loved* her. I'll send you the video I took."

Lennox glared at the lights overhead as Will talked him through his day. Overall, it had been good. He'd gotten lost a lot, but he'd hung out with a few of the people he'd met during his visit over the summer and spent most of his day avoiding his room while his roommate moved in. Eventually, the question Lennox had been wanting to avoid was asked.

"So how was your day?"

"Nothing special." Lennox sat up and examined the room around him. Spots dotted his vision when his eyes fell on the sheet music someone had left behind. Will was silent.

"No, come on. I want to hear. Mine wasn't too bad except for my roommate." Will made a noise as if he was gagging on an unwashed sock.

"At least you're not rooming with two women."

"*What?*"

Lennox flipped through some of the sheet music before he answered. He recognized the names of a lot of classical pieces, but not the parts. He'd never touched a cello or a saxophone.

"Some sort of mix up. They're both nice enough," Lennox said, squinting at some marks written with pencil over four bars. Were those *hearts*? "I'm supposed to be in a new room tomorrow."

"That still sucks. Doesn't your orientation start tomorrow?"

"Probably." Lennox shrugged and flipped to another page. He hadn't bothered to look yet. Ava and Danielle would no doubt drag him along to whatever was planned.

Will continued to worry over the phone, and Lennox sighed and looked away from the sheet music for something else to distract him. Then he noticed someone just outside the room, peering in at him. The guy squinted at him as though he'd forgotten to wear his glasses and then motioned to someone out of Lennox's range of vision.

Curious, Lennox stood up as Benson, his R.A., came jogging into sight. The other guy opened the door slowly and motioned toward the music with a small smile. Lennox got out of his way as Benson followed him in.

"Will, it's fine. Honestly, they should have my roommate situation figured out tomorrow, okay?"

He could almost see Will nodding. "Okay, I should get going. My first class is at nine. Text me?"

"Yeah, love you."

"Love you too."

The guy was still sorting through his sheet music when Lennox put his phone back in his pocket. He grinned at Lennox as Benson took a seat on the couch.

"Sorry to interrupt," the nameless guy said. He was a head shorter than Lennox and just as skinny with dark, straight hair and brown eyes. "I always forget something when I come here to practice."

Maybe he'd just go sleep with Ava and Danielle and hope they weren't up all night dancing. Clearly, he wasn't going to get any peace in here tonight.

"I've got a proposition for you," Benson said. He patted the couch beside him as the other guy took a folder out of his backpack and stuffed the sheet music into it. "This is Troy Nguyen. He's a junior, lives across campus in an older dorm."

Lennox squinted at the floor and tried to think of something intelligent to say. "I'm Lennox."

Troy offered his hand, and Lennox shook it in a bemused sort of way.

"So Nat—she's our hall director— said it might be more than a day. All of the freshman rooms are full, and upper classmen usually pick their own roommates, so they're not sure how they're going to proceed. But... " And here Benson nodded to Troy. "...I've got a possible solution. I'm not sure if you or the residence hall council will all agree, but— "

"I've got my own room, even though it's technically a double," Troy explained. "I can't really afford it this year, though, so if you're interested, you could room with me."

The invitation surprised Lennox. He eyed Troy, but was saved from replying by Benson.

"You two can give it a shot for a few nights," Benson said. "They still might insist on putting you somewhere else, but Nat said you'd end up in limbo after tonight since they won't let you room with Ava and Danielle longer than that."

Lennox glanced from Troy to Benson and back. It was a tempting offer, considering the dance party he'd left behind.

"What do you think, Lennox? You're still hanging with my hall for orientation, but you want to give this a try?" Benson gave him a hopeful smile, and Troy fidgeted with his folder of sheet music.

"Sure. Where's your room?"

TROY'S DORM WAS ON THE other side of campus. Lennox returned to his room long enough to get his backpack and for Ava to give him her phone number, and then followed Troy onto the street. Even at eleven o'clock, students still milled around outside. In the distance, Lennox spotted a small group of guitarists seated together harmonizing.

"You like Boston so far?"

"Seen one city, seen them all."

Troy laughed. "I figured that, too, until I left Wyoming. Boston's probably my favorite. New York is nice for a visit but it's too much for me. D.C. is all museums. Chicago was very gray. Is this your first city, too?"

"No. My audition was in Baltimore. My boyfriend took me to Pittsburgh to see his baseball team over the summer and he's going to school at NYU."

"This one's me."

Troy led him up some steps into a red brick building. This one was smaller than Lennox's own dorm, more like a large house with additions on the sides and back. No front desk or attendant greeted them. Lennox found himself in a hallway with numbered rooms along both sides.

"Come on, I'm on the top floor."

Lennox almost laughed. Troy's version of a top floor was the third. He thought of Will back in New York, climbing a dozen flights of stairs to reach his room. The hall off the stairs was narrow and only held a few doors, but the walls were covered in various sorts of art and flyers for bands and events.

Troy's room was smaller than the one Lennox had left behind, but it had space for two sets of furniture. Lennox set his backpack and pillow on the bare bed and examined Troy's side.

He saw a lot of band posters, a whole crate of vinyls, two guitars, a cello case, and several other instrument cases stacked against the wall. Troy's bed wasn't lofted into the air, but it was on stilts that raised it several feet. Beneath the bed, Troy had created a cave with cushions and what looked like a stack of music books.

"Make yourself at home." Troy tossed his backpack under his bed and hoisted himself onto it. "Is that all you brought?"

Lennox frowned at his duct-taped backpack. "I travel light."

"No kidding." Troy watched him. "Well, that wardrobe is empty. The one that's got the drawers."

Lennox took his time unpacking. He set his sheet music on his desk and used a drawer of the wardrobe for his clothes. Troy didn't bug him or peer over his shoulder the way Ava had.

"So what instrument do you play? Or are you a music tech major?"

"Piano. Some guitar too."

"Awesome. I'm mainly saxophone."

"And a fuckton of others?" Lennox nodded at the stacks of instrument cases.

"Oh, well, some of those aren't mine. Bandmates."

"You're in a band?"

Troy nodded. "Yeah, three. Who *isn't* on this campus?"

A spark of interest lit for Lennox as Troy told him about his bands. He'd expected a musical haven, but to hear Troy speak, it sounded like something much greater than what he'd envisioned. All summer, Lennox had thought of classes and practicing for concerts. He'd assumed that once class was over, everyone would go back to doing other things instead of continuing to play. Except his mother, he'd never met anyone who craved the same deep connection to music as he did.

Twenty minutes later, Troy was still rattling off lists of local and on-campus bands.

"And then the Frights! They actually had CDs when they were still here. Last I heard they'd broken up after they graduated."

Lennox climbed onto his bed while Troy lounged on his own across the room. Their beds ran parallel against opposite walls. Troy yawned and plugged in his phone.

"Have you gotten any of your books or classes set up yet?"

"No," Lennox said, surprised by his own truthfulness. "What are those tests I have to take?"

Troy snorted. "Placement tests. My freshmen R.A. scared the shit out of us with horror stories about people failing them and getting kicked out."

"They're easy, then?"

"They're just to see how advanced your musical knowledge is in different areas so they can put you in the right courses. Like, if you know theory really well, you don't want to take the first level course because you will bore yourself into a coma or worse."

Lennox sighed in relief. That was nice to hear. He'd probably end up in all beginner courses, but at least he wasn't going to fail a bunch of tests before his real classes even started.

"So half of my classes are decided by that?"

"Yeah, you get to pick a few, but a lot of the first year is decided for you and by your auditions."

"I'm auditioning again?"

Troy rolled to face him. "Kind of. They use the one from admissions and then give everyone the same piece and tell them to learn it during orientation and then do some improvisation with it. They gave my year the *Star Wars* theme. It was fun."

"Cool. Well, goodnight."

"Night. Ugh, I don't want to work tomorrow. The bookstore's going to be a nightmare."

Lennox set his phone alarm for breakfast. He had a welcome presentation at nine and Ava had already texted him four times to ask if he'd join her. He responded to her and then to a text from Will timestamped from an hour ago:

Just breathe, okay? You're going to do great tomorrow. Love you.

He smiled and sent his own response.

You're going to be great too. Have fun in your first classes!

..ıll six

MONDAY WAS A FEW POUNDS of snow short of an avalanche. Will was late to his first class—not unsurprising for him. He'd made a habit of first-day lateness since he was a kid. Only this year, the door to his lecture was locked when he arrived seven minutes late. Nobody had warned him about that. His second class was somewhat better, since he actually attended it. The hall it was in, however, was cavernous. To make matters worse, the class was his required math unit, and he'd only found a seat in the back where he couldn't hear anything. Will decided twenty minutes in that if he folded his house in half it would fit in the stadium-style lecture hall. He didn't think that was the sort of math his professor was discussing thirty feet below.

It wasn't until he found his way to the dining hall for lunch that Will ran into some familiar faces. Tyra and Jake were at a small table near the entrance. He'd met both of them during his summer overnight at NYU. Tyra spotted him first.

"Will! I've been looking all over for you!"

She hugged him and pulled back blushing as Jake grinned at him from the table. Tyra's cherub cheeks and ringlet curls made her look twelve. Will hadn't believed she was almost a full year older than him when they'd first met in July. Jake Clark was a ginger beauty. He wasn't Will's type, but he was all fine angles and defined features and muscles. New York fit him better than his expensive, tailored clothes.

Will grabbed something to eat and joined them at their table.

"Any good classes yet?"

Tyra rolled her eyes at Jake's question. "Honestly, I'd be better off sitting in my room eating these books and vomiting them back up."

Will smiled. "I missed my first one; second was math. Nothing great is going to happen in that one."

"Mine were okay," Jake said. "I'm actually done for the day. Two this morning and then three tomorrow. Either of you taking a lab?"

"No."

"No way."

Jake frowned. "I might drop mine. It's zoology, so I thought it'd be cool, right? Get to dissect like fish and birds, maybe a feral cat, but it's so gay. The whole syllabus is about bugs and worms."

Will set his cup down at Jake's words. Nobody back in Virginia had ever used his sexuality in that way. For the most part, they used harder, crueler slurs. He flicked through his memories of that brief trip when they'd all met, but he couldn't recall mentioning Lennox or that *he* was gay.

"Oh, my god, my history class was *awful*. The professor was like a bunny, hopping all over the place," Tyra said. "It was so gross. History's stupid."

Jake hummed in agreement, but Will's frown deepened.

"Really? It's one of my favorites. You can learn a lot from it."

"Yeah, about stuff that's outdated and doesn't matter to us now." Tyra rolled her eyes and twirled her fork in her spaghetti. "We should all go out soon. My sister said New York is the place to be if you want to go clubbing. My roomies are going out for a girls' night this weekend."

Jake punched Will on the shoulder, suddenly roaring with enthusiasm. "Bro, let's go to a *strip club!*"

Will wasn't embarrassed by the idea—Lennox had mentioned it as part of their city-living to-do list—but he didn't think Jake would be interested in the same strip clubs. How had he missed filling them in on that part of his life?

"Maybe we'll get you a girlfriend, Will," Tyra said, and he couldn't mistake the purposeful way she leaned forward or the heat in her eyes. The gaze wasn't that different from Lennox's a year ago. The only difference was the effect it had on him.

"I'm taken." Will cleared his throat and dropped his gaze to his plate.

Jake hooted and demanded details and pictures of his "babe." Tyra wilted as she finished her meal.

"No, come on, man. You can't say you've got a girl and *not* show me a pic of her. You an ass or tit man?"

Now Will was blushing. He'd never been asked such a question. New York City was the last place he'd expected to hear that. In Virginia, Will had been "the gay kid" at school ever since he'd come out. Everyone had known when they'd looked at him. He'd been obvious.

In New York, that didn't seem to be the case.

"Come *on*." Jake persisted. "One titty pic."

Tyra glowered at him and almost upended the table when she kicked Jake under it.

"Stop being a pig, would you? She's his girlfriend, not a painting you can ogle."

Even Will was irritated on behalf of his nonexistent girlfriend. Lennox was going to love hearing about this tonight. Will pulled up a picture of Lennox on his phone, all unruly curls and happy dimples, and turned it for Tyra and Jake to see.

"Lennox, my boyfriend."

Tyra's mouth fell open as she yanked his phone from his hand. Jake stared, his eyes flickering back and forth from Will to the picture of Lennox.

"Boyfriend?" Jake straightened in his chair.

Will did his best not to flinch, but he squeezed his fists shut and prepared himself for whatever would happen next.

"All right, guess you're an ass man."

Jake got up to dump his tray, and Tyra stood and handed Will his phone. "He's gorgeous."

Will and Tyra followed Jake into the atrium outside the dining hall. He shrugged at her.

"Well, see you! Text me about clubbing!"

"Later, Will." Jake punched his shoulder once again, and the pair disappeared into the crowd waiting outside the glass doors. Will made his own hesitant way into the same crowd, getting jostled and bumped as he tried to slip into the flow.

A HARROWING RIDE ON A subway car dropped Will in yet another new location. He craned his neck for a sign on the street. Lennox had warned him about not paying attention when it was crowded, and now here he was in... somewhere.

A flutter of panic caught him, but Will bit it down and did the first thing that came to mind.

He called Karen.

"Will, how was your first day?"

"Um, well, I'm lost." He paused and then added, "Again. Somewhere new this time. Maybe."

Karen chuckled. "Give me some landmarks or street signs."

Will walked to the closest street corner. "East 144th Street and Wales Avenue."

"Why are you in the Bronx?"

"If I knew that I wouldn't be calling you."

"Honey, you took the six instead of the N or R." Karen gave him directions back to the subway station as he retraced his steps. "Get on a six headed for Manhattan. Downtown. Take it to Astor Place and you're a few blocks east of your dorm. Call me when you get back, okay?"

"Yeah, thanks."

Forty minutes later, Will huffed his way up the last few stairs in his building. He shoved through his hall door and opened his room to—

"Heal! Heal me, fuckhead! I'm— What the fuck, dude?"

Will shut the door behind himself and grimaced. Mountain Dew bottles littered the floor around the trash can; the air was heavy with Cheetos powder. Jackson's dark hair was past his shoulders and sleek; his limbs were short and gangly. Still, he didn't stink like the boys' locker rooms in high school, not yet at any rate. He at least seemed to bathe, even if he didn't leave their room.

"Hey."

Jackson ignored him, or rather, couldn't hear him over the catastrophic explosions coming from his headset. Will set his bag on his desk chair, started to pull his books and laptop out, and then changed his mind. He grabbed his phone charger and headphones and left for the study room down the hall.

The room was a narrow rectangle, just a few desks and chairs set beside the slimmest window he'd ever seen. Will settled in and called Karen back. They talked for a bit, catching up on his classes and the city. She handed him off to his dad, and the same conversation unspooled. He hung up quickly after they wished him luck for the rest of his week. Somehow, putting on a chipper voice about his less-than-ideal first day seemed like lying to them.

He texted Lennox to see if he could Skype and was greeted with an instant ping from his laptop. Will picked up the call when it flashed on his screen a few seconds later. Lennox smiled at him, one of the brightest Will had seen from him in the last few weeks.

"Hey!"

"Oh, my god, is that your cute boyfriend?"

Will jumped at the loud voice in the background. Lennox's side of the screen tilted. He seemed to have picked up his new laptop and darted across the room.

"No. Fuck off, Ava!"

"I just want to *see* him!"

The picture on Lennox's side went dark, then showed dark-blue jean fabric.

"Give me a second, Will."

Lennox's voice was muffled, but his argument with Ava continued with what sounded like a wrestling match and a door slamming. The laptop screen tilted again, and Lennox reappeared, panting, with a different scene behind him.

"Sorry. She dragged me over here after we got our new laptops. I wasn't sure how to set everything up, so I figured I'd get her help."

"Where are you?"

"Boston, North America, Earth."

"I meant are you in your new room, smartass."

Lennox shook his head, and part of Will was relieved. His stomach twisted with guilt at the feeling. He was glad Lennox was having a difficult time just as he was, that he wasn't the only one having to adjust to all the unexpected hiccups.

"I *do* have a new room. Maybe temporary, but I'm not rooming with Ava and Danielle anymore."

"Your loss!" A door slammed again and Lennox glared at something off the left side of his screen.

"She's, uh. You did warn me about the dick jokes though."

"You didn't."

Lennox nodded. "It was a dick *and* tit joke actually, and she ate it up. I think I'm stuck with her now." He grimaced, but Will saw a sparkle of fondness in his eyes.

That was a relief, too. Lennox was making friends, or a friend at least. That was better than he'd hoped for.

"So how were your classes?"

Will frowned. "Kind of awful? I missed the first one because I got lost. Second was math. The third was journalism, but I don't know. It was a little intimidating. *Everyone* was talking about internships and things they'd already done, and all I've done is our dumb school newspaper."

"Hey, that's still something."

"Lennox, it was four pages stapled together."

"Experience is experience," Lennox said. "And I'll help you with math if you need it. I've got those weird entry tests tomorrow. Troy said they aren't graded though; they're just placement tests."

"Troy?"

"My maybe-roommate. He's a junior, so he's already done all of this. Majors in like four instruments or something ridiculous. You'll meet him when you come visit."

"Better than meeting my roommate. I don't think he's left the room for *anything.*"

"Not even lunch?"

"Why would he, when he can live off Cheetos and Mountain Dew?"

Lennox shuddered and ducked out of sight. He reappeared with his phone in hand. "Sorry, it's Lucy. We're having dinner at her place, and she's showing me somewhere to get bedding or whatever."

"Finally." Will rolled his eyes and pulled his books out of his backpack. "I should get started on some of this homework anyway. What time are you free tomorrow?"

"Um, I think we're done around two, if Ava doesn't drag me somewhere—or Troy. You won't *believe* all the bands people on campus have formed, Will. It's the coolest shit, like I walked into a gay bathhouse and found twenty clones of you."

Will snorted. "Only *you* would fantasize about that."

"What? You saying you wouldn't be interested in twenty clones of me?"

"I'd end up murdering at least two of them."

Lennox stuck his tongue out. "All right, I have to go meet Lucy. Talk when I get back?"

Will agreed, and they settled on a time range. Lennox shut the call off, but not before Will spotted a woman—Ava, he assumed—peering around the edge of the Skype window. She gave a loud shout and tumbled out of sight as the screen went black.

* * *

THE NEXT FEW DAYS WERE like a clunky wooden roller coaster. Will's Tuesday classes were better than Monday's. He wasn't late, but only because he got up much earlier to make time for getting turned around on the city streets. Every avenue seemed to touch the sky with the same line of buildings that seemed to be caving inward. Will couldn't keep his directions straight. He raced around with a knot of anxiety itching in his chest until he found the right place.

Wednesday morning, he made it to all of his classes, but it was another disappointing day. Tyra and Jake ate lunch with him again and talked about clubbing and if any cool parties were happening soon. Will wasn't remotely interested in either; he'd rather find a good park to walk or a sports field than go out drinking.

Lennox's week was packed with events at Berklee. They texted a lot and Skyped again on Wednesday, but Will longed for a real conversation with him, one that didn't involve their campuses or meals or him getting lost for the twenty-second time—a few peaceful hours of quiet conversation curled up in the same bed murmuring silly thoughts or brave ideas into the darkness of their paired solitude. No interruptions from his roommate blasting aliens or dogs or *whatever* to smithereens on his computer. No Ava hollering and hovering on Lennox's end, or the creepy feeling of Lennox's new roommate being able to hear half of their conversation.

"Hello?" Will held his phone to his ear as he paused at a "don't walk" sign.

"Hey, nephew, how's city life?"

"Nobody reads the "don't walk" signs."

The rest of the crowd kept going right past him, ignoring the "don't walk" sign on the empty road that stretched in both directions. His Aunt Mia chuckled. All week he'd been expecting a call from her. Aunt Mia was his dead mother's sister, who lived in Pittsburgh, and while they didn't see each other more than a few times a year, they'd talked all the time when he was growing up.

"Why would they? Your eyes are better than those signs."

"But they're here for a reason."

He could almost hear her rolling her eyes. "Yeah, for tourists. Come on, you're a city boy now. Cross that street."

"I'll wait." The "walk" sign flashed on, and Will began to walk. "I'd rather be late for classes than get hit by a taxi."

"You aren't a real New Yorker until you've been clipped by at *least* four taxis. Karen told me."

"Karen's a liar, then."

Will waited for the next walk sign to cross to the park a few blocks up from his dorm. His aunt chattered away about her own life, catching Will up on her latest dates, her job, and a Paris vacation she was planning for the summer.

"Maybe you and your cute boy can come along," Aunt Mia finished as Will took a seat on a bench. "The city of *love* will be sickeningly charming with you two around. You still there?"

"Yeah, just finding a seat in the park." Will rubbed his nose. A lot of people were out today enjoying the cooler weather that was promised for the weekend. "And I don't think Lennox would care much for Paris. Maybe London or Berlin."

"Eh, London's too posh for me. We could do Rome. So, how is it then? I was expecting you to cut me off and talk for an hour about how great college is."

Will hesitated, and that was all Aunt Mia needed. "That bad?"

"It's fine. I don't know. It's different than I thought it'd be. Classes are weird, and I keep getting lost and I'm not sure about the people I met when I visited over the summer."

"Sounds about right for your first week."

"But half the week was horrible!"

"First week of college is rough for everyone. Second week too. It's a big adjustment."

Will nodded. His dad had said that when Will had let something slip in their conversation yesterday. Maybe he was panicking too soon. He hadn't had enough time to figure out the city or college.

"Honestly, if you haven't cried at least once this week, I'll be disappointed. I cried like five times my first week of college. Your mom was responsible for a least two of those."

"Really?"

"I'm not a liar like Karen."

Will chuckled. "She isn't. It's going better for Lennox than for me. He had a mix-up with his roommate, but since then..."

Since then Lennox had only gained momentum. Every text and call and Skype session grew in cheerfulness on Lennox's side. He'd taken his entrance tests, gotten his music piece for a new audition, made a few friends—promising friends, unlike Will's group. Tyra and Jake had seemed nice enough, but their comments from that first lunch together still hung around Will's ears. Their common interests had evaporated.

"You're worried about him? After everything you've told me?"

"Of course. He's been through too much, and I don't know if he can handle—"

"He can." Aunt Mia's laughter followed her words like the tinkle of a wind chime. "I know you love him and you worry about him, that's natural. But Lennox can handle himself. That kid hits the ground running and he just goes, better or worse. He's never been able to stop. You aren't like that."

"I could be," Will said, trying not to sound petulant. He sat sideways on his bench and rested his arms on his knees. "That's how you have to be in New York."

"No, that's how New York *is*. You live life at a more thoughtful pace, Will. That's why you've got to adjust more than Lennox."

Will frowned. Maybe he was more thoughtful than Lennox, but that was a good thing. He considered his options more, figured out what was best instead of rushing into situations he couldn't handle.

For years, he'd been preparing himself for New York. So what if he hit a few bumps along the way?

..ıll seven

"So then, Dion says 'you sound like a lightsaber,' and they had a tuba battle right in the middle of the auditorium. Professor Hocks conducted the whole thing!"

Lennox laughed at the end of Troy's story. Troy seemed to have an endless supply of Berklee stories from auditions and classes and ensembles and bands he'd been in since his freshman year. He never stopped introducing Lennox to this new world. It was refreshing in its own way, and Lennox was surprised by how glad he was to listen. Will would like Troy. They both navigated the world with that same gentle patience that put Lennox at ease.

"You should come jam with us sometime. The Rock Lobsters, I mean. We could always use a second guitar." Troy sat up on his bed and let his legs dangle over the side.

"Maybe."

Lennox stared at the scattered papers on his desk. Friday afternoon. Today he'd meet with his advisor one-on-one for the first time and figured out his course schedule.

"Did I tell you about the time that—oh, hang on." Troy's phone buzzed "It's Benson. He says the residence hall committee has given us the okay on rooming together, if we're on board."

And that was the one thing Lennox didn't understand about this whole roommate fiasco. Sure, he'd been placed with two women by accident. It was bound to happen every now and then. But switching to room with Troy shouldn't have been nearly as complicated as it had been. Benson had talked to all the hall directors, who had called Troy in before deciding in their big committee.

"Sounds good." Lennox stood up and shuffled his pile of papers together. "I've got to go meet with my advisor. Let me know if there's paperwork or shit we have to fill out."

Troy stood, too, as Lennox stuffed his papers into his backpack. He wrung one of his wrists and then the other. Every time their conversation got quiet, Troy did that.

"Look, I'm sure you've probably been wondering about, like, how complicated they made all this. I've been rooming alone for a reason."

"So you can have all the sex you want without a nosy roommate?"

"Well, sure that's part of it, but I'm trans and I can't change the gender marker in my home state," Troy paused and chewed on his lip so hard he winced. "Berklee can change it in their records, but there's a lot of legal stuff around who I can and can't room with. It's pretty ridiculous, honestly, because I'm just a guy, right? But if—"

"You're rambling, doofus. So that's all?"

"Um, yeah. That's it, I guess."

Lennox shrugged. "Have I at least been using the right pronouns?"

A faint smile lit up Troy's face. "Oh, yeah, you're good. He and him, that's me."

"Cool. Well, I've got to go meet with this weirdo to get my schedule figured out. Will's been crying all week about not knowing when he can call me."

Lennox headed across campus. He was still sorting out which buildings were where, but his campus was a lot simpler than Will's. Everything was grouped together. He found the building that housed the piano department and then combed the empty halls until he found the office number that matched what he'd been given: Dr. Tyrese Austin, 2534.

The door was open, but Lennox hovered outside. Dr. Austin's office was in a cramped hallway in one of the oldest buildings on campus. Two other doors boxed in Dr. Austin's, but they were both shut and covered in sign-up sheets for office hours and notices about upcoming events.

All week he'd been dragged to events he'd never have gone to on his own. Ava had insisted. Troy had told him he'd find it all useful. They'd both been right, not that he'd ever tell them—or even Will. Everything this week had been refreshing. New. The cusp of an exciting life he still tottered on the edge of.

His shoe squeaked as it scuffed the floor.

"Hello?" A man's head appeared in the doorway. He had a thin, dark face and short dreadlocks more plentiful than a centipede's legs. "Lennox?"

"Uh, present."

The man chuckled and waved him into the office. Lennox stepped into a cramped room, where the walls were lined with bookshelves stuffed with sheet music and books. The centerpiece was a desk; its surface was painted like the keys of a piano.

"Have a seat. I'm Dr. Austin."

Lennox sat across from him in the only available chair. The office was decorated with what looked like album covers hanging on the exposed wall. One small window overlooked a small courtyard that had held a barbeque event the previous evening. Ava had dragged him to it, and Lennox still refused to admit he'd enjoyed the food and festive atmosphere.

"So, Lennox, how's your first week going?"

"Um, fine, I guess."

"Making new friends? Not missing home too much?"

"Sure."

Dr. Austin watched him before turning to his computer.

"All right, not a chatterbox, that's fine. Let's see what your tests say about your class placement."

Lennox waited, tapping his fingers on his thighs. Dr. Austin hummed while he scrolled and clicked around on his computer screen and finally printed out several sheets of paper that he spread out on the desk.

"So, these show your scores on the entry tests and the recommended level you should start at for the core music curriculum." Dr. Austin turned his computer monitor around to face Lennox. It displayed what looked like a spreadsheet. "You're into level three for Ear Training, the highest level for Harmony, and mid-level for Arranging. Then the intro class for Music Tech."

Dr. Austin scribbled something on his notepad. "What majors were you considering?"

"Composition."

"Great. All right, so these are the classes you need to sign up for based on the test scores, and then you'll also do a private instruction class with me. You'll build your schedule around that. Do you want to pick your classes now or on your own?"

Lennox shifted. He had no idea what he was doing. He didn't even know how to access the screen Dr. Austin had pulled up with class lists. Troy might know, but he couldn't keep bugging Troy when he should be asking the people offering help. Lennox tried. "How do you get to that screen?"

"Oh, the class schedule? It's on the website. This particular one is part of the portal. Do you know how to get to that?"

"Not really. I'm sort of bad at the website stuff."

"Really? Most kids your age make me feel stupid when I'm in the same room as a computer."

Lennox glowered. "Don't rub it in."

Dr. Austin only smiled and waved him closer. "Come on. Drag your chair around here. I'll show you everything. We'll get you signed up for classes, too. How's that sound?"

Dr. Austin spent close to an hour walking him through how to access the portal. They ran through lists of available classes, signed him up for courses, and then picked the last few he needed to fill out his schedule. He also got placed into an ensemble based on the professors' ratings from his improvisation earlier in the week. Dr. Austin printed a copy of his schedule as well as his book list and sent him on his way with several pieces of sheet music for their first private lesson.

The sun was setting by the time Lennox left the piano department building. He set out across campus, eyeing all the people milling around, talking, laughing, some sitting on the grass playing their instruments. His phone rang in his pocket. Lennox pulled it out, expecting Will, but it was Otto.

"What do you want, asshole?"

"Don't be a dick," Otto's voice said through a buzz of static. "Can't I call you and make sure you haven't murdered half of Boston?"

"Only if you want to be my boyfriend."

"Ugh, no way. That's Will's job. Oh, Abe says hi."

Lennox nodded. "Tell him he's a dweeb. You two heading back to Virginia now?"

"Tomorrow. Well, he is. I might stay longer."

"I thought you hated Minnesota."

Lennox turned down the street to his dorm as he talked. Otto had done nothing but whine and moan about spending the summer in Minnesota on the reservation with his grandparents. The last he'd heard, Otto would be joining the army when he got back to Leon Monday.

"I need more time, I think. Mom's here to take us back, but I'm going to stay. Go to North Dakota with my grandparents."

"But what about the army?"

Otto was quiet for so long Lennox thought he'd hung up on him. He made it into his dorm and up the stairs by the time Otto replied.

"I'm not going to join."

"Guess your mom's pretty happy."

Otto ignored him. "How's Boston? Classes? Whatever you're doing."

"Good so far. Just got my class schedule. Still have to buy books."

"Gross."

Lennox opened the door to his room. Troy was gone, but a form was on Lennox's bed. He glanced at it and saw it was a roommate form.

"How's the roommate stuff?"

"Fine. Troy's pretty cool. Will's not having so much luck, though. As of yesterday, his roommate still hadn't taken a shower."

"So?"

"You're nasty. Look, I've got some stuff I've got to read through before I get my books tomorrow. I should go."

"Yeah, me, too. Time to force Abe to go to bed. Later."

"See you."

Lennox hung up and plugged in his phone at the desk. He filled out the consent forms Troy had left and was just about to go to dinner when Troy returned, two unfamiliar people in tow.

"Oh, good! I was hoping you'd be back. Lennox, this is Alex and Sadia."

Lennox had already heard about these two from Troy, but meeting them was different. Alex was a stocky woman a foot shorter than him. Most of her head was shaved except for the long, teal and purple French braid in the middle. Like Lennox, she had several piercings. Sadia was the opposite in her hijab and dark jeans and shirt. Her voice, however, carried across the room and probably to the street below. She must be a voice major.

"Troy says you play piano?"

Lennox nodded. Everyone at Berklee seemed to ask about instruments first. "Guitar, too. Some percussion."

"Sweet! We're going to dinner and wanted to invite you," Alex said. She waved a guitar pick at him. "Maybe find a practice room, somewhere to jam?"

Troy gave him an encouraging nod, and Lennox found himself agreeing. He'd never played with anyone outside of band class. They went to dinner together, met Ava, who dominated the conversation, then returned to the practice rooms in Ava's dorm that Troy explained had the best space and equipment.

"My friend Duncan says this one has the best piano," Sadia said as they picked an empty room. Lennox remembered it from his brief time here. It was a larger room with several instruments kept in it. A piano and a drum set were in adjacent corners, along with an upright bass.

Lennox took a seat at the bench and opened the cover. The piano was beautiful, finely carved, well-crafted, and in much better condition than Mr. Robinette's piano had been. Troy plucked at the strings on the upright.

"Give us a melody, Lennox. Or Alex."

Alex had taken up the guitar nearby. She nodded at Lennox. "Let's see what you can do then."

"Er, what vibe are we going for?"

"Jazz?"

"Funk?"

"Rock?"

Lennox rolled his eyes. "Lot of help you shitheads are. Fine."

He played a few chords to test the keys and then picked up a quick, rockabilly rhythm. Troy came in first, thumping along with the upright bass and grinning. Ava backed them up with a solid beat on the drum set, and Alex eyed Lennox's hands shifting along the piano keys.

"G, C, D?"

Lennox nodded. He was too stunned to speak. Perhaps it was foolish, but, even after almost a week, he wasn't used to people knowing music as well as he did. Ben, Will's father, had understood quite a bit, but he'd been flummoxed by piano chords. Sadia took up a microphone and found an amp.

They spent the next two hours playing together. Lennox marveled at the collective skills of his friends—and at the fact that he considered any of them a friend. They traded instruments toward the end of the night; Lennox tried out the guitar and had a wail on the drum set. He'd never had so much fun or learned quite so much while playing. Everyone had their own sounds and favored rhythms, their strengths that they brought and passed on to the group. Band class in high school had never been like this.

"We should do this again," Sadia said. They were walking back to Lennox and Troy's dorm. "Still on for our Saturday morning jog and brunch, Troy?"

"Uh, yeah." Troy tugged at his stomach. "I need it after the summer I had. You in, Lennox?"

"Jogging? No way. I'm sleeping in tomorrow."

Alex raised her fist and it took Lennox a second to realize she wanted him to bump his own against it.

"You are my kind of guy. These two are fitness nuts. Don't let them drag you into madness," Alex said. She hooked her arm through his. "So I hear you got a cute boyfriend."

"Is that how you're introducing me to everyone, Troy?"

Troy waved back at him. "You never shut up about him!"

"I barely talk!"

Alex and Sadia said goodnight at the door to Troy and Lennox's dorm building. They went upstairs together, still talking and laughing.

Troy opened the door to the room. "That one bass riff—I wish I'd written it down. I'm terrible at transcribing music."

"I probably could." Lennox imitated the finger-stretching motions for an upright bass. "You remember the notes? Chords? I'm not sure how it works on an upright."

"Yeah, I've got sheet music from classes that you could figure it out from."

Lennox's phone rang. Troy shrugged. "I get first shower then. Tell your boy hi!"

Lennox flicked him off as he pulled his phone out. Troy ducked into the bathroom and shut the door.

"Hey, babe."

"Hi. Uh, real quick, is it the avenues or streets that go to the higher numbers?"

"Streets, Will. Are you lost again?"

"No? I'm just... hovering."

"On a street corner? Will, it's after eleven."

"I'm fine. I'm just a few blocks away, but I can't ever read the map on my phone." Will's breath rasped as if he was jogging down the street. "Okay, I'm almost to my dorm."

"Good. Don't trip and die. Let me know when you're in your room. I got my schedule."

"Finally!"

Lennox listened to Will puff his way up flights of stairs, grumbling and complaining the entire time.

"I am *never* getting used to this. I'm going to have a one-floor house someday. No stairs ever again."

"You're going to need a lot of land for a one-floor house. Especially if you still want that baseball field in your backyard."

"I'll build my house behind a high school. Use theirs. Ok, I'm— ugh." Will's end grew scratchy as if he was rubbing tin foil over the phone. "He never *leaves*. Hold on."

The thunderous sound of gunfire filled Lennox's ears and then faded fast. A door slammed shut.

"I swear I don't think he's gone to a single class."

Lennox laughed. "You can't know that if you're in classes at the same time."

"He doesn't. He hasn't left the room. He just eats Cheetos and drinks one of his hundreds of cans of Mountain Dew. I'm so sick of video games."

"Maybe he only showers on weekends. Otto does that."

"If you ever do that I'll never touch you again."

"You're sure grumpy."

"Well, my room smells like dung and armpits," Will said. Another door closed on his end. "What's your schedule, then? And your classes? I want to hear how it went."

Lennox fell back onto his bed and kicked off his boots. "Dr. Austin was cool. Kind of cute. I might have to leave you for an older man. No hard feelings."

Will scoffed. "Yeah, and I might leave you for a woman."

"I mean if she loves baseball as much as you do, I won't blame you."

"Everyone here is just really cool." Lennox rolled onto his stomach and bit his pillow. "I'm glad I came here. I know classes haven't started, but I'm really liking it so far. It's still too much half the time, but it's good."

Will was quiet. The pause lingered with Lennox, but before he could acknowledge it, Will spoke. "I'm glad. Berklee's got you written all over it."

Lennox nodded. "Anyway, my schedule has me free after five on Mondays, after four for the middle of the week, and I've only got one short class at one o'clock on Friday. I figure that'll come in handy if I want to sneak off for a longer weekend with you. Could even skip it and come down Thursday night."

"Won't be much fun with my roommate lurking all day and night."

"We'll just have to be raunchy enough to convince him to leave. What days are best then? Tuesdays and Thursdays?"

"Yeah, I'm done earlier those days. We can Skype while we do homework."

"Okay. I miss you."

"You're horny."

"That, too. How about a quickie over the phone?"

"Lennox, I'm sitting in a hallway."

"More risk, more fun."

"No, I'll see you next weekend. Does your roommate leave?"

"Yeah, Troy's gone like half the day. He works on campus, has a bunch of stuff he does. I'm sure he'd be okay staying over with a friend so we could have an uninterrupted night. I'll ask him about it."

"And with no video games blowing up in the background, what a dream that'll be."

...ıl eight

WILL'S SECOND WEEK STARTED ON a brighter note. He spent Sunday afternoon strolling the city with his new friends—Jake, Tyra, and a group they'd gotten together. They took to the hills and ponds of Central Park. Will was glad to be back in a green space. The buildings all but disappeared the farther into the park he went. It was nice to breathe again.

Once classes started on Monday, though, he was less pleased. One week and he was already behind in his math class despite trying to sit closer to the front. His journalism class wasn't faring well, either. Their first assignment was a mock-investigative article, and Will hadn't the faintest idea of where to begin. Nothing the professor discussed seemed to be the journalism Will was familiar with: not interviews or finding an interesting topic. All week had been devoted to discussions of social media articles with biased political leanings and half-truths.

He spent lunch with Tyra and Jake and roamed the halls of the student lounge, checking out the flyers for clubs and events. NYU had a little to offer, but most of what he saw was for off-campus events: concerts in parks, festivals, a lot about Halloween, cider and beer crawls. Nothing said anything about baseball or writing groups, but he found one that caught his interest: LGBTQ Alliance.

Tuesday evening, he started out early and found himself in the student union. The ballroom doors were propped wide open. A huge crowd of young adults filled the space, some were unstacking chairs, but most were lingering in groups of three and four. Will shuffled to the side of the main door, eyed the crowd, and spotted an open seat.

"Is this one taken?"

The woman to his left shook her head, and Will sat down, tucking his backpack under his chair. He smiled as he turned to her, but she was busy with her other neighbor.

"Are you lost, honey?"

Will turned to the man on his other side and thought he was staring at a giraffe. He was gangly with knobby joints and wearing an entire outfit in animal print. The man simpered at Will.

"Sorry? I'm here for—"

"Lacrosse meeting is in the other ballroom."

Will flushed. Why did everyone keep thinking he was straight? He was as gay as could be. "I'm here for the LGBTQ group." Will held out his hand. "I'm Will."

"André." The man grasped his fingers daintily and let go at once. He turned to the people on his other side and whispered something. They all snickered. "You *sure* that's what you're here for?"

Will gritted his teeth and nodded. "Yeah, I'm gay. Have a boyfriend and everything."

One of the other men leaned toward him. "In that outfit?"

They all laughed, and the man next to him made a big show of shifting his chair away from Will's. Will looked at his clothes: sneakers, loose jeans, an old baseball shirt. He'd even worn his Pirates hat. Nobody had ever *not* assumed he was gay, not back at home. The meeting started, but Will couldn't focus on what was being said.

Somehow he made it back to his dorm without getting lost. It was a mercy to find Jackson already in bed. Will climbed into his bed and plugged in his phone. His head was buzzing.

He'd always been the gay kid. Everyone in his town had figured it out, probably before he had. Sure, his interests weren't stereotypical, but it had still been obvious, hadn't it? He'd done nothing to deny his sexuality.

Yet in New York City...

Was he not gay enough? What did that even mean? Will sat up and rubbed his face before calling Aaron.

"Was wondering if I'd ever hear from you again." Aaron yawned in his ear.

"Yeah, sorry. Been busy. Listen, am I gay?"

Aaron snorted. "You're dating a guy."

"I don't mean, like, sexuality wise. Do I act, like, gay? Or look gay? What does that even mean?"

"Uh, I dunno. Where's this coming from, man?"

Will told him about the LGBTQ meeting. "They treated me like I was wearing a Santa Claus outfit to a Hanukkah party. I *am* gay, but the way they looked at me— "

"It's different in New York," Aaron said. "Look, I didn't even know being gay was a thing until you told me you were. Like, you're my definition of what gay is. But New York... that's a whole other ball game."

"I guess. Since when have I not been gay enough, you know? It's always held me back at home."

"Forget them, dude. New York's a big place. I'm sure you've met other people who aren't assholes, right? Just stick with them."

Will turned their conversation to Aaron's baseball team and classes. He seemed to be doing well. The baseball program at the University of Virginia had a marvelous team of coaches and excellent training programs. Aaron's life was on a good track, just like Lennox's. Why couldn't his own be moving upward?

* * *

FRIDAY TOOK TOO LONG TO arrive. Will skipped his last class and caught an earlier bus to Boston. He texted his dad and Karen to tell them he was on his way to see Lennox and promised to let them know when he arrived. He slept during the journey, since he'd hardly slept the night before. Jackson had been up most of the night, marathoning some new video game.

Lennox's beaming face was there to greet him. A rush filled Will at the sight of him. It wasn't until they were tangled up in each other's arms that he recognized the feeling as happiness. Will pulled Lennox's mouth to his and kissed him.

"Mmm, missed me more than I missed you, did you?"

"Just not used to going so long without a kiss." Will stepped back and took Lennox's hand.

"Want to get lunch first? Lucy's been raving about this pizza place nearby."

Will let Lennox steer him along the streets. It was brighter here than in New York, less claustrophobic. Having Lennox beside him helped too. Everything about Lennox filled him with light and wonder: the sway of his curls in the autumn breeze, the curve of his smile in the corner of Will's eye, the touch of his fingertips on Will's arm.

"And me and Ava busked over there the other day."

"Busked?"

"Like, street musicians. We played for money. I actually made enough for lunch to be on me today." Lennox kissed his cheek and chuckled. "What? Why are you so quiet? That asshole keep you up all night with his fucking video games again?"

"Oh, yeah. I'm glad I'm here, though. Two weeks is too long without seeing you."

"Well, my room is ours for most of the weekend, so the sooner we eat..."

They took their pizza to go. Lennox steered him to the far side of campus to give him a tour on the way. Will recalled a few buildings from his day here months ago, but it was much less commercial than his own campus. Boston didn't stretch its never-ending fingertips to the sky quite the way New York did. The vibe from the people was different too. Lennox pointed out various buildings they passed, telling Will their names or what class he had there or what event he'd gone to with his new friends.

"Ava keeps dragging me into the studios here to record with her. It's free reign until October. Then everyone has to sign up for times."

"I guess that makes sense. Where's your dorm?"

"That one."

Lennox pointed out a smaller red brick building across the road. The walls angled up and met in a steep point several floors above the front doors. Will followed him inside and upstairs to the top. A hall lined with obnoxious posters and flyers greeted him. It was empty, but Will could hear the patter of a drum and the whistle of a flute. This was exactly the sort of place Lennox belonged.

His room was simple with a clear distinction of whose side was whose. Lennox's was the bare walls and tussled blankets. Troy's was covered in posters and boasted a stack of instrument cases and an organized desk.

"I see you got bedding."

"Lucy made me. She wouldn't let me have dinner until I bought it."

Will ran his hand over the rumpled fabric—black with music notes and white guitar outlines. The pillow case was decorated with piano keys.

"Well, it's very you."

"Yeah, she wouldn't let me buy anything else."

Will set his backpack down at the foot of Lennox's bed. He felt awkward and out of place. It wasn't the same overwhelming feeling of New York bending in around him, but Lennox's room wasn't his. He stood there the way he had in Lennox's motel room a year ago, trying to decide if he should sit when the only option was the bed.

"You can sit your cute ass on the bed. Jeez, Will."

Will sat; his eyes examined everything. This was Lennox's life now. He didn't recognize any of it, not the bedding or the textbooks, only the ratty backpack at the desk, still duct-taped together. "Sorry, I'm just—this is your life now. I want to see as much as I can."

"Well, have some pizza and then stare at me naked for a while. How's that?"

They sat on Lennox's bed for the next hour with the pizza box open on their laps. Lennox told him all about his first week of classes, from his jazz ensemble to his private instruction to his ear-training test the first day. He's been doing well. This was everything Lennox already understood—a world he saw in the dust from the stars that drifted behind his eyelids.

"See? I told you classes would be a breeze for you."

"My music tech one isn't." Lennox wiped his hands on his jeans and chewed his last bite of pizza. "I don't know anything about all of the technology and recording programs they use. I've got Ava with me for that one."

"You'll learn." Will rested his head against Lennox's shoulder. "I wish mine were going better."

"I'm sure they'll pick up," Lennox said. "Or next semester's will be more interesting. You're stuck doing a lot of those liberal arts core classes right now, aren't you?"

Will nodded, but still he didn't believe it. Everything had fallen into place for Lennox in only two weeks. After a summer of worrying, here he was thriving and doing better than Will had dreamed possible. A pang of jealousy cut through him, but it was stopped by doubt. Did he think so little of Lennox to believe he would screw all this up?

"So, sex?"

"Wow, what a seductive offer to get me in the mood." Will kicked his shoes off and slid down the wall. "Movie and cuddles? I really just want to nap with you right now."

Lennox nodded and pulled his laptop from his desk. They curled up together on the bed. Will's head was buried in Lennox's neck as the laptop murmured from Lennox's chest. He'd hardly shut his eyes when he was awakened by muttering voices.

"Sorry, I forgot my charger."

Lennox's body shifted against his. "It's fine. We're just napping."

Will peered around Lennox at the man across the room. Troy. He was tiny, lithe. His dark hair swept his eyes, but did nothing to hide his disarming smile. He and Lennox whispered a few more words—something about music notation—before Troy crept out of the room. Will didn't even hear the door close.

"That Troy?"

Lennox startled. "Yeah, that's him. He's pretty cool. We should go to lunch with him tomorrow. You'll like him."

Will yawned and curled closer to Lennox. At least one of them was making friends with his roommate. "Is he coming back tonight?"

"No, it's just us until I text him tomorrow." Lennox nuzzled his nose against Will's hair. "I love having you back in my arms. That sounds so fucking cheesy, but it's true."

"I wish this bed wasn't so cramped."

"Well, if you weren't such a big boy…"

Will snorted as Lennox's hand rubbed over the zipper of his jeans. Lennox undid the button, too, but stopped at Will's giggles.

"What?"

"You're awful. You're getting worse every day."

"I'm cute, like, 'gonna ride your dick into the sunset' cute."

Will laughed harder. Lennox pinned him down and tickled him, finding that one weak spot along his ribs that made his lungs spasm with breathless laughter. Their lips met amongst the tickling and wrestling. Will stilled at the touch, the warm caress, and the sureness of Lennox's kiss. This was his place in the world. Every certainty he needed was right here.

"So is this a yes to sex finally, or should I start groveling?"

Lennox kissed his neck and nudged Will's jaw with his nose.

Will giggled. "Yes, you goof. Come here."

ON WILL'S FIRST NIGHT IN Boston, Lennox teased the happiness from his skin, eased him into comfort that had been absent since they'd left Virginia. He stripped him bare, from the outside in. Music filtered in from the hall and the open window and supplied their own crescendos with urgency. The stillness of the Boston night curled around him as Lennox rested against him afterward. Will slept well. In the dim haze of a starry dusk, he awoke to Lennox shifting against his side.

"Len?"

"Sorry." Lennox shifted, and Will felt his erection press against his own thigh. "I'd say that's morning wood, but I'm a greedy horndog, so it's absolutely not."

They spent dawn having sex. Will was surprised by his own libido, but a few touches from Lennox brought back everything he'd seemingly forgotten. He hadn't thought of sex once since they'd parted, not carnally, yet now he couldn't believe he'd gone weeks without.

By early afternoon, however, they were both worn out. The sheets were damp with sweat and musk. Will's skin felt sticky, and his lower back ached from moving his hips. Lennox nibbled on his earlobe like the brush of a butterfly's wing.

"We should probably eat something." Lennox hummed and snuggled closer.

Someone knocked on the door. "Knock, knock, lovebirds. Is it safe to enter?"

Will pulled the blankets over their hips as Lennox sat up. He glanced at Will for an answer, and Will nodded.

"Get your ass in here."

Troy entered, jacket slung over his shoulder and hair a wild hive. He grinned at them and went to his side of the room. "Sorry to interrupt. Needed to stop by and get my violin. Never know when you're going to need it, right?" He grabbed a case from the pile beside his bed.

"We're about to get something to eat," Lennox said. "Wanna join us? This is Will, by the way."

"Figured that much out myself since you're naked in bed together." Troy waved at them. "I'm Troy Nguyen."

"Nice to meet you."

"Likewise. So you two thinking brunch? Lunch? There's this sweet pho spot a few blocks over we could hit up."

Will had no idea what pho was, but they all agreed to go. Walking the city with a group was a new experience. For weeks, he'd been stumbling along by himself, getting confused in crowds and turned around by his own swirling thoughts and lackluster sense of direction. Yet with Lennox and Troy, the blocks made sense; their easy conversation was a balm for his unrest. Lennox's life was peaceful. That was all Will had wished for since he'd first known him.

But the sights and sounds and friendship carved into Will's chest. How come he hadn't found this yet? And why did the vision of Lennox's happiness here dig into his heart to a depth he hadn't realized was there?

..ıll nine

SAYING GOODBYE TO WILL ON Sunday was hard. Lennox walked him to his bus, sat with him until the last moment, and waited for the same anxiety he'd carried to Boston two weeks ago. It didn't come. Seeing Will step out of his physical life again was difficult, but it didn't crush his insides with a sledge hammer as it had before.

He had plans with Lucy for the afternoon. He had dinner with Alex, Sadia, Ava, and Troy to look forward to as well. Lennox was okay, better than okay. The last time he'd felt this carefree was before Will, before his mother died, before he'd left his sister against his will.

Lucy's apartment was a perpetual junk pile. She kicked an overflowing bucket of recycling out of the way and dumped a stack of magazines onto the floor so he could sit with her on the couch.

"I can't believe you didn't let me see Will while he was here." She stuck her stinky foot in his face and handed him a Wii remote.

They started a game of Mario Kart. Lucy was quick to pick the Bowser character, and Lennox flicked back and forth between the mushroom-headed Toad and Princess Peach. He selected Toad.

"We were busy, like, all of Friday night and Saturday morning. Giving our dicks some exercise, you know. Then he wanted to go to a White Sox game."

"Red Sox. Jesus, Lennox, don't let the locals hear you make that mistake. They'll castrate you."

"Will'd never let them." Lennox shoulder-checked her and sent Bowser careening into a wall. "It was nice to see him."

Lucy bumped him back, and they both spiraled off the track. She glanced at him while their characters were fished out of the chasm.

"Nice to see him," she mimicked. "You make it sound like it wasn't a big deal to see him after weeks."

"What? I mean, it felt different, but not like that."

Their race continued, bananas flying and red shells beeping. Neither of them spoke until Lucy zoomed over the finish line by blasting him with another shell inches from a first-place finish.

"Different how? You don't love him as much?"

"I still love him the same, maybe more. That's not what I mean. It's— I don't know." Lennox set his controller down, even as Lucy queued up another race. "My life has been in a shamble for, like, a fucking decade. I've had nothing. Just my sister and then only myself. I shut everything out and shut everything inside of me off. He reminded me of why I shouldn't. But I never felt like I had anything to show him or teach him. And now I do. He sees me differently now that I'm here. Does that make sense?"

Lucy nodded. "I think so. You're both growing up, building lives without each other in a lot of ways."

Lennox twirled his remote's wrist cord between his fingers. "I'm scared by how excited I am."

"I was, too, when I first got here."

"It's not *starting* a new life that scares me." Lennox shook his head and clutched his knees to stop his hands from shaking. He didn't know *what* it was. Maybe it was the thrill of finding a world that welcomed everything he was and built his potential into something greater. Maybe it was the knowledge that this time he was the only person who could take this all away. No, he wouldn't self-sabotage, not this time.

"Everything's too perfect and it's terrifying?"

Lennox shrugged. That was closer.

"Maybe it's good you've got such low expectations of perfect," Lucy said. She messed up his hair and smiled. "Might help Will drop his a bit."

"What do you mean?"

Lucy frowned as if she'd said too much. She didn't speak.

"Spit it out."

"It's just something I talked about with Will. When you guys visited in the spring. It's nothing."

"Bullshit! What?"

Lucy scrolled through the list of available races. "So how about Rainbow Road? We can burn up in the atmosphere. Hey!"

Lennox held her control out of reach. "Tell me."

"Look, he was just worried about you. About both of you."

Lennox stared at her until she elaborated. "Fuck, okay. He was scared about what might happen when you weren't, like, relying on him so much anymore. If you two would be okay."

"That's it?" Lennox laughed. "But that's good, isn't it? Takes some of the worry and weight off him if I'm not dragging him down so much."

"Yeah, I suppose." Lucy took back her control. She forced his own back into his hand. "Come on, let's see how many times I can lap you."

Her abrupt shift made Lennox pause the conversation in his mind. Even as the next race began and Lucy slammed her Bowser kart into his Toad, he hesitated to ask more. She hadn't seemed very confident in that answer. If anything, she'd seemed more concerned by his own response.

Lennox left with a weight on the back of his neck he'd forgotten since Berklee had captured him in its musical fantasy. He couldn't explain it. What was there to dread right now?

College was going great. He'd made a few friends. His classes were wonderful. Dr. Austin was teaching him so much more than he'd realized he needed to know. He and Will were still in love and happy together. So much of his life was happy, but maybe that was right. After everything else he'd endured, maybe he did deserve this chance.

* * *

LENNOX HEARD FROM KAREN AND Ben before he spoke to Will again. They called him Tuesday evening while he was holed up in a practice room across campus. He almost didn't pick up the call. Building a relationship with Karen and Ben—Will's parents—was weird. Were they friends? Did they have a parent-child relationship? Was it that unnamable relationship between a person's significant other and their parents?

"Hello?"

Karen's smile was apparent from her voice. She made him stammer through everything about his first few weeks and insisted on hearing about classes and friends and the city. For once she didn't chide him when he cursed every four words. Maybe they had an odd-aunt and nephew relationship, like what he'd seen between Will and his Aunt Mia.

"So, how's, uh, Virginia? And, um, Oyster?"

Karen sighed. "Quiet without you two. I think Ben's in mourning. It's been hard on him, letting go of Will, but he's adjusting. It's easier for me. Oyster's miserable between all the rain we've been getting and you two being gone. He's slept on Will's bed every night since you guys left."

"What a bum." Lennox leaned back against the wall and pressed random keys on the piano. "Will came up last weekend."

Karen asked about that, too. Lennox felt as though he was drowning. He'd never done this before—held a phone conversation about his own life. Why did she care so much about him now that he was on his own? He wasn't her kid. Not like Will.

"Did you two leave the room at all?"

"Had to eat some time." When Karen didn't immediately respond, Lennox prattled on to help his jitters. "Went to lunch with my roommate. Saw a baseball game. A day in the city. Fun stuff."

"That's good. I'm glad you're doing well. We've been worried since we haven't heard from you," Karen said. "I know it's weird, you and me and Ben. We care about you, though. You aren't just Will's boyfriend or some kid who lived with us for a few months. I count you as part of our little hodge-podge family, okay? That order to call home once a week meant you, too."

Karen passed him off to Ben after he agreed to call once a week. Ben's conversation was shorter and more about if he'd been shaving and what music he was learning. That was easier by far. They hung up after another ten minutes, and Lennox went back to his room. Troy was climbing into bed when he arrived.

"Ava stopped by. Something about coloring her hair? I think Alex is responsible."

Lennox tossed his backpack onto his desk and stripped to his boxers. "Alex's hair *is* about eight different colors."

"Yeah, well, if you join in be careful. They'll convince you that you need, like..." Troy waved his hands around as Lennox got into bed. "...a pterodactyl buzzed into your scalp."

As Troy made screeching dinosaur noises across the room, Lennox chuckled and rolled toward him. He'd never imagined friendships like the ones he'd been making. Everything about his life had been void of other people for so long. Sure, he'd met Otto last year, but that relationship was different from the atmosphere at Berklee. They'd met in hardship. Same with Lucy. Even his relationship with Will had begun on a foundation of anguish and heartache.

"Watch them like hawks if you go, that's all I'm saying."

Troy turned off his desk light and snuggled into his bed. Lennox lay awake, watching his back and then the flicker of the streetlamp outside the window.

* * *

TROY WAS RIGHT ABOUT THE hair dye. After classes and lunch on Friday, he followed Ava to Alex's place. Alex, Sadia, and a few other women Lennox hadn't met lived in a house a few blocks off campus.

It was an older row house with rounded bay windows, a small porch, and crooked shutters.

Ava swung her bag of hair bleach and dye the entire way. "You should dye yours."

"No."

"But you'd be so cute with rainbow curls. And Alex can cut your hair, too. It's pretty long."

"I like it as long as my boyfriend's dick."

Ava snickered as they stomped up the porch steps of Alex's house. She knocked and they were hurried inside by Alex, who already had her hair smothered in hair bleach and a plastic cap. Lennox's eyes watered at the smell.

He sat on the edge of the bathtub while Alex helped Ava mix her own bleach and then brush it into her hair. By the time they were both covered in caps, Lennox was convinced they had straw growing out of their scalps and told them as much.

"Don't be a jealous piss-baby." Ava stuck her tongue out at him.

"Why would burning nostrils make me jealous?"

Alex pinched his cheek hard. "Come on, have some hair-dyeing fun. That's what college is all about."

Lennox glowered at her. "What? Rainbow hair dye?"

"We've still got some left," Ava said, wafting the smell from the container toward him. Lennox grimaced. "Not too late to join."

"Ugh."

"We've got every color of the rainbow for you to try."

Alex pulled out bottle after bottle, and Lennox turned his nose up at them until...

"What about bubblegum pink? You'd rock some pink streaks in your curls."

His eyes flickered to the bottle, and that was all it took. Ava and Alex had him convinced in less than five minutes. Alex painted random curls with the bleach, carefully separating them from the rest. He stopped her when she started on the ones around his ears.

"Don't. Gonna cut that soon."

She did that for him, too. While they all waited for the bleach to burn their skin, Alex buzzed the sides of his head and up the back, fading into the longer curls left up top. Troy was going to roll his eyes so hard.

Two hours later, Lennox went back to his room. Troy did roll his eyes, but he whistled and climbed onto his desk chair. He tugged Lennox over to examine his new pink curls mixed in with the brown.

"I mean, I warned you, but it looks good. Alex should quit music and dye hair professionally. Damn."

Troy tugged at a curl, and Lennox winced.

"What? You don't like it?"

Lennox stared into the mirror Troy handed him, and the truth was, he did like it—a lot. The cut looked wonderful on him, and the pink wasn't too much. Yet he still hesitated before answering. "I mean, I like it, but I don't know. It stands out."

"What's wrong with that? Half the campus has crazy hair."

Lennox set the mirror down and didn't say anything. He couldn't really explain it. Dyeing his hair had seemed too expensive in high school. It wasn't like his piercings. Half of those he'd done himself, and the rest, well, juvenile detention centers offered many souvenirs.

"You okay?"

Lennox startled when Troy's hand touched his shoulder.

"Lennox?"

He stepped away, stumbled, and fell back into his desk chair.

Troy didn't come closer, but he watched him with concern. "I'm sure Alex can change it back."

Lennox shook his head. He shook his entire upper body until the echo of old jitters and pangs faded. He took a deep breath, then a second, a third. Troy wasn't looking at him as if he was scared of him, but Lennox couldn't stand the pity and uncertainty he saw there either.

He couldn't explain himself. Not to Troy. Not to anyone here. They couldn't know about all of that—all the negatives from his life. Berklee was bright and cheerful; a stellar universe fantastic and new.

Lennox ran across campus and down streets and only stopped when he reached the waterfront. His lungs heaved in the crisp autumn air. He didn't know where he was—a park by the water. The sun was a ruby-red taint on the sky behind him. He found a spot along the rocky shore and sat. His sweatshirt stuck to his back. He tried to control his breathing and couldn't. Lennox crossed his arms over his knees and pressed his forehead against them. He flicked his tongue against his teeth as he had for so many years, but the clinks of his old tongue ring didn't follow. Over the summer, he'd taken it out, left one reminder behind.

Only Will understood that. Lennox had never given him the full story. He thought of calling Will. Then Lucy. Karen. Even Otto or Ben. Someone from that darker reality he'd forgotten to leave behind. His hands were digging through his pockets before he remembered he no longer owned a pack of cigarettes. If he'd brought his wallet he might have remedied that.

Instead he sat and watched the ruby sun set over the city's skyline. Lennox thought, tugged gently at a few pink curls of hair. He did like it, and somehow that worried him; it reminded him of the hole still closing in his tongue.

..ıll ten

OCTOBER BEGAN MUCH AS SEPTEMBER had. Will's classes were still wreckage on his daily landscape. He'd failed his first math exam, even with help from Lennox. His history class was ripping apart all he'd ever been taught about American history. Worst of all though, was his journalism class. After a month, they continued to talk about news in ways Will didn't understand. Professor Bates handed back their first assignment, a mock-investigative article, and Will was horrified by the D- scrawled under his conclusion on the last page.

"How'd you do?" The woman who always sat beside him leaned over.

Will rolled his paper up before she could see. His face must have given him away, though. She nodded and showed him her own D with a ribbon of comments below.

"Yeah, me, too. Can you read his handwriting at all?"

Will flipped to the last page of his paper and glanced at the same swirly ribbons.

"No."

"Whatever, I'm dropping this."

She left, and Will sat there as the students around him whispered about their own papers and headed for the exits. Will flipped through each page, but they were all blank except for his own typed words. The only comments were at the end—three short, illegible lines. He waited until the most of the class had left before walking down the steps to the front of the lecture hall.

"Professor Bates? I had a question about my paper."

Professor Bates was close to his father's age, eighty-percent bald but pretending otherwise. Will eyed his comb-over. It looked like the lines of one of Lennox's music staffs.

"Questions are for office hours."

"Okay, I just wanted to know what your comments say. I can't make out your handwriting."

Professor Bates brushed past him for the door. "Come to office hours. They're posted outside my door."

Will stared after him, his D- paper still in hand. Fuming, he shoved it into his backpack and left through a different door. All he wanted was the comments read. It wasn't his fault the man's writing imitated chicken tracks.

He ended up on a subway train going north. Thankful that the car was almost deserted for once, Will slammed his backpack down on an empty seat. Instead of getting off at the next stop and taking a train back to his dorm—and Jackson's throbbing headache of video games—Will continued north to a stop at Central Park.

After a lap around half the park, Will stopped at a pond to catch his breath. Central Park was an island in the miserable stench of the New York streets. He missed the clean air of his country home in Virginia and the warm weight of Oyster leaping into his arms to play and snuggle. He missed *Dumpsters*. What he wouldn't give to see someone toss their trash in a Dumpster instead of onto the sidewalk!

Will took his phone out, then stopped. Lennox couldn't help him with this one. He didn't want to worry his dad either, and Karen would tell Ben. None of his Virginia friends would have any answers either. Just last week Roxanne had boasted about her stellar first grades, Natasha had faded from contact, and Aaron was as busy as ever with baseball.

Aunt Mia picked up on the first ring. "Are you lost again? Because I definitely can't help you navigate New York."

"No, just wanted to talk." Will grimaced and dug his paper out of his backpack. He watched an electronic boat zip past. "How's Pittsburgh?"

"Cold as ass, but delightful otherwise. Got a date with Victoria again in a few hours."

"Was she the banker or the ex-surfer?"

"BMX, not surfing. We're going to the gym."

Will snorted. "You call that a date?"

"You will when you're my age. So how's New York treating you?"

He stopped laughing then. Aunt Mia hummed on her end of the phone.

"About the same, I guess."

"What about those kids you were hanging out with? Meeting anyone else?"

"Oh, they're fine, yeah. I tried going to that LGBTQ group, but..." Will swallowed and shook his head. "...I didn't feel like I fit in there. I got my first paper back for journalism."

"I bet you could find groups off-campus to try. Maybe a local baseball program. How'd you do on your paper?"

Will hesitated.

"That bad, huh?"

"No! I mean, I got a D-, but I can't even *read* what my professor wrote, and he wouldn't tell me what it said. Just to go to his stupid office hours."

"Ouch. First papers are like that. FaceTime me; maybe I can read it. My own handwriting is absolute shit."

They switched their call to FaceTime, and Aunt Mia's freckled face beamed at him. Will showed her the squiggles on his paper, and she huffed.

"Constant... dinosaur... pentagon. Yeah, I have no idea, I just wanted to see your charming face. Turn me around!"

Will did as she asked, and her smile fell once she got a good look at him.

"You look awful, kid. New York really treating you that bad?"

Will shrugged. He didn't have any concrete answer for that question these days. He'd been in love with the idea of New York City for so long, but being here was different. It was floods of people and trash piles on the streets and harrowing subway rides that left him disoriented. It was grungy steel walls and only two, very distant friends.

He told her all of that and then some. Every bit of hurt and anger came pouring out of him: the anti-gay comments from his new friends, the anger at what his professor was teaching on top of his falling grades. The only thing he couldn't bear to mention was the jealousy he felt when he listened to Lennox talk about his new, wonderful life in Boston. That wasn't fair to Lennox. After everything Lennox had been through, he deserved a better life. Will wouldn't make him feel guilty for that.

"I told you it's going to be rough, but—and hear me out on this, okay? Maybe you should apply to Sarah Lawrence again. Or a smaller school." Aunt Mia sighed and what sounded like a chip bag crinkled. "Going from rural Virginia to New York City? That's a huge jump, Will. Maybe you should take a half-step back and try something smaller first."

"But I've wanted New York for so long," Will said. "Ever since I was a kid and Karen first told me all about it."

"Yeah, and ten years on, it's still here. New York will still be there waiting five years from now, too." When Will started to argue, Aunt Mia cut him off. "Look, just consider it. New York can still be a goal, but really think about what you want from your college years. Smaller classes, more hands-on time with professors and classmates, or the huge classes you have right now. Not everyone does well in giant lecture halls."

Will left Aunt Mia to her gym date. He sat in the park for a long time, considering her words and all that had happened during his first six weeks of college. The city was too much. That was true, but he'd figure it out. He'd never given up on Lennox, and he wouldn't give up on New York, either.

* * *

PROFESSOR BATES' OFFICE HOURS WERE sparse and full. Will signed up for the first time he could swing—a ten-minute session after fall recess. He made his numb way through the rest of his week with only the excitement of Lennox's long weekend visit to keep him going.

"Did you finish that math problem, Will?"

Will snarled at Lennox's face on their Skype call. He scratched out his third attempt at the same math problem in his notebook. It was Wednesday night before their fall recesses. He was just glad their recesses overlapped. Aaron and Natasha both had theirs the following week. Roxanne didn't have one at all.

"No. I mean, I've *finished* it three times, but you keep telling me it's wrong."

"When's that assignment due?"

Will sighed and shut his book. "Next week. My math class is cancelled on Friday. All I have is journalism and I'm starting to hate that class."

"Isn't that your major?"

Will shrugged. He wasn't sure he wanted to study it anymore, not if it meant more of Professor Bates and sensationalist news instead of real journalism.

"I might change it. I don't know. What Bates is teaching isn't what I thought journalism would be about."

"What do you mean?" In the background, Will heard Troy on his saxophone.

"Like, it feels like law school. All we talk about is ethics and rights and what we can and can't do. Laws and laws and more laws. It's not fun like writing articles for the newspaper in high school was.

Everything's about laws and restrictions. I don't care about the history parts. I just want to write."

"Sounds like you got a moldy professor."

Will laughed. "Moldy?"

"Gross, you know. What are you thinking of changing to? Creative writing? Going to write me some smoldering porn?"

"No. I'm not sure what else I might be interested in besides writing baseball articles. Definitely not math." He shoved his book off his desk and to the floor. "Aunt Mia said I should consider other options, like trying Sarah Lawrence again."

"Well, you did like it better than NYU."

Will nodded as sirens wailed on the street below, echoed off the buildings and then faded slowly. His head throbbed at the cacophony. "They never gave me an answer. It's like they got my application, thought it was a joke, and tossed it."

"I doubt that's true. You're fucking fantastic."

"That's how it seemed."

Will picked up his laptop and carried it to his bed. Lennox made a face at Jackson's back, but for once Jackson's gaming was quiet. He still had his headphones on, but, as some magical spell swept the screen, all was silent in their room.

"I really want New York to work," Will confessed. "I don't know what else to do."

"You mean besides me?"

Will rolled his eyes and curled up under his blankets. He pulled them over his head, hiding himself and Lennox from view.

"Look, I can't tell you that you should stay or leave or what major to pick, but you don't seem happy, not like you were in Virginia."

Will frowned. Now that Lennox had said it, it seemed obvious. His happiness had dimmed since he'd arrived in the city, while Lennox's had only grown brighter. Was he going to be confined to a small-town life? The very thought made him queasy.

"I'll call Sarah Lawrence tomorrow. See what became of my application."

"Cool. I'll see you after that. Should be there around seven." Lennox flexed on screen for him. "You ready for me?"

"Ha, never, you dork. I love you."

"Love you too."

WILL HOLED UP IN HIS room once his classes were finished for the day. He spent almost an hour convincing himself to search for Sarah Lawrence's admissions office phone number and then another twenty minutes to call. Part of him didn't want to know the answer. If they'd gotten his application and rejected him, then he was stuck—stuck in New York City where he longed to feel at home, but felt more like an outsider every day.

"Thank you for calling Sarah Lawrence admissions office. This is Annabelle; how can I help you?"

Will swallowed. He almost hung up. "Hi, I'm calling about an application I submitted."

"Okay, what term was it for?"

"The current one," Will said before rushing ahead. "I never received any sort of response."

"And after you applied you received a confirmation email that the application was successfully submitted?"

Will pulled up the email on his computer and gave her the confirmation number, then his name. While she looked everything up, Will paced his room. Jackson wasn't there for once. It was a relief not to have him whooping in the background, even though his sweaty, Cheetos stench hung in the air and had saturated every piece of fabric in the room. Will shoved the window up to let the cold air in.

"Okay, Mr. Osborne, it looks as though everything processed and your application was accepted. Unfortunately, since the semester has already begun, you'll need to reapply if you wish to attend Sarah Lawrence."

"I got in?"

"Yes, you did. It's uncommon for acceptance letters to get lost in the mail, but it does happen. Is the following address correct?"

A hollow numbness spread through his body. Will sank onto his bed. Annabelle read out an address—the wrong address—and repeated her question.

"Mr. Osborne?"

"That's—no, that's not my address. I've never heard of Walborn Avenue."

On autopilot, he gave her the right address, then listened with dead ears to her talking. He could reapply. The spring semester deadline was in November. She could submit his application from the one already in their system.

Sarah Lawrence had accepted him. Yet here he was, fumbling along New York City streets as if he'd never been taught to walk.

"I'll think about it," Will said at her prompting.

"Okay, just make sure you submit your application by the fifteenth if you decide to apply for the spring. We look forward to having you join our community."

Will hung up; his phone slid right out of his hand. His arms shook. How could he have messed up the address? Had their system glitched? Even then, if he did reapply, what would he study? His one journalism class had sucked all the enthusiasm out of him. Nothing else seemed any better.

Will left to meet Lennox. The city was damp and cold. Rain splattered the ground and poured down the steps at the subway station. Will picked the correct train for once and emerged just up the block from the bus stop. He stood inside the station entrance and texted Lennox to meet him there.

Lennox appeared with a shower of rain and that goofy grin that increased in brightness every time they spoke. A pang of anger shot through Will at that smile—at how much Lennox had grown while he stalled out. Will tried to shake off the feeling.

"Hey, handsome. You waiting for someone, because you are—"

"I don't even want to know how you're going to finish that." Will accepted a warm kiss that billowed hot breath onto his face. "Hi."

Lennox found his hand and squeezed. "Did you call Sarah Lawrence?"

Will nodded as they walked down to the subway. Lennox pestered him while he purchased a subway pass and then as they piled into a car with the rest of the city.

"Well? What did they say? Are our trips about to get more complicated or—"

"I got in. They accepted me and mailed the damn letter to some address that doesn't exist, and I don't know. Okay? I just don't know."

Will ignored Lennox's surprised face and rested his forehead against the pole he'd wrapped his arms around. He'd much rather hold on to Lennox, but right now he could barely look at his boyfriend. Frothing anger simmered in his belly.

They made it back to his dorm without another word. Lennox took his hand, but Will couldn't bring himself to hold on very tight. As Lennox set his backpack down, he caught Will by the shoulder.

"What's up?"

"The ceiling. Probably caked in Cheetos powder like everything else in here."

Will sat at his desk. He still couldn't bring himself to look at Lennox. He couldn't explain why. Just a glance made his stomach knot with anger.

"No, don't be an ass. You're not yourself."

"I'm always myself," Will said, his eyes on his desk. "Hard to be anyone else."

Lennox stayed quiet, unzipped his jacket, and toed his sneakers off. "Look, I don't want to argue, but are you mad at me for something?"

The truth stuck in Will's throat. He was and he wasn't. Lennox was peppy and happy and that same untamable avalanche he'd been a year ago. All at once Lennox was everything and nothing, and it made Will feel skinned and exposed.

"Will?" His bed creaked as Lennox sat down. "For fuck's sake, at least look at me. If you're pissed at me, then fucking tell me why."

Will shot up. A rage he couldn't explain filled him. Just the sight of Lennox—with his adorable pink curls, his bright hazel eyes, that same luminous smile—made him furious.

"Pissed? Why would I be pissed at you, huh? How could I *possibly* be mad at you? With your stupid college where you're making all your fucking friends. And the classes you're acing, and everything just falling into place like you've been working at all of this since you were a kid. Why would *any* of that piss me off?"

Lennox stared at him. Regret cut through Will, but he stamped it down at the fierce look Lennox leveled at him.

"You pushed me to do all of that, dick breath. I get you aren't having an easy time here, but don't blame me for that. I spent all summer telling you to worry about your damn self instead of me so—"

"Whatever. *Move.*"

Will shoved past Lennox's outstretched arm and slammed his door behind him.

..ıll eleven

Lennox sat in Will's room for over an hour. Will didn't return. His insides ached as he ran over their argument again and again. He shouldn't have risen to the bait. The moment he'd met Will it had been clear something was wrong. Will had been cold but for that one kiss. None of his usual bubbling light had greeted Lennox. Nothing happy had come from Will at all.

Lennox tucked his feet back into his shoes and grabbed his phone. He hadn't explored much of Will's dorm. On his last visit, he'd spent the weekend between Will's room and the occasional trip to the bathroom down the hall. Still he searched. Door after door passed by as he walked. He checked the bathroom, but everything on the hall was quiet. Lennox went back to the staircase and checked the other two halls off their landing.

He found Will in the second one, curled up at a wobbly desk in a small study room.

"Will?"

Will sniffed and rubbed his nose along his sleeve.

"Come back to your room," Lennox said. He rested his hands gently on Will's shoulders and then massaged at the tension when Will didn't pull away. "Come to bed and we can talk."

"I'm an asshole." Will wiped his eyes with his snot-trailed sleeve.

"So am I. It's why we work, now come on. Let's go get comfy and talk about this."

Lennox led Will back to his dorm room. Darkness swallowed them as the door shut behind them. Will went right to his wardrobe, opened it, dug through his clothes, and kept wiping at his nose and eyes. His eyes were puffy, lined red from his tears. Lennox climbed into the bed and watched him.

"I'm sorry." Will peered around the wardrobe door, but still didn't make eye contact. He pulled his sweatshirt off and traded it for a thermal shirt.

"I'm sorry, too." And Lennox meant it. Mostly. He was sorry for rising to Will's cruel bait and sorry that nothing Will had wanted or expected from college had happened so far. Will climbed into bed and settled into Lennox's arms, but his torso was rigid.

"I'm not mad," Lennox told him. He wrapped his arms tight around Will's body and held him. "Relax, we're fine. I'm here. Nothing between us has changed."

Lennox felt Will go limp against him as he mulled over his own words. What else did Will have to ground him besides this? His classes were terrible, and he was failing half of them. So far his only friends hadn't amounted to much. His attempts to connect with others had been met with derision and laughter. And New York— that sunrise Will had chased for almost a decade—was a sunset, still sinking past the rim of the earth.

"I didn't mean it. About how you shouldn't be happy and doing well at Berklee. I'm just... this is a lot harder than I thought it'd be. And, sometimes, seeing you doing so well makes me feel like I'm a big failure."

"You aren't," Lennox said and he made Will twist to look at him. "You just picked the wrong school. Just like what you told me about people going through a bunch of majors. Sometimes you have to experience it to know it's not right."

Will shook his head. "I want to be here. I *do*. New York has been my dream forever, and if I can't handle it, then..."

"Then what?"

"I don't know. What good are dreams if I pick ones that are too much for me? I'm just a stupid country boy from some hick town who won't ever make it in the city. So what if Sarah Lawrence accepted me? It'd be just as bad there. I'd be so close to New York that I'd still feel like I'd failed because I didn't make it here."

Lennox brushed Will's hair with his fingers and let him curl into his chest. Dreams were such an odd phenomenon. His own little fantasies were new—putting together college bands, playing a solo at a campus concert, maybe joining a symphony or rocking out for a roaring, moshing crowd. For most of his life he'd never made time for them. The dreams he'd dared to think up as a kid had become tattered and worthless. His dad's drinking had seen to that.

"Maybe you have to work at this one in a different way," Lennox said. "Build up to it before you're ready for New York. Or shelve it like you did with your box back at home."

"I've run out of dreams to shove in that stupid box. I don't feel like my life is going anywhere or doing anything, but I don't know what to want besides this right now."

"Take a semester off. Or focus on your friends and finding better ones. Just take your core classes for now until you think of another major to try."

Will shrugged. "I'm sorry."

"You already said that."

"I know, but I feel like I need to keep saying it. I'm just jealous. I didn't mean it."

"Course you did. If you hadn't meant it in some way, then you wouldn't have said it. It's fine. Everything has been easier for me. You're right. It's been so close to perfect it terrifies me."

Lennox kissed his forehead. Will squeezed him tight and shivered. Beyond words, Lennox didn't know how to help him. After all that Will had done for him, he'd give anything to make his life happier, to make sure that he returned all the caring and encouragement and commitment that Will had given to him.

* * *

THEIR LONG WEEKEND TOGETHER WAS happier after that. Every day, Will's spirits seemed to rise. Without homework or classes or that nasty gamer roommate of his, Lennox watched Will transform back into the boy he'd come to New York with. His smile blossomed as they joked about the billboards in Times Square. His eyes glowed when they rented a paddle boat at a pond in Central Park. Will's laughter was louder and truer with every meal they ate.

Yet, Lennox found Will's joyful transformation to be unsettling. He'd missed this bold, shining boy; he'd ached for him during their weeks apart and yet… Will was still Will, and somehow that seemed wrong.

"No, no, no, let's play Zombie Dice." Back in his room, Will handed him the cardboard cylinder complete with artsy zombies drawn on the outside. "It's quick and fun."

Lennox agreed to the game Will had picked out at a shop in Brooklyn. The day had been Will's first true adventure outside of Manhattan. They'd gone into bookshops and bakeries. They'd eaten breakfast at a Russian pastry shop, and then had a late lunch at a Vietnamese place that shook and rumbled as subway trains passed underneath. Will's enthusiasm brought Lennox right back to Virginia, to shifting through stacks of movies in Will's living room or listening to Will gently explain baseball statistics and positions.

They managed to play two rounds of the game before Lennox had Will's shirt on the floor. He'd done his best to treat it like a stripping game, much to Will's chagrin. All weekend they'd avoided sex. At least, it had seemed like avoidance to Lennox. He expected part of the reason was their argument, but a lot more of it seemed to be Will's mood.

"Let me have you once before I go back," Lennox said as he pressed Will onto the floor and kissed his neck. "Three weeks is even longer when you double it."

Will stopped laughing. He nudged Lennox off of him and scratched at his chest.

"What?"

"Can we not talk about tomorrow? I don't want to think about you leaving again."

"Okay, I'm sorry." Lennox kissed his cheek, then his neck. Will leaned into him, but the happiness Lennox had stoked so carefully all weekend had dropped. Like a punctured balloon, Will was falling into a dozen pieces.

"Let me make love to you all night and all day tomorrow. I'll stay here, with you."

Will was pliant and accepting as they made their way to his rumpled bed. Lennox craved his affection, wanted nothing more than the happiness they'd shared for so long, even if that meant he *was* that happiness. Will had been that for him for a while, and he could do the same.

As the city night came to life around them, the low rumble drifted up to Will's closed window. Lennox removed Will's clothes and trailed kisses over every freshly revealed inch of skin. He took his time to build ecstasy. Will panted into his kisses and shook as their bodies rocked together. Sweat freckled his skin like stardust, and Lennox kissed that, too. He kissed him as if he could draw the fear and loneliness and despair right through his lips and into himself.

Lennox held Will as he slept and watched the fluttering of his eyelashes and the part in his lips. Will deserved the world—however and wherever he chose to make it his own. He couldn't give Will that, not every moment or memory, not the conversations or the tentative starts of friendships Will hadn't forged. But he could be here more for Will. Somehow, Lennox would help make that happen, even if it meant giving up part of his own world.

TOO SOON, SUNDAY MORNING ARRIVED. Despite Lennox's assurances that he could stay one more day, he was ushered to his bus at midday. Will gave him his best-worst smile as they parted. Lennox climbed onto his bus and watched until Will was out of sight. His stomach clenched and gurgled. His love for Will still felt right, and nothing about leaving him did.

Lennox spent his bus ride with his headphones on while he worked through one of his music notation assignments. Boston greeted him with a cloudy, charcoal sky and slow, fat raindrops. He hurried to campus to beat the storm and got drenched.

Troy was easing his way through a new cello piece when Lennox stumbled in.

"If you want to be Aquaman for Halloween, they have drier costumes."

"Shut up."

Lennox grimaced and hung his damp backpack on his desk chair. He pulled his leather jacket off and hung it on his wardrobe door and then peeled his shirt off too. Even his underwear and socks were soaked. Lennox found his warmest sweatshirt and pajama pants in his backpack. After he'd pulled the sweatshirt on, he realized it was Will's. He'd left it during his last visit.

"It's too fucking cold for rain."

Troy hummed the tune he was trying to play and marked something on his sheet music. "You'll get used to it. It's not even real winter yet. This is nothing."

"Yeah, but winter means snow instead of icy-ass rain."

Lennox curled up under his blankets and breathed in the scent of Will's cologne that still lingered on his sweatshirt. He missed him already. Yet it was bearable in a way Will's yearning for him didn't seem to be. He considered calling Karen for advice. She was older and had probably been through difficulties in relationships before. Her advice might help them, but calling Will's mom—particularly when Lennox didn't know how much she knew about Will's hardships—was stupid. He couldn't break Will's confidence like that.

"Hey, Troy?"

"Yeah? Hey, could you play this measure on the piano for me? Like, I *think* I've got it right, but it just feels off."

"I'll trade you that for some advice."

Troy set his bow down and, even as he collected his sheet music and handed it to Lennox, he seemed to realize something major was going on.

"You okay? You and Will manage to leave his room this weekend?"

"Yes. No. Both." Lennox skimmed the sheet he'd been handed to where Troy's heart marks ended. "I mean, I'm fine. It's Will mostly. He's having an awful time in New York. His classes are shit, and he's got almost no friends. I don't think he leaves his dorm except for class. He's scared to go out and explore because he's worried he'll get lost."

Troy nodded. "Is he thinking of trying a different school?"

"Maybe. The one he really wanted never answered him, and when he called them last week he found out he'd gotten in."

"Ouch. That blows, dude. I mean, I applied for Julliard in New York City. I got waitlisted. Same with a school in California. It hurt, you know? But then I came here and I don't regret it for a minute."

Lennox shrugged. "I want to help him, but I don't know what to do. He's been there for me so much since we met, and I want to do the same for him now."

"Honestly? I don't know that there's much else you can do. You can be there to listen and to bounce ideas off, but it's his life. You can't make any of the decisions he needs to make for him. All you can do is support him and help him find new interests, or help him look into different schools he might like."

Lennox frowned. That wasn't the answer he'd wanted to hear. Yet wasn't that exactly what Will had done for him all last year?

"I just wish I could fix everything for him. He's so much happier when I'm there."

"Yeah, but your life is here now."

"I could visit more, though. See him every weekend instead of every two or three. Get him out into the city so he finds his city legs. That sort of thing."

"And what about the rest of the week? When are you going to practice if you're there all weekend?" Troy shook his head. "Look, you care about him a lot, I get that, but you can't split your life up like that. You can't let his happiness be that dependent on you, Lennox. That's insane. It's not healthy."

"We could make it work," Lennox said, but even as he spoke he felt the truth of Troy's words digging holes into his own. "Just a few months. If I can get him more comfortable there, then he'll start going out on his own. Come spring semester, he'll be fine."

"Who's he going out with? You won't be there. You *can't* be there every second and you can't make friends for him either. And, look," Troy said and he grabbed both of Lennox's hands until Lennox met his eyes, "you want to help him, but he's got to help himself too. You guys have hit that freshman mark."

"What the hell's that mean?"

"Half the people who go to college are dating someone. Everyone thinks they can make long distance work and that visiting helps, but eventually... a couple months and they've broken up. The longer it takes, the nastier it gets. People build new lives without each other, and it hurts to see how much your worlds don't connect anymore, how much you both can change so quickly. It happens."

"That's bullshit. Me and Will aren't like that. We've been through too much awful shit to call it quits because things are difficult for a while."

"Lennox, I'm not trying to—"

"No, fuck you, man." Lennox tossed Troy's sheet music at him. "And it's a fucking F sharp, not an F, dipshit."

Lennox tugged his blanket around his shoulders and left. He paced up and down the dorm halls. The halls were as silent as they always were on a Sunday evening. Most people were at dinner or taking advantage of open practice rooms across campus. Lennox ended up in the study room down the hall.

Rain continued to fall in kaleidoscopic curtains. If he'd kept his shoes on and the rain wasn't so icy, he'd have gone out and washed away every buzz of anger and spark of uncertainty and hurt. He was used to all of that, and yet every hurt seemed fresh and new, as if he was eight years old again with his knees and shins damp from kneeling and his pant legs stained with blood. The day his mother died had been a steady numbness, but the weeks and months that followed had felt like this: unsure, stressful, more about others in his life than himself, about Lucy, his father, now Will. He wouldn't lose him too.

He'd visit Will again this coming weekend. No matter what Troy said, if he was there for Will, then Will would find his feet again. Will wasn't comfortable in the city, and he was. He could sacrifice a few weekends of this first semester for Will. Giving up a small amount of what he'd gained—even temporarily—would help each of them in the end.

...ıl twelve

WEEKENDS BECAME A FAST SANCTUARY as October wore on. Will welcomed them in a way none of his classmates did. For them, weekends meant parties and drunken strolls through a massive city that wrapped each of them in their own collection of sights and smells and sounds. His weekends were defined by Lennox: the pair of them sharing a scarf as they walked Fifth Avenue; the coconut scent of Lennox's new body wash; the constant companionship and warmth of his love and friendship.

New York was wide open—until the weekend ended. Then New York thundered down on him as if he was caught in relentless ocean waves. Every strike for the surface shoved him farther down; his lungs shriveled in his chest. His classes washed his mornings out from under him. The torrential rains of October turned the buildings and sky a deep, unfriendly gray. Will sloshed his way through half-flooded subway staircases, longing for the snow at the foot of the Appalachians and for the warmth of Lennox's breath on his neck, tickling him awake on frosty mornings.

Halloween approached, but Will's excitement for costume ideas ended with Lennox's call to say he couldn't come that weekend. "Hey, hot stuff."

"Is that really the best nickname you've got for me?"

Lennox's laughter constricted Will's chest, even over the phone. "I could call you Mr. Big Dick."

"Ugh, no."

"Bubble Butt? Tented Sheets? Oh, Cum Bucket has a horrible, nasty ring to it."

Will rolled his eyes as he splashed across a crosswalk—another empty crosswalk because the rest of the crowd had kept going past the "don't walk" sign and into the empty street.

"If either of us could be nicknamed Cum Bucket it would certainly not be me."

"It would be the condoms." Several piano chords hummed over the line. "So, listen, I can't come this weekend. Ava needs a pianist to back her up. She's performing at the big Halloween party on Friday night, and I said I'd accompany her."

"Oh, that's great. I'm sure it'll be fun."

"Yeah, Troy's going to dress me up as a Disney character. Dr. Facilier? He's trying to get me to sing the guy's villain song, too, but I'm no singer."

His eyes burning, Will leaned against the nearest building. Listening to Lennox's life was such a tragic wonder sometimes. He was grateful. Truly it was wonderful to see Lennox thriving in his new life, but it started an ache as painful as horses trampling his chest.

"I figure I'll spend half the night playing instead of partying, *but* I thought maybe you could come up here if you don't have any other plans."

As a crowd of people went past, Will pressed himself harder into the building. He'd had plans—plans he'd built on Lennox being here for the third weekend in a row—brunches, a stroll through Central Park, and watching a Halloween parade that was being advertised all over campus.

"No, I've got plans. Big Halloween party this weekend with Jake and Tyra."

"Really? That's great. Have fun, yeah? I'll see you the weekend after. Got to come down there for some birthday sex."

Will nodded. Lennox's birthday. He'd forgotten that too. He'd been so distracted by trying to find one sliver of New York that made him feel at home. "I should get going. Got to, you know, figure out my costume and stuff. Love you."

"Love you too."

Will shoved his phone into his pocket and glared at the rain-speckled windows and at the dripping trees in the park across the street. The rain had stopped on his walk back to his dorm. A chilly wind whipped down the car-lined street.

He had no real reason to be mad at Lennox, and yet he was. It wasn't fair to expect Lennox to come see him every weekend. Will knew that. But he wanted Lennox here nonetheless. With Lennox at his side, the city didn't seem quite so daunting. The roads were like the halls of Eastern High; the buildings were like their old classrooms with this year's new batch of students. Nothing could worry him with Lennox by his side.

WILL TEXTED TYRA AND JAKE that evening. They met for dinner and Will was relieved to hear they had Halloween plans for Saturday night and that he was invited. He hadn't seen much of either of them since Lennox's weekly visits had started.

"It's a dance club," Tyra said. "Will, it is *so* cool. We even managed to get shots last time. They didn't bother checking I.D.s at all. They're having a Halloween party this weekend. Think we can finally drag you out with us?"

Jake shoved four tatter tots into his mouth. "It's going to be so lit, Will. You can't miss this one."

Will's plans brought giddiness back into his life. He spent that evening at a Halloween shop with Tyra, searching for a costume and rolling eyes at the cheap, bland outfits lining the shop's racks.

"I think I'll be the sexy pirate. Here, you can be the normal pirate."

Will frowned at the boring pirate outfit, but he went into a dressing room to try it on. The shoulders were too tight and the pants too short, but Tyra insisted he looked great. While she continued to search for alternatives from a sexy zombie to a sexy nurse, Will wandered the aisles. He noticed Frankenstein's monster, Beetlejuice, and several bulky Power Rangers costumes that looked more like

Transformers. At the back of the shop, next to the makeup kits and hair dyes, Will found a section of glamorous high heels, towering wigs, and a shelf of guides for drag queen makeup.

"Wow, Tyra, come check this out!"

Will lifted a wig onto his head and his knees bent from the weight. He glanced at himself in a nearby mirror and laughed. Lennox would kick him until his shins gave out, not because he would think Will looked idiotic, but because of how much taller he'd appear with a foot-tall wig on his head. He took the beehive wig off and tried on the rest. By the time, Tyra joined him with her chosen costume, Will was flipping through a book, and the wigs were back in place.

Tyra made a face at the pictures in the book he was reading. "It's weird, isn't it?" she said, misreading the wonder on his face. "Like, why would any man want to wear women's clothes? Do they even *make* them in your sizes?"

Will frowned and put the book down. He was dazzled by this corner of the shop. He itched to find something that fit and send a picture of himself in it to Lennox. Tyra dragged him up to the counter to pay and then led the way onto the street. Night had fallen as much as it ever did in the heart of Manhattan. The avenue was still crammed with taxis, and dozens of pedestrians filled the sidewalks.

"Like, it's weird," Tyra repeated as they walked to the nearest subway entrance. "I know I'm from middle-of-nowhere, Nebraska, but I can't believe they have that in a shop."

"It's not weird, it's as normal as everything else. The wigs were pretty cool. You'd never be able to do that with your real hair."

Tyra gave him a strange look. "Will, you wouldn't... do you like that stuff?"

"And if I do?"

Tyra didn't answer.

Certain the stop was two blocks to their right, Will followed when she led him down the correct stairs one block left and two down. They swiped their cards and walked down a flight of stairs to the tracks.

Tyra frowned the whole way, swinging her hair and shopping bag. "You're just messing with me, aren't you? I mean, you wouldn't *really* dress up like that, would you?"

Will was saved from answering by the squealing brakes of their train. Tyra departed for her own dorm once they were up on the street again. In his room, Will tried on his costume in front of his wardrobe mirror. It was nothing special, just a generic pirate outfit half the city would be sporting—good enough for a club. As he changed into his pajamas and got into bed, a line of drag queen wigs danced before him. They'd looked good on him, made him feel powerful in some still-unexplored corner of his mind. Jackson's video games thundered across the room. Will shut his eyes. He imagined the fierce makeup, the weight of those towering wigs, the stiff muscles of his calves as he strutted in those monstrous heels. He saw Lennox kneeling at his feet with his fingers inching toward the dainty panties snug over his throbbing cock...

Will glanced across the room; his upper body was as flushed as if he was boiling. He pulled his blankets over his head before dialing Lennox. "What would you do if I dropped out of college and became a drag queen?"

"Would you spank me while you fucked me?"

Will's flush deepened. He blamed the heavy air under the blanket. Lennox had asked that of him once, and Will had, grudgingly, agreed. He'd managed two weak pats on Lennox's bare butt before pulling out of the deal.

"You *know* how I feel about hitting you."

Lennox's eye roll was obvious from his tone. "I'm *asking* you too. It feels good in that context. So what brought this up? And just how hard are you right now?"

"What makes you say that?"

"Will, you're panting into the phone."

Will's flush burned hotter, and his dick twitched. He was aching. Seeing Lennox weekly had brought back his sex drive. He freed himself from his pajama pants and poked his head out to glance at Jackson, whose headset was sealed to his ears and who was facing away.

"I am not."

"Yeah, and now you're pouting and heavy breathing. Are we about to have phone sex? Because I'm sitting in a practice room that's got an entire wall of windows."

"Like that would ever stop you."

"If you're in the room with me? Definitely not. Sitting here looking like a lonely, horny asshole jizzing on the piano? I'll pass."

Will took his cock into his free hand anyway. "Then just help me get off. What are you wearing?"

"A Winnie the Pooh outfit."

"Lennox, come on, please."

"I'm just wearing my usual. Jeans, shirt, my jacket."

Will stroked his cock even as the heat in his stomach lessened. Nothing would make him happier than to have Lennox under him right now, on his stomach, ass in the air, groaning and panting for Will to fuck him deeper. Every desperate moan or lustful cry from Lennox made his body pulse with need.

"But *you*, you're outside my practice room," Lennox said slowly. "Decked out in your very first drag queen outfit. Your legs are so damn hot in heels, Will."

"Yeah? I, I look okay?"

"You're gorgeous. Even better when you bend me over the piano..."

Will came in minutes, doing his best to not get cum on his blankets and failing. He ducked out of his cocoon, grabbed a handful of tissues, and wiped himself. Across the room, Jackson was still oblivious.

"I can't believe I just did that with him in the room."

"Pervert. I say as I sit in a practice room with an erection. I blame you."

"I accept that blame entirely."

"Hear, listen to this piece I'm doing for class tomorrow."

Will heard Lennox count off. A sharp melody met him, across the miles and the waterways. Will smiled without Lennox beside him for the first time in months. He curled up under his blankets and let Lennox's symphony lull him to sleep.

* * *

SATURDAY EVENING BROUGHT A TORRENT of rain to New York City. Even in his dorm, Will shivered as he changed into his costume. The flimsy pirate garb didn't do much more than hang on his body. The shoulders were still too tight. Tyra had been texting him incessantly since noon, asking for makeup advice and opinions on hairstyles. For whatever reason—and Will did his best not to connect his sexuality to it—Tyra seemed to think he was an encyclopedia of proper makeup techniques and how to braid hair.

"Why are you wearing that under your costume?" Tyra plucked at his thermal shirt and then gave him a twirl of her sexy nurse outfit.

"It's way too cold for nothing else."

"That's what coats are for. Come on, we're going to be late."

They met Jake and his friends outside the subway. Jake gave a scattered flash of introductions—Ally, Brent, Cassidy, Malcolm— before they boarded their train. Will had no idea where they were headed. Tyra had told him the name of the club and nothing else.

Every subway car was crammed full of people in costumes. Tense from the drunken laughter and the shouts all around him, Will wedged his way toward a pole with Jake and one of the other guys. Picking up more people than it let off, the train careened through Manhattan. As Jake and his friend laughed, Will held the pole and did his best to stay calm.

"Bro, look at that chick. Damn, that's a fine ass."

Will glanced at Jake's friend—was that one Brent? Jake had said everyone's name, but he hadn't bothered to point to each person. Probably-Brent wolf whistled at a pair of women a few feet away, both dressed—like Tyra—in a costume that had definitely had the adjective sexy in the title. One shot them a look of disdain. Jake chuckled and shoulder-checked Brent.

"Ha, better luck never with her, man."

"What about you, Will?" Probably-Brent shoulder-checked him, too. "Think you can get her?"

"Dude, I told you he's taken."

Probably-Brent huffed. "So? Bitch is hot."

Jake muttered something to him, and Will looked away. Neither of them said anything else to him for the rest of the ride. They left the subway with half the crowd, climbing to the street into a part of the city Will wasn't familiar with.

Tyra squeezed his arm even as Will's stomach clenched with nerves. "This is going to be great! I'm so glad you finally came along."

A long line led away from the club's entrance. They queued up to wait. Will stared at the line of people in costumes. Most of them seemed to be half-dressed. He swore he saw at least three nipples. After twenty minutes, they reached the front, had their I.D.s checked, and went inside. Will's heart stalled when they found the main dance area. The room vibrated from the thump of the music; flashing lights flickered in all directions.

"Awesome crowd! Wow, look at that guy!"

Tyra pointed out a buff man with pencil legs, gave Will a wink, and strode off to introduce herself. Will watched her go. Apparently, introductions here meant grinding. He swallowed and eyed the mass of sweaty, half-naked bodies humping each other to the thrum of a bass line.

The rest of his group shoved their way onto the dance floor. Will found the bar along the wall and grabbed a seat. Lennox would know the proper etiquette for ordering a drink or how to get the bartender's attention. He didn't have a clue what to do, except avoid the dance floor.

After a while, the bartender came over. "Can I get you something?"

"I can't," he blurted. At her squinty look, Will added, "I'm only nineteen."

"Shirley Temple then?"

Will accepted the bright red drink. He expected a nice, long chit-chat with her, but the bartender floated away to serve someone else. It would have been nice of her to say out loud that he didn't belong here. Someone pointing that out would have made him feel a little less crazy for wanting to leave already.

Another forty minutes passed before Will spotted anyone he'd come with. Tyra and her buff guy came stumbling out of the crowd. He hadn't seen her at the bar, but it was clear she was drunk.

"Will! Willy, Will, Bill boy! Hi."

"Glad you're having fun."

She hugged him like a polar bear on narcotics and then planted a sloppy kiss on her buff guy. "You got a condom, Willy Bill Booty?"

Will stared.

The guy laughed and pinched her ass. "No worries, baby. They've got them in the bathrooms."

"Great!" Tyra blew him a kiss and dragged the man off, presumably toward the nearest bathroom.

Will continued to stare at the space she'd occupied a moment before. *This is the straightest night of my entire life.*

Will texted Aaron to tell him exactly that. Aaron pinged right back, first to send him a lot of sad-face emojis, and second to give him a picture of a brightly lit baseball field with a glowing scoreboard behind left-center field. The sight made his throat tight. He'd give almost anything to be at that field right now. He missed baseball, maybe more than he missed home or his parents or Oyster or even Lennox. For fifteen years, baseball had been a large part of his life, and now only a void inhabited that space.

He shoved his phone away and spotted the rest of their group down the bar, throwing back shots. Jake could give him directions back to campus. He didn't really want to find Tyra.

"Jake?"

"Dude! There you are. Here, man. Do a shot with us."

A shot glass was forced into his hand. Probably-Brent counted off and they all gulped the amber liquor down. Will set his full shot glass down on the bar top.

"Hey, I'm going to head out. What line is it back to campus?"

"What? Already? We're just getting started!"

A chorus of agreement went up around Jake. Nobody seemed to care much for leaving. Tyra was still missing with her buff guy, but Will just wanted to go home, to curl up in his bed with Lennox and Oyster. Even his dorm was better than this.

"You can't leave! No, come on, don't be a baby."

"Yeah, you're being a pussy, man," Jake said, punching him on the shoulder.

A flare of anger filled Will. "That's really rude. Look, just tell me how to get back. You guys can stay."

"Just have your shot," Probably-Brent said, pushing the full glass toward Will. "Come on, bro. Loosen up."

"I'd rather go back to campus."

Nobody offered any directions, but conversed and threw back drinks. Will turned to leave, and Jake caught his elbow.

"No, come on. You can't leave yet, dude."

"Well, I am. I'm going back to campus."

Jake mumbled something to Probably-Brent, who nodded.

"Let's hit up this late-night coffee shop a few blocks over. How's that?"

The rest of their group groaned.

"What? We're supposed to *party*."

"We can't get shit-faced over coffee."

Jake elbowed one of them, but nodded toward the door. Will led the way. The street was even busier than earlier; people staggered around in various states of drunkenness. Jake nodded toward the far corner.

"Few blocks that way," he told Will as the rest of the group hovered in the doorway, pulling on coats. "Down on Hoover Street, two, maybe three, blocks to the right. Gonna have to single file this."

Will wedged his way into the crowd. He glanced back and saw Jake, then kept going. The crowd didn't thin until he'd gone four blocks, but he still didn't see a sign for Hoover Street.

"How many more blocks?"

Nobody familiar was behind him. A pair of women loitered outside another club, but Jake and the rest were nowhere in sight. Will walked back toward the club, checked the street signs, and turned down more blocks, searching for them. It took him twenty minutes of fruitless, panicked searching to realize what had happened.

They'd ditched him.

Will found a restaurant still lit up and stood outside of it. He wanted to go back to the club and punch each of them in the face. Why couldn't he have one wonderful night in this stupid city without Lennox? Why hadn't he found a single friend worthy of his time? Was there some terrible reason nobody liked him?

Will took his phone out and flicked open the map, but he hadn't the faintest idea of how to read it. He was sure he was the blue dot, but beyond that he was hopeless, especially with tears in his eyes.

Karen could help, so could Aunt Mia. He had an entire list of people who might help, but he couldn't stomach the idea of breaking down before any of them, especially Karen. She couldn't know all of this. New York was supposed to be his dream. He couldn't tell her what a nightmare it was.

"Hey, Will." Lennox picked up, same as he always did these days: bright, cheerful, with a lilt in his voice that meant he was gushing with new tales.

Will's voice croaked when he spoke. "I, I'm lost again."

"Will?"

Will's breath stuttered as the tears fell, thick, warm, and then icy from the chilly wind.

"What's wrong?"

"I... They were all *drunk* and they ditched me at that stupid club, and I'm, god, I'm so lost. And I didn't want to wake Karen and worry her."

"Whoa, slow down. Babe, hey, you're okay. What's the nearest street sign?"

"Um, I don't know. That's... I'm on West End Avenue?"

Will kicked at the sidewalk as Lennox pulled up a map on his phone. He'd saved the location of Will's dorm the day they'd arrived there despite Will rolling his eyes at him. Right now he couldn't have been more grateful.

"Okay, start walking. What streets are you crossing?"

"Seventy-ninth? No, that's seventy-eighth."

Lennox had him name a few buildings, and then turned him left toward Broadway.

"Are you sure? I've never been to this area. Or I don't think I have. I don't know. They just made like we were leaving and then ditched me, so I started walking and got turned around and— Oh, am I near Times Square?"

A few brilliant, glowing billboards lit the street Lennox had directed him to.

"Like, thirty blocks up, so no, not really. You should see a subway entrance, though."

"I don't— Wait. Yeah, I see one."

Will jogged toward the familiar sign over a stairwell leading underground. Lennox gave him a few more directions on which lines to take.

"Call me when you get off at your stop, okay?"

"Okay, thanks."

Will sniffled again, and a bubble of anger filled him as they hung up. He hopped onto the subway train Lennox had said to catch and was thankful to see it so empty. Everyone must still be drinking and partying. That wasn't him. It never had been. Being healthy for baseball had always come first.

He curled up on a seat and pressed his cheek against the window. Why didn't anyone like him anymore?

..ıll thirteen

WILL STAYED IN BED ON Sunday. For once, Jackson had left their room and taken his computer with him. His room was quiet, or as quiet as New York City allowed. On the street below, he heard the sound of car horns and people, the clang of buses as they drove past, someone piling up trash bags for collection. Will was glad he couldn't smell it from up here, not even through the open window. Yesterday's chilly rain had turned into a cloudy Sunday afternoon.

Lennox texted him at midday. Will replied a few times, but stopped. His body ached. His head was wooly and numb. More than anything, he wished he was curled up with Oyster on the couch at home while his parents laughed and cooked dinner, or with Lennox sitting on the floor in front of him, his back resting against the couch, his curls tangled in Will's fingers, and his head blocking half the television screen, or with Aaron playing baseball in the sharp chill of a Sunday in early November

The following week was a haze of city streets, classes, and to-go meals in his room. Tyra and Jake both texted him, joking about Saturday and inviting him on another adventure the following weekend. Will ignored them. They weren't anything like he thought they'd been. Saturday night had given him proof of that. On Tuesday afternoon, they caught up to him at lunch.

"Will!"

"There's our guy."

Tyra and Jake grinned at him, as if nothing was amiss.

"Ah, come on, man, don't be a baby about Saturday."

"Yeah, everyone was drunk. Shit happens. Ha, it was so much fun. Wish we could have seen your face!"

Jake bumped Will's shoulder with his fist when Will didn't respond. "What, dude? It was a joke, man. Don't be a bitch about it."

Will passed his to-go container to the server and asked for servings of everything.

Tyra frowned at him. "Like Jake said, don't be a bitch, Will," she said. "If you drink next time, then you won't get left."

"Man, you gay guys are always so touchy about shit." Jake grabbed a tray and sneered at him. "Whatever, man."

Tyra followed Jake away. Will accepted his food, filled a cup with soda, and went back to his room. Jackson was blasting away on his computer. He didn't even look up when Will entered, nor when he turned and left a few minutes later. Will curled up in the study room down the hall; his food was forgotten back in his room.

He felt like crying, but couldn't bring himself to tears again. Will pulled his phone out, intent on calling Lennox, but the text picture from his boyfriend made him stop. He opened it and found three pictures and a video. Lennox with his friends, dressed in the goofiest clothes Will had ever seen. Purple checkered suit jackets, bowties the size of watermelons, and a variety of ridiculous hats that would have made him smile on a different day. The video was short, and clearly sent from Ava after she'd snatched Lennox's phone.

Will couldn't bring himself to spoil Lennox's day after that. He sent a cheerful reply and went back to his room. He ate his cold food, watched Jackson go to class, and then curled up in bed, skipping his own. He skipped Wednesday's classes, too. Then Thursday. He didn't get out of bed until it was time to meet Lennox Thursday evening.

Cheer returned to him at the sight of Lennox, with his pink curls and infectious grin. Lennox dropped his backpack at Will's feet, looped his arms around Will's neck, and kissed him until the lack of air choked Will's lungs. Will smiled into the second kiss, then the third. He giggled at Lennox's warm breath and the brush of their noses.

"In case I wasn't clear, I've missed the fuck out of you. And actually," Lennox said, a teasing smirk on his lips, "I'm hoping to fuck into you as well."

Will laughed loud and clear then; the vibrations made his throat hurt. They took the subway across Manhattan with Lennox's arms around Will's waist as the car swayed and the people crowded closer. His lips kissed the knots of tension in Will's neck until they stepped onto the street.

"Please tell me your jackass roommate followed through on going home this weekend."

"He did."

Lennox's hand slipped into the back pocket of Will's jeans and stayed there until they were upstairs in his room. He shut the door, locked it, and backed Will up to his bed. They tumbled onto the blankets together.

Will shut his eyes and let go then, opened himself to every emotion and sweet kiss that Lennox graced him with. His clothes were stripped away; his skin seemed to burn off too. A rage of flame lit him, churned warm and throbbing in his belly. Lennox held Will's head in his palm as he rocked into him, his hips steady and sure, then rushing and hard at the insistent press of Will's feet against his ass.

Will didn't remember when he came, only the broken cry and spark of tears it brought, the warm press of Lennox's mouth cleaning his chest and stomach, and then the blissful pleasure of Lennox still inside him, still cradling his head and bringing him home once more.

Night had fallen around them by the time Lennox rolled off of him. Will curled into his chest. Words didn't come to him. His thoughts buzzed like a beehive.

Lennox kissed his damp hair. Will felt the smile on his lips.

"I'm still in love with you."

Those words were wonderful, but not enough. He wanted this every day; he needed Lennox holding him every single night.

"I'm here whenever you want to tell me what's wrong."

Will nodded against Lennox's chest. He traced patterns on his skin and smeared beads of sweat into Lennox's chest. Will couldn't bring himself to explain it, or anything else he wished for right now. Lennox couldn't leave Berklee, and Will refused to give up on New York City. Somehow he was going to make his life here.

"It's just those idiots I went out with. That's all."

Lennox slid down in his arms until they were eye to eye. "Forget those fuckers, all right? Piss on them and then go back to that queer group you talked about. I'm sure you could make lots of friends there."

Will buried his head against Lennox's neck. No tears came, but the familiar comfort of Lennox's embrace soothed him. He couldn't bring himself to reply because it was more than that. All of this was so much more than Tyra and Jake being jerks. It was the snide people at that queer group, the unfathomable classes, and the competitive journalist hopefuls. It was the disinterested professors and the yearning for home that never left except when Lennox warmed him. It was the vast uncertainty and boisterous noise of New York City that still woke him at night and startled him in the streets.

None of that made it to his lips. He buried himself in Lennox and fell into a deep sleep.

WILL WOKE TO THE BUSTLING rumble of the city. New York was frothing with shouts and screeches and horns. Lennox wasn't anywhere to be found. His insides curled to ash at his absence. Had yesterday been a dream? Could the last three months have been one miserable, hostile dream? If he'd awakened in his room back home, he might have believed it.

He grabbed his pajama pants and a sweater, and found a note stuck to his phone.

Went to grab breakfast. Back by ten, sleepyhead. -Lennox

While he waited Will got comfortable among his blankets. He set up his laptop for an afternoon of movie watching. They'd stay here today. Celebrate Lennox's birthday just the two of them. Will could recharge on some happiness and then...

Lennox went back to Boston.

Will wished he wouldn't. Everything was better when Lennox was here. His life felt more solid, his day-to-day schedule slotted back into something comfortable from last year. New York was exciting with Lennox by his side. They were together again; smiling, happier than when separated. Every day should be like that.

Lennox returned, flecks of snow dotting his still vibrant pink curls. "Finally awake, huh? I got you a strawberry cream cheese croissant."

Will unwrapped his as Lennox climbed under the covers with him. The center was still warm, the cheese creamy and melty in his mouth.

"Mmm, this is really good. Where'd you get it?"

"Shop in Brooklyn. Ava's sister lives there. She's been insisting I give her a second opinion before she tries it herself. Apparently, Ramona's taste buds aren't fully functional."

Will ate another bite and leaned his head on Lennox's shoulder. "Happy birthday."

Lennox kissed his temple. "Do I get birthday sex or does last night count?"

"Mmm, guess we'll see. I was just going to snuggle up and watch movies with you. If that's okay. I don't feel like going out today."

Lennox nodded. He squeezed Will's free hand and selected a movie at random on Netflix. As the opening credits rolled, Lennox shifted his head to catch Will's eye.

"Have you been out at all since..."

Will frowned. "For classes."

"Did you go back to that queer group this week? You never answered that text."

Will shook his head and made a point of adjusting his laptop screen.

"Will, you can't stay locked up in your room all the time. I mean, you're in New York! There's so much to see and do."

"Yeah, and nobody to do any of it with."

"Will…"

"Can we just watch the movie?"

Lennox stopped pestering him. They made it through the atmospheric horror movie that Lennox had picked and then through a short comedy. Just as Will's stomach was rumbling, Lennox suggested finding a good pizza shop for lunch.

"Can't we just order in?"

"Come on, it'll be fun. Look." Lennox pulled up a map of nearby pizza places and waved it at Will. "See? They've got menus and everything. We can take a romantic stroll. It'll be fun, Will."

After ten more minutes of begging, Will agreed. They bundled up in coats, gloves, and scarves. The snow had stopped, hardly a dusting had fallen. Grimy slush lined the streets, and Will grimaced at the sight. Snow was prettier back home, not muddy and full of random wrappers and garbage.

"See? It's not so bad."

Will could see what he was trying to do, but it didn't matter. The truth got knocked a little deeper into him with every visit from Lennox: He didn't belong here. The only reason these strolls were bearable was because Lennox was with him.

"Only because you're here."

"So when is that next queer group meeting?"

"Lennox, I'm not going back. I don't… I wasn't gay enough for them or whatever. Just forget it."

"Not gay enough? What the hell does that even mean? You have a *boyfriend!* What else do they need?"

"A feminine lilt to my voice, an enjoyment of makeup, and a more-than-modest understanding of fashion."

"What the fuck does that have to do with sexuality?"

Will shrugged. "They weren't nice. Not the kind of people I want to spend time with. Not like your friends in Boston."

"This is the place." Lennox dragged him into an open door. "Oh, wow, look at that one! Is that feta cheese?"

They picked out their slices and grabbed a table toward the back. Lennox stuffed his face. Will picked at his pizza. It was tasty, but he wasn't very hungry.

"I'm sure that queer group has people more your speed," Lennox said after his second slice. "I mean, I got lucky. Troy and Ava and Alex and Sadia are great. Part of that's because we're all going to school for music. Kind of have built-in shared interests. Do they have other NYU clubs? Like for newspapers or baseball or even like Netflix Anonymous?"

Will snorted. "Maybe. I just... It's more than that. I've loved New York for so long, but ever since I got here..." *It's only perfect when you're here.*

Lennox frowned and finished his fourth slice of pizza. Will took his to go, and they went back to his room to continue their movie marathon. He didn't know how else to explain what he was feeling. After all these years, how did he tell everyone he'd finally gotten his dream and that it was the absolute opposite of what he wanted? Except when Lennox was here. His body seemed to come to life with Lennox at his side. The city was less daunting, and he had someone to spend time with, someone else to talk to about his struggles.

While Lennox took a shower, Will clicked off Netflix and searched for music schools in New York City. Julliard was the first that came up. That school had been in the pamphlets Will had given Lennox last year. Yet Berklee had caught Lennox's eye—a more modern school, less classical and formal. Did New York have a school like that? Lennox would transfer for him, wouldn't he?

..ıl fourteen

AVA WAS OUTSIDE LENNOX'S DORM Monday morning with two
cups of nasty coffee. She forced the second one into his fist. "Oh,
stop making that face. Yours is hot chocolate, god."

They went outside together, taking their time walking to their
shared class across campus. It was Lennox's largest class by far, a
seminar for their music technology course. He was glad to have Ava
with him. The internet and computers were becoming more familiar,
but he still wasn't as quick as his classmates.

The lecture hall was empty. They took their usual seats in the
third row and pulled out their laptops.

"How was your birthday? Did you get lots of birthday-boy sex?"

Lennox gulped a burning mouthful of hot chocolate.

"Oh, come on. Don't leave your sex life up to my imagination,
because I am the kinkiest shit this side of the Atlantic."

"It was fine. Yes, there was sex," Lennox added at Ava's continuous
winking. "It was nice, but Will's so miserable there all alone."

"He *still* hasn't made any friends?"

"I think he's given up trying, honestly."

Ava frowned. "Poor guy. Is he going back for the spring?"

"I don't know. I think he wants to."

"But *why*?"

Lennox shrugged as a few other students entered the lecture hall.
"New York's this idea he's wanted for a long time, and he finally got
it. I guess he just doesn't want to give up on it. Or himself."

"Sometimes you have to." Ava kicked her feet up on the row in
front of them and finished her coffee. "Or find better dreams for who

you are now. I mean, you said he's been aiming for New York since he was a kid. When I was seven I wanted to be a cattle wrangler. Then I met a cow and thought it was the dumbest, cutest, grossest creature on the planet."

Lennox didn't say anything. Nobody at Berklee knew how dark and difficult the last decade had been.

"I mean, didn't you have crazy dreams when you were a kid?"

"Does eating daily count?"

Ava made a face. "What?"

"Rough childhood. Um, I just don't know what to do to help him."

"I don't think there's much you can do that you aren't already." Ava tucked her empty coffee cup under her seat. "You can be there for him and tell him to try something besides New York or a different school, but you can't make friends for him or anything. He's got to do that on his own. And maybe stop taking being there for him so literally. I miss hanging out with you on the weekends."

"He needs me."

"He needs to make his own friends or try somewhere else if the city isn't for him."

Lennox glowered, but was saved from replying by their professor entering. The rest of his morning flew by. Professor Grumpkin handed back their midterm exams in his harmony class. A large blue A and a smiley face marked the top of his. Harmony was the only class he was solo in, and even then the people on either side of him were friendly.

Was New York really that hostile? Or was Will in a string of terrible luck?

Dr. Austin greeted him for his private instruction after lunch. They dove right into the piece Lennox had been working on—the one he hadn't practiced since last week. Being in New York from Thursday to late Sunday afternoon had meant sacrificing quite a bit of practice time. For once, it hadn't seemed worth it. Will had been no happier when Lennox had left than when he'd arrived.

"Not up to your usual standard," Dr. Austin said when he finished. Lennox dropped his fist onto the keys. "Hey, don't beat up the piano. Have you been practicing? Starting to get strained from your work load? What's going on?"

"I'll practice for next week, I promise."

Dr. Austin smiled and handed Lennox his sheet music. "I don't want promises, Lennox. I'm not your dentist. I want hard work and dedication. That's how you get progress. Now, what's distracting you?"

When Lennox didn't answer, Dr. Austin twirled a dreadlock and sighed.

"You don't have to tell me, but I do know you've been through a lot. Part of the reason I insisted on being your private instructor was because of that essay you wrote. Everyone here plays phenomenally well, but they don't all have rough childhoods. You're a lot like I was as a kid. Family pulled apart by circumstance, raised myself and my siblings, got into a lot of trouble thinking I was an adult when I wasn't."

"That's not why I got in trouble. You *don't* know me."

"No, you're right. I don't. But I'd like to. I'd like to know who you are in your own words, so we can get into the deeper part of music that connects to each of us differently. I've only got you as a student for four years, but educational relationships can become much more."

"Are you *hitting* on me?"

Dr. Austin threw back his head, dreadlocks swaying, and roared with laughter. Lennox flushed and slapped his sheet music folder on the piano keys.

"Lennox, I am, regrettably and woefully, as straight as they come. My wife is quite ashamed of it, actually."

"That doesn't make any sense."

"Of course, it doesn't. We aren't good enough friends for me to explain that story just yet, but I'd like us to be. You have so much potential, and I want to do my very best to help you grow that potential into actuality. One of the best ways I've found to do that, both as a student and a professor, is through friendship."

"What does friendship have to do with playing music?"

Dr. Austin smiled, that charming, robust grin that made Lennox feel like the stupidest and greatest person ever to set foot in the room. "A lot. Haven't you played with your friends on campus? Didn't seeing their abilities teach you anything?"

Lennox shrugged. Maybe they had, but he couldn't bring himself to notice that. Not with Will in such distress.

"Look, I'm not saying we need to make friendship bracelets and have sleepovers with cake and ice cream. I just want to know more about you, so I can do my very best to teach you how to place yourself in your music every time you sit down at a piano. Does that make sense?"

"I guess."

"So, who are you, Lennox?"

I'm just some kid who got lucky. In life and in love. "I'm no one special."

Dr. Austin shook his head. "I think that's where you're wrong."

"I think I know myself better than some hippy professor."

"That's the guy I want to see more of, that voice right there." When Lennox didn't respond, Dr. Austin continued, "Do you know who I think you are?"

"You already know who I am. I'm Lennox. I'm just some kid that plays the piano. I'm not anything—"

"Special. So you've said. In my experience, saying something a lot means you want to believe it, not that it's true."

"Whatever."

"Ah, petulance. We'll make a fine pianist of you yet. So, assignment for next week."

"Practice the piece again, I know. Get it right."

"No, get it wrong. Make mistakes, all that jazz. Actually, jazz. Find a jazz piece we can play around with next week, but your real assignment is this: Who are you? Who have you been? Who do you want to be?"

Lennox swallowed. He'd left all of his darker impulses behind in Virginia where they belonged. "That's the past. It's not important anymore."

"If it defines who you are right now, then it does. I expect an answer next week and I'd prefer it be in words," Dr. Austin said. "If there's one thing I do know about you thus far, it's your insistence on explaining yourself with music. I'll see you for ear training."

Lennox went back to his room, heavy with Will's problems and his own lies. Well, he supposed he wasn't actually lying to anyone here, but it felt like it. He wasn't being honest. Not to Troy or Ava or Dr. Austin. They knew this new Lennox he was still discovering, but hadn't seen any part of the boy he'd been back in Virginia.

"Damn, you look miserable." Troy greeted him by lobbing a balled-up sock at his face. "Bad birthday sex?"

"No. Why do you and Ava care more about my sex life than your own?"

Troy snorted and tossed a second sock at Lennox, who caught it and threw it back. "Ugh, I hate laundry day."

"Come on. I need to do my own too. I haven't touched it in, like, a month."

Lennox stuffed all of his laundry into his backpack while Troy picked up his hamper. They walked to the basement and dumped their clothes into a pair of free washers. The room was long, bright, and narrow, just a row of five washers and six stacked dryers at the far end. Lennox took a seat at the table in the corner by the door and pulled out his laptop. A pair of boxers were stuck around it—Will's. He tossed them into the washer too.

"So how was your weekend, birthday boy?"

"Fine. What about you? You were nowhere to be found yesterday."

Troy grinned. "Sometimes I get lucky, too, you know."

"Well, good, 'cause I totally jerked off on your bed."

"Dude, gross!"

Troy gave him a shove, but then they were both laughing again. This was nice. Berklee and his friends and this *life* he'd settled into was the kindest he'd ever had. Yet Will wasn't here to share it.

"No, really, how was your birthday?"

"It was fine. I'm not big on birthdays or parties."

"And Will?" Troy hadn't let that go for weeks. Not since Lennox had started disappearing to New York City every weekend.

"He's bad. I thought me being there would help, but he wasn't any happier when I left than when I got there."

Troy nodded. "Look, I know last time I tried to give you advice on this you blew up at me, but..."

"I'm not giving up on us. *Us* isn't the problem. Will's just— He's stuck right now. And I can't help him get unstuck until he's starts doing that himself."

Troy gave him a steady, quizzical look. "You two have been through a lot, haven't you? I mean, shit, when I was a freshman, I went *wild*. I was a mess, but you're not."

Lennox snorted. "I am. More than Will's ever been, and don't give me that look just because he's having a hard time right now. It's true. If it wasn't for Will—for us—I wouldn't be here right now."

"Have you talked to him about ditching NYU?"

"Mentioned it, but I don't want to pressure him into something. He's wanted—"

"New York forever. Yeah, I know. You're a broken record about it. Look, he can force it all he wants, but it's not for him. That's the truth. If he keeps pressing, he's going to mess up a lot more of his life than one semester of college."

Lennox couldn't find it in himself to disagree. New York, no matter how much Will wanted it, wasn't working.

* * *

FRIDAY AFTERNOON, LENNOX MET WILL at the train station. Will's smile was exuberant. He almost chipped Lennox's teeth when he pressed their mouths together.

"You seem happy."

And Will, surprisingly, was. Relief settled in Lennox at the bright smile and cheerful conversation they started on the walk back to his dorm. They talked about Karen and Ben, Oyster's latest adventure into the neighbor's yard, even Aaron's baseball team at UVA. Something had sparked this sudden bliss, and Lennox hoped it was a new friend, or a better class experience—anything that might help him carve his own space into New York.

"Is Troy around?" Will peered into the empty bathroom in Lennox's room.

"Out for the night. He wanted to take us to a drive-in movie on campus tomorrow."

"Great." Fumbling in his haste to get Lennox naked, Will grabbed him by the belt buckle. "So, sex all night? I mean, I'm sure you won't object, but it's always good to ask."

"Have I ever said no?"

Will spent the evening taking him apart. Lennox imagined himself as a piano, keys plucked and pried up, new ones gently settled back into place. Will had brought him to many new highs over the last year, but this was some new desperation, Will's desperation for something nameless, carving into him, bleeding pleasure into his body.

Night had already clouded the sky when they'd begun, but a deeper darkness filled the room when they finished. Will curled into him, breathing heavily, but seeming content. Lennox didn't know if he needed to bring up his long-standing suggestion that Will leave New York until he was ready, or if something had finally gone Will's way.

"How was your week?"

Will huffed and kissed his neck. "I didn't fuck you hard enough if you can still talk."

"I spent the last, like, hour telling you what to do." Lennox brushed Will's damp hair off his forehead and kissed his nose.

"You're a very demanding bottom."

"I am and now I demand to be told about your week. And suggestions for dinner."

Will hesitated. Lennox saw the shift in his gaze and recognized Will was stalling. He wasn't hiding something, that wasn't it. Yet whatever Will had to say was important enough to scare him.

"Well?"

"Classes were the same, I guess. I skipped a lot of them again."

"Don't you have finals soon?"

Will shrugged. "Right before Christmas, then I'm on break until next semester, but I've been thinking—about New York and me and us. You know, what's best for the future."

"Are you going to try Sarah Lawrence again? Or take a semester off?"

Will frowned. "What? No, I mean, I'm going to look into other majors, but I'm staying. New York's my dream; I'm not giving up."

Lennox sat up. He'd have to bring it up himself then. Will's persistence was admirable, but at this point it was foolish too.

"Will, I think it's awesome that you're so insistent on making this work, but... babe, it's not. You've been falling apart for weeks. And I can't keep coming to visit every weekend either. My finals start right after Thanksgiving; I need to be here to practice."

"I know." Will said it with such certainty, it startled Lennox. "You need to be here to finish the semester. I get that."

"Cool, but I don't know if you forcing yourself to stay in New York is the best idea. I... Will, I want to spend some of my weekends with my friends. Have you visit me here too."

"What if we lived together? In the same city?"

"I mean, that'd be wonderful, but if you're staying in New York..."

"I want you to come to New York with me."

Lennox stared at him. He wasn't sure if he'd stopped breathing, if the pounding in his ears was his heart ready to explode or his lungs screaming for oxygen. Will sat up, tucking his feet under his butt. He grabbed Lennox's hands and rubbed them between his palms.

"Just hear me out, okay?"

"But—Will, Berklee's in Boston. Everything I've been doing is here."

"I know, I know, but Julliard is a fantastic school. Like, the very best. It's right in the heart of New York, like NYU. We can both take a semester off, get an apartment, find part-time jobs, then start back up in the fall. Maybe Oyster could even come live with us. He'd *love* it. Karen and Dad never stop talking about how lonely he is without us."

"Will, he'd hate the city. He spends all day running around the backyard, and I can't just ditch Berklee."

Will squeezed Lennox's hands tighter. "But, we'll be together. We won't have to figure out schedules or not see each other all the time. Sex as much as we want too. And you said you thought your mom went to Julliard. You could go to the same school she did! We can be New Yorkers together, and then after school we'll have so many job opportunities there, we'll be set."

Lennox pulled his hands away. "No. I can't do that. I *like* Berklee. This is— You *wanted* me to come here. All last year, you were egging me on to dream for this, and now that I have it you want me to forget it?"

"I, I want this for us. We're happier when we're together."

Lennox shook his head as he climbed out of bed. "That's not true. I mean, it *is* in some ways, but... Will, I can't *remember* the last time I was as happy as I am at Berklee. I've probably never been this happy in my entire life."

"Not even with me?"

Will got out of bed, too, and pulled his boxers and jeans on. His hands were clenched as he searched for his shirt.

"That's not fair." Lennox pulled his own pants on. "Of course, you make me happy. I love you, Will, but, except for you, my life was absolute shit last year. It was even worse before that. I'd do anything to make you happy again, but me leaving Berklee isn't going to do that."

"Having you with me makes me happier."

"For a little while. I can't be your whole world, Will, just like you can't be mine." Lennox handed Will his shirt from the pile on the floor. "Look, let's just calm down and talk this out."

"What's to talk about? I want us to be together in New York and you don't."

"What's to talk about," Lennox said, gritting his teeth, "is that having me by your side isn't going to fix what's wrong. I think you should try Sarah Lawrence or take a semester off. Maybe New York isn't right for you, not now."

Will glared at him, yanked his shirt on, and got it stuck on his ear.

"Don't be stupid. New York's my dream."

"A dream that's treated you like shit for almost three months. It's not *working*, Will. I want you to be happy, I do, but New York isn't making you happy. Your classes suck, you haven't made any friends who aren't assholes, you won't even leave your room to explore! I'm not saying you should forget New York, but work your way up to it. Try Richmond or D.C. or even Pittsburgh with your aunt. Try a smaller school with smaller classes. New York's always going to be there when you're ready for it."

Will paced. Lennox sat on his bed and watched. He'd never expected Will to ask him to move. Will had encouraged him to come here. A year ago, Lennox could see himself agreeing to move to New York. Even a few months ago, he'd have done whatever Will had asked of him. But that was before auditions and graduation and Berklee.

"I just want us to be together. To start our lives together and be happy. Yeah, in New York. I know it's asking a lot, but I just want to see you more." Will stopped his pacing and faced Lennox with his arms curled around his chest and tears hanging on his eyelashes. "I want to be with you all the time, for the good days and the horrible ones. Please, come to New York."

Flashes of the last year swept through Lennox's mind: Will curled into his chest crying after his dad's heart attack, hushed confessions of love, wrestling with Oyster, college letters, a summer full of swimming and light-hearted sex, nights under the stars. Everything came right back to Will, who stood in front of him, half-shattered like a windshield in a hailstorm.

Was this what a breakup was like? He couldn't bear the thought of Will leaving his life, but, as their eyes met, Lennox didn't doubt his answer. "No."

"You—fine." Will grabbed his bag, his tears running down his cheeks.

"Will, don't leave, come on. Please."

"Why? You clearly don't want me around."

"That's bullshit and you know it."

"Then come to New York!"

"Damnit, Will, I'm not giving this up! Not even for you. You shouldn't want me to either. I'm staying at Berklee."

"Yeah, well don't come crying to me when they kick you out like your fucking grandfather did. Or like my *dad* wanted to last year. Remember that? How I convinced him to let you stay?"

A flare sparked in Lennox at Will's words. "Then don't come crying to me when your jackass dad has another heart attack, or did you forget who got you through that?"

Will paused in the doorway, still crying, but his face was red hot like an ember. "You think you're such a badass, but you're the same scared kid they dragged into juvie. You think I don't know why you put up all those fucking walls? You were too scared to deal with that, and you're too scared to do this now!"

Lennox slammed the door in his face.

..ıl fifteen

"NO, NO, DON'T...I DON'T WANT—"

"Lennox."

"Stop, let me go!"

"Lennox, *Lennox!*"

Lennox's face smashed into something hard. His chest clenched. A light flickered on somewhere over his head. Troy's face swam into view. He held his phone's light over Lennox.

"You were shouting in your sleep again. Here, your nose is bleeding."

Troy pressed a fistful of tissues to his nose. Lennox grabbed them and held on. He blinked once, twice. He felt his eyelids blink off time with his breathing. Troy left his vision and then the overhead lights came on.

"You okay?"

Lennox didn't answer. He held the wad of tissues against the cut on his nose and refused to meet Troy's eyes. It was Sunday night. This was supposed to be the end of a wonderful weekend with Will, but Will hadn't returned Friday night. They hadn't spoken since. Troy hadn't asked about it yet, but Lennox recognized the glint in his eyes.

Troy helped Lennox to his feet and back onto his bed. Lennox glanced at the tangled mass of blankets and sheets. He'd ripped his pillow cover off, and it was now hanging on his still open laptop.

"Sorry. Maybe I should invest in a muzzle, yeah?"

Troy sat on his own bed, but he didn't laugh. He wrapped his own blankets around himself like a shawl and watched Lennox.

"Stop fucking staring."

"No, man. This is— I mean, I'm not mad. People have nightmares. I used to have this insane one about a talking bear trying to eat me, but you're scaring me. Not, like, horror movie running from Freddy Kruger scared, but I'm worried. You and Will fight, and now…"

Lennox looked away. All weekend he'd woken up from jumbled dreams. Troy insisted they were nightmares, but Lennox refused that word. He couldn't bring himself to call them memories either. Troy's concern was genuine. Will had taught him to see that truth in others.

"It's nothing."

"Liar." Troy pushed himself back against the wall; his feet hung over the edge of his bed. "I don't want to push, but give me something: the best way to wake you, anything."

Lennox grabbed at his hair. He couldn't explain. Everything would be ruined if he did. If his old life bled into this, it would all shatter around him.

"Ruined? How's telling me something going to ruin anything?"

Lennox yanked harder on his hair. He'd said that out loud. So far, Lennox had managed to keep all of his secrets from his Berklee friends: his dead parents, his estranged grandparents and sister, his arrests and the eighteen months with an ankle monitor, his time in a juvenile detention center. Everything painful and difficult was tucked safely behind Virginia's state line.

"Lennox. Hey, come on, look at me."

When Lennox finally raised his eyes, he was doing all he could to not cry. The flashes of memory in his dreams had been terrible enough, but telling Troy anything was impossible. He hadn't even told Will all about his time in the juvenile detention center, yet that single jab from Will had unlocked all those months of torment.

"I can't mess up Berklee."

"And what? You think having nightmares instead of talking is going to make the next four years easier?"

Lennox shook his head. He pushed back on his bed and pulled his legs up to his chest. Troy continued to watch him, but Lennox stared at his hands. His hands were all he'd seen in tonight's dream. As he'd been dragged around that first night at juvie, he'd seen his hands in the cracks of light under the too-high blindfold that stunk of sweat and grime.

His hands were still the same—thin, smooth, nimble. How long could he keep it from someone sharing his room? From anyone he expected to be friends with long-term? "I ever tell you I was in juvie?"

Lennox heard Troy shift on his bed, but he kept silent and that made it easier to keep talking.

"Stupid shit that got me in there. That's what I've been dreaming about, being back there. Something Will said when we fought brought it all back. That's all."

Troy cleared his throat. "How long were you in there?"

"About a year." Lennox got up and shut the lights off. That was enough. Anything else would turn his throat raw. He got back into bed and curled up.

"I got arrested at a protest last year." Troy's bed creaked across the room. "Just a one-night deal. I got dragged along by some friends, didn't even want to be there, but next thing I knew I was in handcuffs."

"No shit."

Troy's dark shape shifted again. Lennox peered over at him.

"Yeah, we all ended up crammed in there together. Sadia, Alex, my old boyfriend. Wasn't exactly fun, but memorable."

"Wish mine wasn't so memorable."

"Yeah, my dad was all cheery about it, but my mom had a cow."

Lennox bit his tongue. A flash of his dad visiting behind a wall of glass, then another of his mother, lying cold in a casket. "Mine are dead."

"They're—what?"

"Dead. My mom when I was a kid, my dad about four years ago."

"Wow. I can't even imagine. I'm sorry, man."

Lennox bit back a callous response. Troy was genuine. Everything he said and did was true to himself and the kindness he carried with him.

"Is that how you ended up living with Will then? After your dad?"

"How'd you know that?"

"Will mentioned it once, just in passing."

Lennox flinched at his name. He should call Will, or text him, try to get them past this argument or to figure out if this was it for them.

"He was all I really had after juvie. Until I came here."

"It was bad in there, wasn't it?"

"I destroyed that place."

"Sounds like the opposite of what you're saying in your sleep. If you want to talk..." Troy's phone light flickered on. Lennox rolled away, but he didn't go back to sleep.

* * *

WILL DIDN'T ANSWER LENNOX'S CALL Monday morning, or the second call after lunch. Lennox fixed his gaze on one of Dr. Austin's dreadlocks during his private instruction and let his mind pull apart each individual twist of hair, each shade of lighter reds and deeper browns. Maybe he'd grow his hair out enough to do that. Maybe then Will would call to tell him how stupid he looked with dreads, how much he missed running his hands through Lennox's soft curls...

"Yoohoo! Hey, daydream with your words right now."

"Right, sorry."

He set his fingers to the proper keys and started to play the piece he'd practiced last week. Dr. Austin grabbed his wrists to stop him.

"Hey, what'd I say last week? Words, not music."

Lennox stared at him. Dr. Austin was as cheerful as ever, but Lennox hadn't a clue what he'd been talking about for the last five minutes. He'd coasted through his day so far. That didn't work very well in this class.

"So, did you come up with an answer to my question? Who are you?"

Lennox shook his head by reflex, but Dr. Austin had learned to wait for him. He didn't have any good answer, nothing poetic or descriptive or prepared the way Will might have. A lonely fizzle of anger filled him at the thought of Will, but it melted into worry.

"I'm just Lennox. That's it."

"It's not." Dr. Austin closed the piano cover, almost snagging Lennox's fingers. He fixed Lennox with his gaze. "See that right there?" Dr. Austin pointed to each of Lennox's eyes in turn. "Your answer's right in there, just off-center. You *know* this. It's who you are. It's who you've been and who you want to be. Just capture that and put it into words, Lennox."

Lennox shook his head again and turned away. "I'm nothing special."

"You *are*. Do you know who I think you are?"

"Another one of your dozens of students."

"I think you are one of the most talented, troubled musicians I've ever had the privilege to teach. You're funny and smart and exploding with life that you're scared to let out, and I think you know all of this, but you're afraid to get too comfortable with that part of yourself."

"That's bullshit."

"Then give me a different perspective. *Tell* me who you are."

"I, I just want to forget who I've been, all right? I don't need any of that anymore. I don't want it."

"You can present yourself as someone else, but you will never be without the person you were."

"I can't be that person anymore, I don't want to go back to that. To any of it, and if..."

"If what?"

Lennox swallowed. If Will left his life for good, would he revert to the boy he'd been last summer? Or worse, the one at the boarding school after juvie?

"Lennox, I'm not pushing you to upset you, okay? I'm sorry if I have. It's just very clear you're holding parts of yourself back, especially when you play. You're still incredible, but that emotional depth I saw in your audition isn't present. I'm trying to help you draw that out."

"Whatever, man. Can we just play?"

"Sure."

Lennox ran through his piece from the previous week, hitting all the accents and crescendos. He played right into the piece he'd been told to bring this week, not pausing to rest, to breathe. The notes poured out of him, from memory instead of ink drops on the papers Dr. Austin had stopped turning. The music shook him, left his arms heavy and trembling and his chest aching as if it was full of quicksand.

"Lennox?"

He couldn't bring himself to look at Dr. Austin through his tears. "What if I go back to how I was without him? If all this goes away, too?"

"Without who?"

Lennox wiped his nose on his sleeve and packed up his sheet music.

"Lennox?"

"Forget it. I'll figure it out."

KAREN CALLED HIM THAT EVENING while he was hiding in his bed skipping dinner.

"Hey, Lennox, how's everything? You didn't call last week."

"Fine, sorry."

It hit Lennox, as he was halfway through answering her questions about his week, that this relationship would end too. If he and Will were over—and Will's continued lack of response said they were—then Karen was gone too. Ben, still a tentative friend, was gone. Oyster was gone. A home for the summer and everything else in Leon was gone as well. He wouldn't even have this phone anymore once they were out of his life. At least Virginia would truly be cast aside.

"Listen, I have to go. Dinner before a long practice."

"Okay, sure! Do well; have fun. And let Will know he needs to call us, okay? I'm sure he's just busy, but he hasn't texted us or called me back, so just pass on the message."

Lennox hung up, then dialed Will's number. Just like the last five calls, he got Will's voicemail.

"It's me again. Please, just text me. Let me know you're okay. Karen called and said to call her because she's worried, too. I miss you. Just let me know where we stand. I don't want to lose you, Will. I don't know how."

* * *

WILL DIDN'T RESPOND. KAREN CALLED like clockwork the following week, but Lennox let her call, and then Ben's that same evening, go to voicemail. He celebrated Thanksgiving with Lucy and Kelly and then threw himself into studying and practicing during the first week of December. Only Dr. Austin seemed to notice the cracks expanding in him, but he was tentative about asking after Lennox's abrupt, tearful departure. For their final private instruction of the term, Dr. Austin had Lennox join him in his office to pick his spring classes.

"So, those are your required classes, and, based on your final grades and rating for your ensemble, you'll get placed in January. Any genre preferences?"

"No, I like everything."

"It's always good to have an expansive knowledge of genres. How about rockabilly?"

"Sure. That's fine."

"I'll make a note, and then there's your private instruction."

"Same day and time?"

"Actually, I want to know if you wish to continue with me, or try a different professor." Dr. Austin slid a list of the other piano department professors toward him. "Ever since I pushed you with my questions, you've been uncomfortable. I'd rather you have the best experience here, even if it's with another professor."

"What? No way. I'm sticking with you."

"You're sure?"

"Yeah. How many other professors have dreads, right?"

Dr. Austin smiled. "All right, it looks like Thursday's best, but we'll settle on a time after break."

Lennox nodded, then checked his phone. Still nothing from Will. It had been almost three weeks, and Will hadn't answered. "I don't know what you want for an answer. About who I am."

"I want your truth. Your answer is yours. There's no right or wrong. I only want to see how you define yourself. Does that make more sense?"

"What if I don't know?"

Dr. Austin reclined in his chair. "We all know, even if we can't put it into words. It's a tough question, Lennox. I'm not expecting a crystalline answer. I only want you to take the time to think about who you are and what you're bringing into each piece you compose or play."

"If I'd known college was going to be such a pain in the ass..."

"Let's shelve it for next semester, but think about it. Think about what parts of yourself you're putting into your music. It's important. Sound good?"

Lennox agreed.

TROY WAS LYING FACE DOWN on his bed when Lennox entered their room.

"Can't I just be a walrus or something?"

Lennox slapped his ass with his music notation book. "Come on, another week and we're done."

"Speak for yourself. Ugh, I can't imagine being a senior next year. I don't want it."

"Let's take a break tonight then. I'm sick of practicing and I don't want to memorize anything else for music tech." Lennox tumbled onto his own bed and buried himself under his blankets.

"What day are you leaving again? I'm stuck until Saturday morning."

"My last final's Thursday night. I'm probably just going to stay here."

"With Lucy?"

"No, in the dorm."

"Dude, the dorms close until the spring semester." Troy sat up. "I mean, maybe if you hide in the ceiling they won't notice, but..."

Panic filled Lennox's throat. He couldn't go back to Will's, not without answers from Will, not without knowing whether or not he was welcome. Lucy might let him stay, but she'd want to know why he wasn't with Will too.

"You could come to my house for Christmas."

"Your parents live in Wyoming. I can't afford that flight."

"Maybe Alex or Sadia are staying in town. They might let you house-sit if they're going home."

"Yeah, maybe."

Lennox traced the lines on the ceiling with his eyes and imagined the deep red walls of Will's room, the fluff of Oyster lying across his ankles, the warmth of Will's body curled into his side. His body ached for that comfort. Yet Will wouldn't answer a simple text, asking if he was okay. He couldn't go back there.

"Do you hear something?" Troy asked.

Troy glanced around and cupped his ear. Lennox sat up. Something was ringing.

Fast as he could Lennox bolted out of his bed and found his cell phone, but the screen was black. Troy stared at his phone too.

"It's definitely a phone, but…" He started digging through his bedding, then through his desk. "Maybe Ava or Alex left theirs here?"

Lennox dug through all of his belongings—nothing. The ringing had stopped, but Troy continued to look around.

"It sounded like a house phone, you know?"

Troy nodded; his face was scrunched up. Somewhere in the room, a phone beeped. "Does our room have its own landline? Is that a thing dorms have?"

They continued digging, following the beep. After five minutes, Troy found it, buried at the bottom of his wardrobe. A red light flashed on the corded phone's cradle.

"Weird. I don't remember putting that in there."

"I'm surprised it works." Lennox picked it up, and the cord snagged on the wardrobe door. "Ugh, what a stupid invention. Who's calling us?"

"Twenty bucks says it's a wrong number."

Lennox put it on his desk after they'd untangled the cords. He longed for Will's voice, but after the voicemail message—announcing that the caller had reached Daphne and Mia's room—he was stunned.

"Hello, Lennox, you should change that message. I had the staff check three times to confirm this was the right room, but they assure me it's your room now. I didn't know how else to get in touch with you, but Lucy and I wanted to invite you for Christmas. You're welcome to stay for the rest of your break as well. There's a lot I'd like to talk to you about."

Lennox played the message a second time, just to be sure he'd heard right. Troy stared at him. "Who was that?"

"My grandfather."

..ıll sixteen

"HONEY, DO YOU WANT SOME soup? A sandwich?"

Karen's voice carried down the stairs to Will, but he couldn't make himself respond. He stayed curled up in his bed with Oyster cuddled into his chest. Being home had been an endless craving since he'd left in August, but without Lennox he was as miserable as in New York.

"Will? Hey, why don't you come upstairs. Have some lunch with me." Karen turned one of his lamps on and then sat on the foot of his bed.

"I'm not hungry."

"Now I know that's a lie," Karen said, and, just as Will started to protest, his stomach rumbled. "Come on. We can eat ice cream and make Christmas cookies."

Will let her drag him to the kitchen. Oyster whined until Karen opened the sliding glass door and let him race into the snowy yard.

"Lennox was right. Oyster would hate New York."

Karen set a tub of ice cream in front of him. "I stocked up. Ice cream's the best cure for a breakup."

"We didn't break up," Will insisted, but he didn't see how that could be true. "We just had a bad fight, and I was a complete ass, and I hate all of this."

She pushed the ice cream toward him again. "You still haven't said what happened."

Will only shook his head and retreated downstairs. He'd been home for almost two weeks, and every day he felt worse. He didn't feel as bad as he had in New York, especially during finals week. He'd missed half his exams, slept all day, and finally decided to just pack up early and return home.

Lennox had been calling him daily, texting him greetings in the morning and well-wishes at night, but Will never answered. How could he ever look Lennox in the face again?

"Will?" This time it was his dad who came downstairs. Ben's hair was whiter; his body was a trimmer, but still as muscular as every memory Will cherished. He pulled Will's desk chair to the bed and sat.

"You gonna tell us what's up, or should I drive to Boston and track Lennox down for answers?"

"It's nothing. It's fine."

"It's not. What happened?"

Will hesitated. So far, he hadn't told either of them anything negative about his semester in New York, not about his classes, or the friends he'd tried to make, or the city life bowling right over him. He couldn't disappoint his parents, but his grades would tell on him soon enough.

"I'm failing, like, everything."

Ben shifted. "I was thinking more about you and Lennox, but okay. We can talk about that too. What's going on with you? You've always been such a happy kid, Will. You're not yourself."

Will shrugged. "Can you please just leave me alone?"

"All right. When you're ready to talk, we're here, bud." His dad kissed him on the head before he left.

"Of course, I'm worried. But we can't force him to tell us, Ben!"

"Well, we have to do something. He's been moping around his room ever since he got here. He hardly eats; he sleeps all day. Lennox won't answer us, and now he's *failing* his classes. Karen, we have to—"

"Be patient. When he's ready to talk, he will."

Will sniffled and curled himself up around Oyster. His dad had left the door cracked when he'd gone back upstairs.

"It's been *two weeks*, Karen. He's had more than enough time to decide what he wants to say."

"Do *not* go back down there. Leave him in peace."

His door snapped shut, and the room went dark. Oyster yodeled at him.

"Shh, it's just Dad and Karen."

Will stayed in his ball of blanket and Oyster's warmth. Being home was so much quieter than New York. He'd missed the quiet, but his room felt cavernous and disjointed without Lennox sharing it.

It was almost midnight by the time he forced himself out of bed, put on his coat and snow boots, and took Oyster into the backyard. Yesterday a light snow had covered the house and yard. Oyster had spent the day outside, leaping through the flurries and then howling at the moon as it drifted in and out of sight.

He couldn't keep moping. Will sat on the deck while Oyster took a lap around the yard, then raised his leg on his favorite oak. At some point, he had to deal with the shambles of his life. He stared at his phone, at the good-night text from Lennox he still hadn't opened.

"At least tell *me* why you're not talking to him." Karen stepped onto the deck and whistled at Oyster until he came back into sight.

"I messed up."

"You only make it worse the longer you wait. Trust me on that."

Will shook his head. "I don't think it matters. He won't forgive me."

"What makes you say that?" Karen dusted off the step beside him and sat. "If I'm proud of one thing you've shown Lennox in the last year, it's how forgiveness works."

"I begged him to come to New York so I didn't have to be alone, and he said no."

Karen was quiet for a long time. Will kicked the snow off his part of the steps. His eyes teared up as he remembered what he'd asked, what he'd demanded.

"I'm glad he said no," Karen said. "His life is in Boston now, and it's unfair to ask him to uproot everything he's building there. I think you know that without me saying it, but why do you need him with you in New York? Everything you've been telling us sounded fine."

Will swallowed. "New York was terrible. I— God, it was such a mess. All of it. Me. Even if I wanted to try again, I doubt I can. I skipped three of my finals. All my friends ended up being assholes. I'm not going back to that. It was stupid to ask Lennox to drop his whole life for something I don't even... It was dumb, that's all."

"Will, it's not stupid to lean on him when things get difficult for you, but I think you need to realize something Lennox found out the hard way a long time ago." Karen patted his knee and made him look at her. "He's part of your happiness, not all of it. Your happiness, that's inside yourself. It's in you. It's in the things you do and accomplish and the relationships you build with *everyone* in your life, not just a romantic partner."

Oyster charged back to them, shaking snow all over Will's arms.

"Why didn't you say anything? We've talked every week since you left," Karen said. She dusted Oyster's face. "Mia's mentioned a bit, but with me and your dad you've acted like everything was fine. We could have helped if we'd known, Will."

"I didn't want to disappoint you guys." He rested his chin on his knees and curled his arms around his legs. "I've talked up New York since I was kid and then I got there. I couldn't handle any of it. And I don't have *any* backups."

"Will, you going for a dream and then realizing it's not what you want could never disappoint me or your dad. Hell, when you gave up on that yo-yo dream, I was thrilled."

"Well, I did break your windshield."

"And three windows." Karen smiled. "It's like when you decided you didn't want to be a professional baseball player anymore. We're sad you've lost a dream, but we're glad you recognize when you don't want to make a life out of something too."

He'd been thirteen when his baseball dreams had been crushed. Karen and Ben had never known the real reason he'd set that aside, but the reality hadn't changed. Being gay and a professional baseball player would never work.

"You're the best mom, you know that?"

Karen shifted. "I'm not your mother, Will."

Her words stung, but Will pushed anyway. He didn't know how to make her understand what he meant when he placed her in that role. Neither of them seemed to be on the same page with that. "You are to me."

"Will..."

"It's true. I can't explain it more than that."

Karen watched him. "I know that. I do, but you calling me 'Mom' reminds me too much of my own. How much I hated the very idea of mothers."

Will frowned. "What do you mean? She comes to holiday dinners and stuff. I mean, she's not my *favorite*, but you seem to get along okay."

"We do now. Mostly," Karen said. "Not seeing her a lot helps. She's half-senile these days too."

For so many months, he'd wished to call Karen 'Mom' officially, but he'd never considered her reasons for refusing. Karen's mother was sharp and rude and never acknowledged his sexuality.

"You're nothing like her, you know. I'd never want to call you 'Mom' if you were."

Karen shook her head. "Give me some time, okay? I can't promise, but maybe someday."

"Okay. If I slip up..."

Karen kissed his hair. "You can't help it. I'm *glad*, honestly. I never thought you'd see me like that. I thought I'd always be a stepmom to you."

Will hugged her. Karen squeezed him back before standing up.

"Enough of us. Call Lennox," Karen said as she led Oyster inside. "Or at least text him. He won't respond to us either. I've filled his voicemail box and I doubt he knows how to empty it."

"What if he doesn't want me anymore?"

"He texts you twice a day, every day, even though you don't answer. Trust me, he does."

* * *

WILL TOOK A FULL DAY to contact Lennox. He sent one simple text after Lennox's "Good morning, I miss you, I love you. I hope you're okay" and then shut his phone off. It was Friday morning and the end of Lennox's finals week. Will wanted to rush to the bus station in Richmond to await Lennox, but Lennox wouldn't be there. Lennox would have made other plans by now, and Will did his best to do the same.

He called Aaron, who was back in town for the holidays. They met at their high school's baseball field; remnants of icy snow crunched underfoot. Will swung his arms in circles to loosen his shoulders.

"How's UVA been?"

Aaron dropped his bucket of baseballs and imitated Will.

"Good. I mean, classes aren't my thing, but some of them are interesting. I might major in history. We had a whole intro class about European history and the professor was awesome. What about you? How glamorous is New York? I'm surprised you even came back."

Will shook his head. "New York was awful. Felt like I was being pummeled with fastballs with no padding."

Aaron winced. "Were your classes interesting? Your friends? Last I heard from you, you were having the straightest night of your life."

"Ugh, don't remind me. They were assholes. Classes were bad. I didn't feel like I fit anywhere. Like, I wasn't gay enough, but then I was too gay for other people. I was smart here, but not smart enough to do well in classes there. I don't know."

Will scooped up his glove and tossed a baseball high in the air. "Are you going back?"

"Probably not. I mean, I failed at least three of my classes, so there goes my partial scholarship. I don't know what I want to study now or what school I want to go to or in what city or anything."

Aaron grabbed his glove and motioned for Will to toss to him. They started a game of catch, increasing their distance every couple of tosses. Will fell into the rhythm like a second skin. He'd missed being on the field, feeling his glove envelop his hand and the smack of a baseball hitting the pocket. Everything felt right with his cleats in the dirt and his eyes on the ball.

"Maybe you could find a school in Boston," Aaron suggested. "See Lennox more. You two are still going strong, right?"

"Uh, well..."

Aaron missed Will's next throw. "No way, you two didn't break up. Roxanne's going to have a cow."

"It's complicated right now."

"Well, uncomplicate it."

Aaron dragged him over to the dugout, forced him to sit, and then pried the last four months out of him, word by word. Will didn't stop until he'd said it all. He told Aaron about all his college missteps, the friends he'd tried to make, every jealous pang at how successful Lennox was in comparison.

"...and I'm mad at him," Will finished. He punched his gloved palm. "I'm mad at him for no good reason, and it's not his fault. I thought everything was going to be great and now I'm stuck here again."

"Trust me, I get the jealousy thing. If I played like you, I could be in the minors right now. Coach says maybe in another year, but I get it."

"I'm not that good. I never pursued it enough to be that good."

"Doesn't mean you aren't."

Will pulled his glove off. "I texted him to say I was sorry this morning, but that's the first thing I've said in weeks. I was such an ass. I don't even want to look him in the face."

"If you want him around, then you've got to." Aaron shrugged. "Look, I'm no relationship expert. I mean, I was the shittiest boyfriend to every girl in our history class in seventh grade. Is he coming back for break?"

"I doubt it."

"Then call him. Or find out where he is and go see him." Aaron stood up. "But do that tomorrow, okay? I want to throw with my old catcher. Those guys at UVA just don't *get* me."

"Fine, but I don't have my gear, so if you bounce even *one* pitch and hit me, you're a dead man."

...ıl seventeen

I'M SORRY. I LOVE YOU.

Lennox spent his entire first plane ride staring at Will's words. His grandfather had insisted on flying him to Richmond instead of having him waste time on a bus or a train. He was sandwiched between two old men with Will's words glaring up at him. He couldn't think of what to say now that Will had answered. Off the plane with his tattered backpack, Lennox wandered with the crowd until he found a way out of the security checkpoint. His sister was bouncing by the doors, scolded by his grandfather, Cameron.

"Lucy, if you don't *calm down—*"

"That's him!" Lucy barreled into him, knocking his backpack off his shoulder and the breath from his chest. "I've missed you," Lucy said, as she stepped back and measured herself against his height. She frowned. "Did you get taller? That's not fair."

Lennox spun her around. Will had asked him the same question last summer, but nothing seemed different. "It's the pink hair."

Lucy yanked on one of his curls. "You look silly, like you've got a bubblegum tree growing out of your head." Her own Afro was wide and cloud-like.

Cameron approached. Lennox swallowed; that old familiar dread trickled down his spine. Accepting his grandfather's invitation had been a quick decision. Troy had been against it, but the prospect of seeing Lucy again had been enough to convince Lennox. Whatever ulterior motives Cameron had couldn't make him regret spending time with his sister.

"Lennox, it's good to see you."

They shook hands and walked to the car without another word. Lucy took over their silence, talking nonstop about her soccer tournament, about her first year of middle school, about everything Lennox had been missing. On and on she went, down the short highway drive and up the old house's driveway. Lennox lost focus on her questions then. He hadn't been back to his grandparents' house in years, but not a lot had changed on the outside: same red brick colonial, same sleek columns on the open porch. Cameron followed the driveway up the right side to where it curved behind the house. The old deck was gone and in its place was a sunroom.

"That's new."

Cameron went inside, but Lucy hung back with him.

"They remodeled for Grandmother while she was sick." Lucy made a big show of putting his backpack on and hobbling inside. "I told Grandpa he should make it an indoor pool now that she's gone."

"Gone?"

Lucy squinted at him, then tossed his backpack on the leather couch that still dominated the sitting room. "Didn't Grandfather tell you? She died right after your birthday."

A muffled explosion went off inside Lennox. His grandmother was dead. Was that the reason Cameron had invited him? He couldn't say he felt remorseful about the news. Gwendolyn McAvoy had never been kind to him. Even when he was a child, she'd been severe and stern.

"Oh, well, that's..."

Lucy nodded. Like him, she'd never had a close relationship with their grandmother. "Yeah. Grandfather's... he's been weird about it." Lucy grabbed his hand. "Come on, you have got to see my new soccer jersey!"

Lennox spent the evening with Lucy, playing soccer in the designated space in the backyard and then making their favorite dinner in the expansive kitchen. The cabinets were new, a darker upgrade from faded white, and a new double oven had been installed.

They sat at the counter together, waiting for their taco meat to cook.

"Grandpa tried to make tacos last summer, but it was like eating shoe polish."

"Nobody makes them like I do," Lennox said. He stirred the meat. "It's close. What are we putting on these?"

Lucy dug through the refrigerator and took out a dozen different options. Lennox turned the heat down. Cameron appeared, still stiff and impeccably dressed. His face looked worn.

"Tacos?"

Lennox nodded. "Favorite of ours. Do you want some?"

His grandfather nodded and watched them prepare their tacos. Lucy's every movement flowed. He put the meat on the shells; she covered each taco in its own toppings. Cameron sat at the island counter with them and ate, something he'd never done before. Meals with his grandparents had always meant a meticulously laid table in the dining room.

After dinner, Lucy insisted on a movie and then fell asleep twenty minutes in. Lennox almost tried to carry her upstairs, but she wasn't a toddler anymore. His sister would be twelve soon. It took some convincing to get her to move to her room.

"I'm not tired." Lucy yawned and her prosthetic leg caught on the stairs.

"You're going to bed. I'll still be here in the morning."

She hugged him tight and took a long time to let go and shut her bedroom door. Lennox went downstairs again, not sure what to expect. Lucy had been a wonderful buffer from his grandfather. Cameron wasn't in the living room, though. Lennox checked the main floor, from the dining room all the way around to the new sunroom. He found him, in a small cloud of cigar smoke, on the other side of the open front door.

"Grandfather?"

Cameron waved him onto the porch. Lennox stepped outside. He wasn't used to the warmth after Boston, but the streetlights were a comfort. As a kid, he'd thought every city was like Richmond, a small hub of historical buildings with row houses and neighborhoods lining the streets. New York and Boston had shown him otherwise.

"How's Boston?"

"Cold." Lennox toed at a stain on the brick porch. "Berklee's great."

"I'm sure you're doing well. You've always enjoyed the piano."

Lennox shrugged and leaned against the column a few feet from his grandfather. "I'm learning a lot."

"And how's, uh, Wayne?"

"Will." Lennox crossed his arms. "He's fine."

"Well, good. That's good."

Cameron took a seat on the porch bench and clipped the end of his cigar into an ash tray. Lennox stayed by the column and waited. Small talk had always been their go-to, and even then it was stilted and awkward. After several more puffs on his cigar, Cameron spoke.

"I'm sure you're wondering about the sudden invitation."

"Well, I can't imagine you were desperate to see me."

"Lennox."

"What? We're both adults. You don't want a gay grandson. No point in sugarcoating it."

"I've never said that."

"You didn't need to." Lennox turned away from the cigar smoke; his fingers itched for a cigarette. "Lucy told me Grandmother passed."

"Heart disease always seems to win in the end. She was ready."

"Were you?" Lennox looked at his grandfather then, at his frail wrists, the skin hanging under his eyes. "You look like shit."

"Lennox, what have I told you—"

"Foul language or not, it's still true."

Cameron shook his head and eyed him critically. "I'm not your parent, Lennox. I suppose nobody ever has been. Honestly, I don't know how I feel about your sexuality anymore. Somehow it doesn't seem as important as it did. You and Lucy are what matter. Gwen never truly got that, but I want this last Christmas with you two, even if I can't make everything right."

"Last Christmas? You taking a drunken-binge vacation or something?" But Lennox understood what that meant. Cameron puffed on his cigar. "Does Lucy know yet?"

"No," Cameron said. He coughed as if one of his lungs was exploding. "I wanted to sort out her future first, so she won't worry about what will happen to her."

Lennox paced, his fingers shaking. "And that's why I'm here. Because you want *me* to raise her. *Again.*"

"Lennox, your father did his best after your mother's death, but you can't have expected that he would be an ideal caregiver."

"You can't be that stupid," Lennox said. "I know you weren't around after he cut you off, but you *saw* what he was like after Mama died. He wasn't even fit to care for himself."

"I'm sure he did his best."

"I'm sure he drank and I figured everything else out. *I* took care of Lucy. I changed her diapers, and watched old home movies of them teaching me to walk and talk so I could teach her. I took her to daycare and picked her up. Do you have any idea how ridiculous it is for a fifth grader to potty train a two-year-old?"

Lennox paced the length of the porch, from the window of the dining room and back to his grandfather. He'd take care of Lucy, of course he would, but how would that work with him away at school in Boston? Now that Berklee was his, he couldn't give it up.

"I knew there was something else with inviting me here. The only person who ever wants to see me just to see me is Lucy. Fuck, I already spent my childhood being her parent. I *raised* her, no matter what the fuck you think Dad did. That was me! I've finally got a life that's mine, and now you want me to give all of that up?"

Cameron sighed, but he didn't appear upset. "I have enough set aside to pay your tuition and for a private school near you for Lucy. This house would sell well, too, I'm sure. The property alone—"

"I don't want your money. I have a full scholarship. I just... You can't uproot her like that, which means I come back here and figure it out." Lennox sat next to him.

"You won't do it?"

"Of course, I will." Lennox glowered at him. "She's my baby sister."

"I'm sure Lucy would be thrilled to join you in Boston. We can talk about options with her."

Lennox watched several cars drive past. "Isn't there anyone else? Just for a few years while I'm in college? Berklee is... I love it there. I don't want to leave."

Cameron was quiet. He set his cigar down and considered Lennox. "On my side? No. I thought of another option, but I haven't seen your mother's parents since the wedding. They may be dead. I'm not sure where they live anymore or have their phone numbers. Nothing. You probably don't even remember them."

"Do you know their names?"

"Either Harold or Henry Hill. Very common. I don't remember her name."

"Maybe Dad left it in his stuff. He must have had something. You still have his boxes, don't you?"

"Lennox, that's such a long shot. Half of what's left is old clothes, trinkets. Your grandmother got rid of all the sheet music, old papers..."

Lennox stood. "It's worth a shot. Lucy and I will see what we can find."

* * *

Lucy's temper sparked at the very mention of their father the next morning. Only the prospect of more grandparents and spending the day with Lennox coaxed her into the basement after breakfast.

She kicked at boxes and then at all of her soccer balls stuffed in their net bag.

"This is boring. Who cares what their address is?" Her next ball ricocheted off the wall and smacked Lennox on the head.

"Ouch! Are you going to help me look or not?"

Lucy glowered at him. "Fine. What are we looking for again?"

"Mama's parents address. Or names. Anything on them."

She sat next to him and flipped open a box he'd already gone through. "Are they nice? I didn't know we had more grandparents."

"Neither did I." Lennox ignored her confused look and kept digging. Some of these clothes must have been his. He didn't recall ever putting Lucy in a white and green dinosaur onesie. His dad's belongings were sparse: old ties and suits that might fit him now, photographs and albums, even a few old trophies Lennox didn't recognize.

"Didn't you ever meet them?"

"Maybe. I don't remember them if I did."

Lucy tossed what looked like a raggedy kite into the air. "Do you think they're nicer than Grandmother was?"

He hadn't considered it. Their dad's mother had never seemed fond of him, not even when he was a child. The only memory he was certain of was a visit for Christmas, before Lucy's birth, when Grandmother Gwen had tugged on one of his long curls and berated his parents for allowing it to be so long and greasy.

"I hope so." Lennox opened another box, this one full of photo albums. "I bet they look more like us."

Lucy's eyes lit up. "Really?"

"Yeah, I've shown you pictures of Mama. She's black, and I'm sure her parents are, too."

Lennox flipped through the top photo album and handed it to Lucy opened to a page of himself and their mother. He couldn't have been older than three, but their smiles matched in a frozen happiness he was still trying to retrieve. Will had brought him close; Berklee brought him closer.

"I wish she was alive." Lucy traced her fingers over the glossy pages. "I don't even have pictures of me with her. Grandmother said there weren't any. She never seemed to like Mama much."

"She didn't. I'm not sure she liked me either."

Lucy shook her head. "She didn't. That's why I didn't like her. Grandmother said a lot of rude things about you."

"Come on," Lennox said. "Let's find an album with you and Mama."

They spent the afternoon going through every box in the basement, from Christmas lights layered in dust to an antique china set decorated with a blue flower pattern. A lot of old clothes were in boxes marked "James." Eventually Lennox found the last box in the corner; its bottom was damp from a leaking crack along the floor.

"Gross, I was *bald!*"

They laughed at the very first image: Mama holding a bald baby Lucy up for the camera. Lucy flipped through the photos eagerly. In every image she grew a little bigger. A few featured Lennox holding his new sister. But the pictures stopped abruptly just as Lucy began to crawl. Her face fell when she saw the blank pages.

"That's when she died," Lennox said. "I should have taken more, but..."

"You're my brother, not Dad. He should have been doing that. And doing all the stuff you did."

Lennox swallowed. "Come on. Let's finish this last box and then get something to eat."

A few more photo albums waited for photos never taken. Knickknacks littered the bottom. A flash of memory from Will's bedroom hit him, but there were no yo-yos or silly middle school notes. Instead he found a mini tool kit, an old box for an internet security program, and a Rolodex.

"What's that?" Lucy grabbed the Rolodex and flipped it upside down. All the cards fell out.

"It's a Rolodex." At her puzzled look, Lennox added, "like an address book."

"Huh?"

"Like the contacts list on your phone."

They collected the scattered cards and the plastic case and carried them upstairs to the kitchen. Half of them were blank, another third was damp and ruined, but Lennox read through all that he could. There were dozens of names he didn't know, one that was definitely Lucy's old babysitter from down the street. His dad's parents were listed, along with over twenty people marked as friend.

"I found it!" Lucy waved a card that was stained with water damage.

"Henry and Josephine Hill. Where's Charlottesville?"

Lennox scanned the address. Every choice kept drawing him closer and closer to Will. Charlottesville was an hour west of his grandfather's house in Richmond, maybe forty minutes south of Will's parents' home in Leon.

"Guess we're taking a road trip."

..ıll eighteen

"WILL, IT'LL BE FUN. THE team's great." Aaron hoisted the last of their baseball bags into Will's truck bed. "I promise they'll be cool about you joining for the day, okay?"

Aaron climbed into the passenger seat, and Will followed suit on the driver's side. Aaron had invited him to tag along for an impromptu workout session with several of his UVA teammates.

"I haven't played in months," Will said. "I'm sure I'll make an ass of myself."

"Better than sitting around with your parents and their pity party."

"They're worried about me, that's all."

"Can't say I blame them, but come on. Baseball, man. The good old days."

Will smiled at that. He'd missed being on the field: the repetitive tossing of the baseball, the warm sweat of a glove on his hand. Just the thought of being with a team on the field again made the knots in his chest loosen. They arrived in Charlottesville within the hour, and Aaron directed Will to the athletic complex. It was four days before Christmas but they climbed out of his truck to a warm breeze and a hot winter sun shining down on their backs.

"Bet Lennox is freezing his balls off in Boston right now."

Will scoffed. "I hope not."

"Have you heard from him since you texted him?"

Will shook his head. He didn't expect to, either. Lennox's daily messages had stopped almost a week ago. His response to Lennox had only brought silence.

"Come on, field's this way." Aaron led the way along a brick path beside a soccer field and then past a dozen tennis courts. An impressive baseball field, fenced, with a towering scoreboard and stands, extended to the tree line. Aaron led him into a locker room. It smelled better than their high school locked room and was very plush. The lockers weren't metal with clanging doors, but well-crafted wood and hung open the way Will had seen in locker room interviews after major league games.

"This one's mine." Aaron waved at one with his name and the number thirty-nine. They changed into their cleats and carried their equipment up a flight of stairs to the dugout. A small group of men were stretching on the field. Several of them shouted greetings to Aaron.

"Hey, Aaron!"

"What's up, Sandyman?"

Will grinned at the nickname. "Glad to see that nickname carried over."

Aaron glared at him through his laughter. "Shut it, Ozzy. Part of initiation. Better than some of the other guys."

Giving both real names and nicknames, Aaron introduced Will. Bert Fields was a thick-muscled, six-foot giant of an outfielder. His deep voice told Will exactly why his nickname was Ace of Bass. Dave Rogers was another outfielder, with a nose that must have been broken at least twice. His smile was warm, though, and when Aaron introduced him as Pooh Bear, nobody laughed. The rest had nicknames based on their last names like Aaron and Will. Alfonso "Brookie" Brooks, Andre "Milly" Miller, Nelson "Gussy" Gustav. Everyone shook Will's hand and greeted him with a smile.

"You're the catcher, huh? Sandyman never shuts up about you."

"He's always had a bit of a thing for me," Will said. The group chuckled. "What are you guys doing today?"

Aaron answered. "Stretches, some field work, keep our rhythm and timing sharp. Maybe some live batting practice."

Everyone dispersed into pairs for stretches. Will teamed up with Aaron; they sat on the ground, legs spread in a V, the soles of their cleats pressed together.

"They seem nice," Will said as he pulled Aaron forward.

"What'd you expect? Triceratops? They're chill. Also, Andre's staring at your butt."

Will glanced over and found that Aaron was right. He turned away, his face warm. When he'd gone to New York, he'd expected flirty men or at least a few glances, but not in Virginia.

"I'm sure you could get his number. He's definitely single."

"I'm taken, remember?"

Aaron shrugged as he leaned back and brought Will forward. "I mean, how taken are you if Lennox and you don't ever talk?"

Will didn't have an answer. He didn't want to consider Lennox leaving his life for good, either.

After stretching, Will tucked thoughts of Lennox away and let himself sink into the rhythm of the game, first, tosses around the diamond, testing his infielders' accuracy and speed on soft grounders, then warming Aaron up to let the outfielders take some fly balls. Will ended up being their main batter. Everyone else wanted to practice fielding, so Will stepped up to the plate for the final half hour.

"Wow! What a moon shot." Aaron hooted as the infielders called each other off to catch the pop fly.

Will stared up at the dark dot that was the ball. Andre caught it at second base and tossed it back to Aaron. His smile was dazzling in the afternoon sunlight, but it only made Will wish for Lennox.

He knocked balls all over the field. Guys called out that they were getting bored until Will aimed one toward them. It wasn't easy when he was so out of practice, but he'd caught for Aaron so long it didn't take him long to recognize his pitches. The backstop was littered with the balls he'd missed when they stopped.

"Nice swing," Andre said. He high-fived Will but didn't let go.

The rest of the guys catcalled as they walked into the locker room. Aaron winked at Will.

"So, this is kind of forward, but do you want to get dinner some time? I mean, if you're, like, single or, uh, interested."

Will's chest fluttered. He wasn't interested, but it was charming to be asked out by a boy, especially one much kinder than Lennox had been when they'd first met.

"Thanks, but I have a boyfriend."

"Oh, okay. Cool." Andre let go of his hand, smiled once more, and walked to the locker room.

Aaron helped Will pick up the missed balls behind home plate. He elbowed Will until he knocked him over.

"Dude, come on."

Aaron stared. "Did you just call me 'dude'?"

Will climbed to his feet and tossed the last few balls in the bucket. Lennox said that word a lot. Half his conversations with Otto over the phone this past summer had been the word dude and little else.

Aaron sat on the bench in the dugout. "Why'd you say no? Andre's pretty great. I mean, you and Lennox are... whatever right now. What's it going to hurt?"

"I don't want to move on from Lennox. We haven't even officially said we are or aren't broken up." Will's eyes followed the last ray of sunlight up the stands as the sun dipped into the trees beyond the outfield. "I'm sure Andre's great, but I love Lennox. I can't just give up on what we've got until I talk to him."

"Then *call* him. If you love him and want him in your life, then show him that." Aaron shook his head. "I mean, damn, Will. When did you start being scared of talking to him? You guys always seemed so close."

Will stayed out on the bench after Aaron went into the locker room. He couldn't put into words what held him back from pulling his cell phone out of his pocket and dialing Lennox's number. Lennox had his trust. He had his heart. Yet whatever this was—besides residue of his embarrassment from their last visit—he couldn't shape it into anything coherent.

"I miss you," Will said as the sun sank deeper into the trees, "and I don't want to."

WILL RETURNED HOME TO A quiet house cocooned in darkness. The porch light was out. Oyster's usual barks and excited yips didn't greet him at the door. He stumbled into the hall and thumbed on the light switch. A note was left on the kitchen table from his dad and Karen.

Gone shopping with Mia. Back for dinner.

He took a shower and made grilled chicken and roasted vegetables for dinner. By the time he was finished, headlights flashed through the living room windows. Oyster whined through the hall and all the way to Will's feet, where he rolled about until Will scratched his belly.

"Hey, boy. Did you go on a nice car ride?"

Oyster howled at him and made his way to the sliding glass door. Will let him out just as Aunt Mia, Karen, and his dad entered the room. Aunt Mia gave him a one-two punch on the shoulder and shook her snow-flecked scarf at him.

"How is it snowing? It was in the sixties earlier!"

"Virginia," Karen said. "Oyster's enjoying it at least."

Will watched the husky hop around the back deck trying to eat the falling flakes. Aunt Mia hugged him tight, then held him at arm's length.

"Yeah, you're definitely taller than me. You can't *still* be growing."

Ben measured his own scalp to Will's eyebrows. "Doesn't get it from me."

"Well, Beth was a midget. You got mutant genes, nephew?"

Will shrugged. He didn't feel any taller except when he tried to look his dad in the eye and found himself looking down. Lennox was still a few inches shorter than him, same as always. Maybe they'd been growing together, and he hadn't noticed.

"How are you? You stopped calling." Aunt Mia pinched his arm and dragged him into the living room. She grabbed a box of cereal on the way.

"But I made dinner."

"Cereal, Will. This is the greatest gift college kids were ever given, besides ramen." She made him sit with her on the couch and popped open the box. "Eat."

"But the chicken and—"

"Eat cereal."

Will crunched down a chocolatey handful of Cocoa Puffs. She seemed satisfied when Karen joined them with plates of chicken and vegetables. Ben disappeared into the master bedroom, and Will heard the shower cut on.

"You know, I was mad to see you weren't with my retrieval crew in Richmond."

Will only stared at her.

"I'm just saying, I bet Lennox is visiting his family there. His sister. I was going to drag us all over there and get you two to sort this out."

"I doubt his grandfather would invite him," Will said, but the conversation turned away from him and into one about him.

"Has he called him at all?"

Karen shook her head, eyes on Will. "He won't do it. Even when I told him he should."

"It's not that simple."

"Everything starts with a word, Will," Aunt Mia said. "You'd think an English major would know that."

"I can't just... call him. This is— It's complicated, okay?"

Aunt Mia sighed and munched on her cereal. Will ate his own plate of chicken and vegetables and then hers too. Baseball all day had given him an endless appetite. Being on the field again surrounded by other guys playing had been spectacular. A tiny part of his life seemed to realign from just one afternoon on the field.

"The only way to un-complicate it is by talking it out," Karen said.

Will ignored her and stuffed a fistful of cereal into his mouth.

"Well, airplanes make me feel gross," Aunt Mia said when the cereal box was empty. "I'm going to use your shower, okay?"

Leaving Karen and Will alone, she disappeared downstairs.

"So, have you figured out any plans for the spring semester?"

"No. I mean, I'm not going back to NYU, but I don't know what else to do. I guess I'll work at the shop, you know. Go back to being a small-town guy. The city isn't for me."

"That city maybe. It was a big leap, Will, for anyone."

Will shook his head. He couldn't go back after how badly he'd failed. NYU wouldn't accept him, he was sure, and without school he'd never cut it in New York City.

"Try Boston or Richmond. Mia's already said she'd love to have you closer to Pittsburgh. You can't stay here. Your life's got so much more going for it, Will. I'm not letting you give up on that. Lennox won't either."

"Lennox isn't here."

Karen gave him a sad smile. "That isn't his fault. You know that, right?"

"Of course, it isn't," Will said and he stood up to leave. "Why would he be here? He's got his own life now."

"His own friends and hobbies and plans? Will, did you really expect his life to not change when he got to Berklee?"

He frowned. "No. Maybe. I just expected that for me, too, you know? I've had this planned for years, and it all fell apart. And he's never thought about his future until last year."

Karen patted the couch next to her. "That's not always how life works, honey."

"But my life's been so easy. I've had everything I needed to set up my future, and Lennox didn't!"

"And you think the future is ever that easy?"

Will sat beside her again. "Shouldn't it be?"

"Just because one part of your life is easy doesn't mean others will be. The future is complicated, Will. Some parts of your life will be rough or hard or downright horrible. Others are going to be smooth sailing. There's no set way for all of it to work out, but remember the same is true for Lennox. Just because you two are together doesn't mean your lives are always going to be parallel."

"I wish it did. I hate being jealous of him, because I *know* it's not his fault, but I can't help it. Everything I was dreaming about, he's got now."

"Well, you can try again. A new school, different city. Take a year off. Figure out what you want to do now while you're young."

"I don't have any other dreams," Will said before he could stop himself.

"I don't believe that's true. Just take some time; experience more of the world. Something will come to you."

...ıl nineteen

LENNOX CLUTCHED THE STEERING WHEEL the entire hour-long drive to Charlottesville. Lucy hummed, kicked at the dash, and thumbed through radio stations as if she was gobbling up candy.

"What about this one?"

Lennox laughed. "They're all fine. You pick one, Luce."

She kept clicking through stations, pausing for a few seconds and then moving on.

"We're almost there," Lennox said as he turned off the highway.

He'd never been to Charlottesville, but it reminded him of Fredericksburg—an explosion of suburbia in rugged rural land and mountains. Lines of shopping centers and neighborhoods greeted them. The GPS directed them into an older neighborhood to a split-level house covered in pale blue siding. A steep driveway led up to the house. Lennox pulled in behind the two cars parked side by side.

"Those cars look ancient," Lucy said. "That means old people probably live here, right?"

Lennox shrugged. Whatever happened now, part of him was terrified. Cameron had gone to a medical appointment this morning, leaving them free to see if their mother's parents were still alive and living here. Lucy was thrilled at the idea of them, but Lennox was sure a ball of snakes had taken up residence in his stomach. One set of grandparents were already homophobic; Lucy didn't have to worry about that.

"Come *on!*" Lucy was at his window, smacking her hand on the glass. Lennox climbed out into the frosty morning and followed her up the steps. At the door, however, Lucy hesitated. She nudged him forward.

"You knock. You're the adult."

Lennox glowered at her. "You're going to hold that against me forever."

"Duh."

Lennox rang the doorbell. Lucy ducked behind him and hung onto his arm.

Minutes passed. Lucy told him to ring again, but he knocked. A few seconds later, the door opened. A small black woman appeared. Her Afro was thick and pale gray; dark glasses hid her eyes. She had Lucy's nose and a cane in her hand. She was blind.

"Yes? Hello, who's there?"

They froze on the porch. Lennox had never dreamed she existed, yet here she was.

"Who's there?"

"Uh, I'm looking for Henry and Josephine Hill. This was the address we were given."

"And who's that? I'm not interested in buying anything."

Lennox caught the door before she closed it. She smacked him right in the stomach with her cane.

"Hey! Don't hit Lennox!"

Something about Lucy's voice made the old woman pause. Lennox rubbed his stomach.

"Lennox? That's not... what's your name, young man?"

"I'm Lennox McAvoy, and this is my sister, Lucy. We're, uh, well we're your grandkids."

Josephine took a step back. Her hand covered her mouth, and then she reached out in his direction.

"Lennox? Oh, my gosh. My sweet boy. And Lucy, too?"

"Present!"

Josephine's hand brushed Lennox's shirt and climbed up his neck to feel his face. Tears fell down her cheeks. "Oh, I can't believe this. Henry? Henry, come here!"

She continued to run her fingers over Lennox's face, over every feature, even his eyelids and then his hair. She pulled gently at one of his curls. "That's really you, Lennox? You're all grown up, aren't you? Henry, for god's sake get out here!"

Another voice echoed from inside the house. "I'm coming, Josie."

An older man appeared in a fetching pair of bright purple suspenders and a rumpled flannel shirt. His hair wasn't as pale as Josephine's, but it was swirled with blacks and grays and whites. His skin was darker, too. "Who's this now? Josie, don't claw the poor boy's face off."

"Henry, this is Lennox and Lucy. Our grandbabies. How did you find us?"

"Grandbabies?" Henry squinted at each of them, raised a finger at Lennox's face. "You're Lyra's— Lord, you could be her ghost."

Henry waved them inside and helped his wife stand out of the way. Lucy hopped right through the door to examine all the pictures on the wall, but Lennox took his first steps inside as if they were his last.

"Hey, look, Lennox! They've got pictures of us! Ugh, I'm still *bald*."

Now Henry gently tilted Lennox's face down to his, then to each side. "Lyra's eyes, her smile I bet. You used to smile so big when she brought you over. Everything but her nose."

"Uh, cool."

Lennox swallowed as Henry moved to Lucy, lifting her into a huge hug. Everything was strange. The walls were decorated with more pictures than an art museum: babies, toddlers, teenagers, family portraits. A dozen pictures of their grandparents lined another wall. The rooms were comfy compared to the stiff air of his grandfather's house.

Henry and Josephine served them a plate of cookies: iced gingerbread, chocolate chip, snickerdoodle, and Lennox's easy favorite, peanut butter cookies with Hershey's kisses on top. Lucy stuffed her face. Lennox tried to cut her off, but Henry only filled the plate higher. They ate their fill of cookies as they talked. Their grandparents—insisting on being called Pop and Nana—wanted to know everything about their lives.

Lucy told them all about school and soccer. She showed off her new prosthetic leg too.

"I got this one over the summer 'cause I'm growing so much. I'm going to be taller than Lennox!"

Pop laughed and Nana hugged her tight. Lennox had deflected from himself so far, but the questions turned to him next: about his childhood after his mother's death, school, what he was doing now. As soon as Lennox mentioned he was going to school in Boston, Henry leapt to his feet.

"Boston? What are you going to school for?"

"Lennox is a musician." Lucy wiggled her fingers in the air as though she was playing a keyboard.

"You kept playing?"

Henry took Lennox by the shoulders.

"Uh, yeah, of course. I love it."

Josephine dragged him into the living room to a well-polished piano. She set him down at it. Henry joined him and lifted the cover.

"Used to play this all the time, at jazz clubs. I was quite the hip fella when I was your age," Henry told him. "Musicians speak to lovely ladies in a way words can't. Bet you know all about that, handsome young man like you."

Lennox grunted; his chest was tight like a wound-up wind-up doll. He played the first piece that came to mind: the jazz piece he'd done for his private instruction final. Henry chimed in after a dozen measures. It was a fun piece, bouncy and fast. Lucy twirled around, laughing, while Josephine clapped along and began to sing.

Henry played a full piece that Josephine sang the words to. They made quite the pair, full of smiles and glowing eyes. Lucy admired them, but, when the song ended, she left for the bathroom, and Lennox could hear her clomping around, no doubt touching everything in sight.

"Oh, you play as beautifully as your mother. She studied music in college too."

"She went to Julliard, didn't she?"

Nana shook her head and reached for his hand as he returned to the couch. "Berklee, in Boston. I'm guessing that's where you're going?"

Lennox nodded. "She went to Berklee, too? But I thought—"

"Oh, she did a few short programs at Julliard," Henry said as he closed the piano. "One between semesters, another when you were young. They had a lot of opportunities, and she loved the city. Nothing like New York. We went up for our anniversary a few years ago. Lot of fun dance clubs, even for our crowd."

"Right. Yeah, New York's great. My b—"

But Lennox stopped himself. Would they reject him, too? He had to make sure Lucy could live with them before they found any of that out.

"So, you're a college man now, all grown up. You have yourself a girl?"

Lennox shook his head, although it was more of a diagonal movement than left and right. Nana patted his leg. "Henry, don't pester him about that. I'm still picturing that cherub-cheeked little boy I remember."

"No, it's all right, uh, Nana." His tongue caught on the last word.

"A boy then? A cute boyfriend?"

"Henry, leave him be! He doesn't have to say if he doesn't want to."

Lennox swallowed. "I do have someone. His name's Will."

"Oh, that's wonderful, but don't you let Henry weasel everything out of you. Boy your age needs his secrets," Nana said. She stood up and grabbed her cane, not the least bit surprised. "I'm going to go drag Lucy out of whatever she's gotten into."

Henry took her place. "Will, huh? He a nice boy? Treats you well?"

"Yeah, definitely. I mean, we've hit a bit of a rough patch, but he's great."

"Rough, hmm? Josie and I hit a few over the years. It happens, but you work through it." He patted Lennox on the shoulder. "What do you kids say to my famous chili for lunch?"

HENRY DID HIS BEST TO fatten up Lennox and Lucy. He dropped four cornbread muffins onto their napkins and insisted they have third helpings of his chili. Lucy ate like a ferocious bear, but Lennox tried to be polite. He was still reeling from how simple his coming out had been: no shock or statements trying to dissuade him, not even a raised eyebrow. Henry and Josephine had accepted him without batting an eyelash.

"And then, okay, I took my leg off, see, like this—"

"Lucy, not at the table."

Lucy frowned and left her prosthetic attached. "But the story's better when I wave it around."

"Not at dinner, okay?"

"Fine."

Henry eyed Lennox. Josephine continued to eat, but her hand found Lennox's. They didn't say anything until the dishes were clean and Lucy was in the living room flipping through television channels.

"As glad as we are to have you two here, I think we're both wondering how this happened. After your mom died, your dad just disappeared with you."

Nana set a cup of hot chocolate in front of him. Henry added whipped cream and nudged it toward him.

"You still do the chocolate chips on top?"

Lennox shook his head. He'd told them a vague outline of his life—one that left out all the difficult parts.

"We wondered, all these years…" Henry dabbed at his eyes with a napkin. "Last I remember, he ignored all of our calls. We drove down to visit for your birthday that year and the house was for sale. Didn't think we'd see either of you again."

"Dad moved us up north, near D.C. He kind of fell apart." Lennox cleared his throat and took a long drink of hot chocolate. "His parents kept us for a few months, then Dad got us back, and we moved right before my birthday. He wasn't the same."

"How's he doing now? You two are still with him, I'm sure."

Lennox shook his head. "He died. About five years ago."

"Oh, honey..."

"It's fine. I mean, he wasn't much after Mama died."

Henry only nodded, but Josephine said, "You've done a good job with her."

"What?"

"Bringing your sister up. She adores you, listens to you."

"I'm all she had."

Lennox drank the rest of his hot chocolate as the conversation continued. They asked all about the last few years and his time in a juvenile detention center. Some of that seemed to surprise them, but they accepted all of his words without question. He talked them all the way through until now, and the request he'd come here to make.

"Grandfather's sick, too. He hasn't said much beyond that it's terminal, and, since I'm in Boston at school and Lucy's here..."

"Of course, we'll take her," Henry said at once. "We've missed too much already. We'd love to have you both."

"Oh, I don't need—"

"You're going to need somewhere to stay for your breaks," Nana told him. "Somewhere not too far from that boy of yours. You haven't told us much about him. Is he cute?"

"Weren't you just telling me a few hours ago to leave him be about that?"

"Hush, Henry." Nana pushed a new plate of cookies toward Lennox. "Tell us. He's kind? A good man?"

"Will's the best."

"You don't sound too sure of that."

Lennox frowned at her dark glasses and noticed the way she tilted her head so that her right ear was directed at him.

"He *is*. We're just… we're in a rough spot, that's all. He's great, I promise. He's sweet and kind and wants only the best for me."

"And you love him?"

From the doorway, Lucy made a gagging noise.

"Shut up," Lennox snapped at her.

"Boys are gross."

"So are you."

"Kids, stop." Henry chuckled. It was impossible to miss the adoration in his eyes. "You know, I've missed getting to say that. It's too quiet around here now that everyone's grown up."

Lucy gaped at him. "Do we have aunts and uncles? And cousins? Do they have puppies?"

She sat down with Pop, but, to Lennox's surprise Nana led him into the living room and then to the front door.

"Am I going somewhere?"

"You're going to see this boy. Will."

"But I've got to get Lucy back to Richmond."

"By the sound of it, you've been her parent long enough," Nana said. She squeezed his arm. "Time for you to have a life of your own and to fix whatever's wrong."

"Nothing's wrong."

"Sugar, you don't talk about someone the way you've been talking about Will if you think everything's fine. Go on now. Get going. We'll call your grandfather, get things settled. Lucy can stay here tonight." She pulled his coat off the hook by the door. "You know the way? The address?"

Lennox nodded, and she smacked him in the side with her cane.

"Don't you nod at a blind woman."

"Sorry. I know the address. I've been using it as mine for the last year."

She touched his cheek then, but only her frown told him anything about what she was thinking. He wasn't used to such kindness. Lennox let her brush her fingers over his cheek for a minute, before leaning away.

"You go on. Let us know when you get there." Josephine pushed him onto the porch with her cane, into the steady orange glow of the streetlights. Lennox climbed into his grandmother's old car and sat.

Should he call Will first? Text him? His fingers went numb from the cold as he sat there, phone in hand, unmoving.

Henry came out with a bag of trash for the can on the curb. He knocked on the window. "You going or not? Josie can be very sharp when she's sure of something."

"I don't know. I want to see him, but…"

"Then go see him, Lennox. Don't waste whatever time you've got together. Fear's not worth that."

LENNOX PULLED INTO THE GRAVEL driveway of Will's house hours later. The trees were dark; the house was invisible until his headlights hit the windows. He flicked them off. Snow crunched under his tires as he pulled in beside Ben's jeep. Nothing looked out of place. The same dark shutters framed every window, the porch was still well-swept and neat, a trail of smoke drifted from the chimney over the garage.

He climbed out, checked the time. Midnight. Both the icy country roads and his half a dozen anxious stops had slowed him down. Lennox stepped onto the porch, raised his hand to knock, then thought better of it. Oyster would wake the entire house.

Will's bedroom window was sealed shut when he jumped down into the window well. Inside, Oyster yipped, and his collar jingled. Lennox knocked.

Oyster gave one brief bark before Will's voice scolded him.

Lennox knocked again.

"Aaarrrooo!"

Maybe he'd have been better off at the front door.

"Oyster, hush!" Will's voice again, louder now. A lamp flickered to life on the other side of the frosted window. Something scraped under the window, and then a dark cloth swept the fog and frost away. Will's sleeve was replaced by his freckled face, sullen and sleepy.

"Lennox?"

"Uh, hi."

Will unlocked the window, and it flapped open. Even half asleep he stared at Lennox in wonder. "You're here."

"Yeah, doofus. You think I wouldn't see you for Christmas?"

"But it's the middle of the night, and Christmas isn't for a few days. I mean, we haven't spoken since..."

They both went quiet. Will hugged himself tight and shivered. Oyster's tail thumped against Will's bookcase.

"Looks like you need a good blanket."

"Well, if you hadn't woken me I'd still be in my blanket pile."

"I meant me."

Will hesitated. "I'm sorry."

"So am I. Can I come in already? It's freezing out here."

Will stepped back. Lennox climbed in and dropped to the floor. Oyster was on him at once, whining and rubbing against his legs. Lennox scratched his head as Will shut the window. He wouldn't meet Lennox's eyes when he turned around.

"You do want to see me, don't you?"

Had this been a mistake? Will had never been so awkward around him. Not once since they'd met over a year ago had Will acted like this. He'd never acted the way he had the last time they'd seen each other in Boston, either.

"Yes, of course, but I... I was such an ass. You should hate me."

"Well, I don't. Doubt I ever will." When Will still appeared unconvinced, Lennox stepped closer and eased his arms around Will's neck. "I love you, Will. That hasn't changed."

Will tried to smile. "I love you, too. But I'm just..."

Lennox kissed him, one gentle peck on his lips, then another on his jaw. "We'll figure it out, I promise. But for tonight, can we just be us?"

"Okay."

...ıl twenty

"Bud, wake up."

Will tried to roll away from the person shaking him. Ben grabbed his shoulder to stop him.

"Dad?"

"Hey, Mia and I are going to go into town to get Karen's present before she gets back from work. You want to go?"

Will grumbled and curled himself into his blankets, tried to snuggle into Lennox, but his warmth was no longer in the bed. He sat up and looked around—just him and his dad. Oyster's nails clicked on the kitchen floor over his head. Had last night been another dream?

"No, I'll stay here."

"Okay, we should be back before her, but if not, and she asks, tell her we went to brunch."

Will nodded and fell back in his bed. He could hear his toilet running. Ben heard it, too.

"That thing running again?"

Will shrugged. For one blissful moment, he'd thought Lennox was here. Who cared about a running toilet?

"Probably time to replace the valve," Ben said.

Ben patted his head and went upstairs. Will curled himself into a ball of blankets and warmth. He'd dreamed last night. Lennox knocking on his window, Lennox snuggling up with him, whispering about all they'd missed of each other, and then falling asleep holding one another. Every bit of that had been one fantastic fantasy.

"Will, I'm gonna leave your door open for Oyster!"

Aunt Mia's heels clicked off beat with Oyster's nails. He heard sets of feet walk toward the front door, and then it snapped shut.

Calling Lennox didn't seem like such a bad idea. Dreams like last night's only made him ache with regret. The bed behind him dipped—Oyster's arrival to the cuddle pile.

"Hey, lover. Can I get some blankets, too?" Lennox's arms dug into his blanket cocoon and pulled him closer. It hadn't been a dream. Lennox was here, in his life once again.

"Did you just call me lover?"

Lennox pressed his face into Will's neck. "Yeah, and did I hear right? We have the house all to ourselves?"

"Us and Oyster."

"He knows when to stay away."

Lennox kissed his neck, then under his earlobe. His breath warmed Will as his damp kisses chilled Will's skin. Will rolled over to face him and was met with a firm kiss that tasted like minty toothpaste.

"I see what your plans are then," Will said, but he smiled and pulled Lennox closer under the blankets.

He sank right into Lennox's kisses, greedy for every touch he'd missed. Lennox traded one kiss for a second, then a third, each longer and firmer. He nibbled Will's lower lip and hooked his thigh over Will's hips.

"We do still need to talk," Will mumbled. He kissed Lennox once more; a bolt of heat ran through his belly.

"Yeah, we've got a lot to talk about, I know." Lennox rested his forehead against Will's to slow them down, but Will only pushed his hands under Lennox's shirt, thrilled at the way his skin rippled at his touch. "But talking can happen all the time, right? I mean, sex is best in an empty house."

"Right. Definitely."

Lennox's hands tugged at his shirt; one leg locked around his thighs. His lips moved over Will's neck before Will managed to ease away to pull his pajamas off. They both stripped under the blankets, fumbling and kicking until all the cold air they'd been trying to keep out had seeped in.

"Ugh, it's so fucking cold down here."

Will smiled. "Come here."

They held each other close, not moving much besides their lips or the brush of their hands. Will reveled in Lennox's passion; in the smiles Lennox kissed him with, and the happiness that filled him with an irreplaceable contentment. Nothing had changed between them.

Lennox arched into him; his hips rolled into Will's. Their cocks rubbed together, and Will groaned.

"What do you need?"

Lennox's hands cupped his face. He kissed him once, and Will shuddered. All he needed was Lennox here with him, to see and feel how much they were still with each other. To have Lennox pliant and open beneath him, sinking into pleasure only he gave. To be *wanted*.

"Will?"

Will bit his lip.

Asking Lennox to step into uncomfortable spaces was always hard. Giving up control was difficult for Lennox, but Will craved those rare moments when he did. Lennox collapsed in exquisite detail. His eyes glazed over; his body moved only to welcome pleasure. All they needed was each other. Their bodies joined in wild freedom as Lennox lost control and Will wrapped it around himself like skin.

Will ached with a carnal hunger. For Lennox to let himself go— for him to willingly give all of himself and his trust to Will—that was enough. He craved Lennox's body shaking as if an earthquake was shattering inside of him. Will had found that breaking point only once over the summer, with Lennox's first prostate orgasm, then intermittently with the others. Some aspect of familiarity had dissolved and given them something grander. Will longed for that breaking point.

"You okay? We don't have to—"

"I want you to let go for me."

Lennox's eyes flickered in the dim dawn. Will expected the usual hesitation, even the abrupt and callous rejection from last spring. Yet this boy—this man—curled up with him wasn't that Lennox anymore. Lennox cupped his face again, his eyes sure.

"I'm yours."

A shuddering breath left Will. Lennox smiled into their next kiss as Will fumbled behind himself for the nightstand's drawer. He pulled out a box of condoms and an icy bottle of lube, then tucked the bottle between their chests. Once Will's condom was on and the lube was warm, he coated his fingers and squeezed Lennox's ass with his clean hand.

"How much do you need?"

Lennox shivered. "Two, maybe three. It's been a while."

Will found Lennox's hole, pressed his finger against it, and rubbed. Lennox jolted. "Still cold."

Will took his time, rubbing the puckered skin and kneading Lennox's ass with his other hand. Lennox tried to kiss him, but he couldn't keep from gasping and panting while he rutted against Will. Will pushed his index finger in first; Lennox was clenching tight and groaning.

"Fuck, faster. I need *you*."

"My fingers *are* me."

"Don't be a smart ass."

He worked Lennox open quickly, thrusting one finger in deep, then adding a second. He scissored them apart as he thrust, letting Lennox squirm and try to work himself down onto his hand.

"I'm ready, come on."

"Are you sure?"

In answer, Lennox removed Will's fingers, grabbed his cock, slicked the condom with lube, and hooked his leg higher over Will's hip. He lined Will up and arched his ass. Will's body jerked, and he felt the head of his cock push into Lennox. He thrust slowly, pausing when Lennox's body began to tense.

"You needed three."

Lennox kissed him roughly at first, but then slower, softer. Will held him by the hips, rolled his own back, and then gave another shallow, slow thrust. Lennox's kisses faltered; his hips eased into the rhythm Will started. They spent a few minutes on gentleness, Will pushing a little deeper with every thrust until his balls were pressed to Lennox's ass.

"Okay?"

A soft hum, another sweet kiss. Lennox breathed with him, pliant and malleable, as Will adjusted the angle of his hips, once, twice, a third time until—

"Shit, just like that!" Lennox clung to him, his cock stiff between them, his breaths sharp.

Will obeyed, reveled in the bliss that eased Lennox's features. It struck him how small Lennox felt with his narrow hips in Will's hands. A flicker of power rushed through Will. Being Lennox's shatterpoint, finding every miniscule pleasure that brought him closer to being lost in ecstasy, was divine. He was a force of passion, guided by the commands of Lennox's body.

Lennox opened for him: his face to Will's cheek, his mouth panting and crying out into his ear.

"Will! Yes, right there. Good, so good. You're all I need."

Lennox's ass tightened around Will's cock. He buried his face in Will's neck and moaned. Will slowed his pace, buried himself in Lennox, and stilled. He was winded and tense from the orgasm shaking Lennox's body, but he could continue, for Lennox and himself. Lennox had collapsed into bliss once before, and he needed that now. They both did.

"Good?"

Lennox nodded, his body trembling. "The best."

Will rolled them, eased Lennox onto his back and kept his cock inside him. He nuzzled Lennox's neck, his cheek.

"Love you."

"In love with you."

Lennox hummed as Will began to move again. Will chuckled and kissed him; his insides shriveled with delight. He belonged here, with Lennox in whatever capacity they found.

Pieces of Lennox crumbled for Will. First his resolve to control his volume dissolved to ash with his first shout. In another prostate orgasm, Lennox's body shook; his muscles contracted along his thighs, his stomach. Yet his feet kept pressing Will's ass closer, driving him into him. His consciousness was the second to go, and Will's own body shivered and quaked to see Lennox's eyes glaze and his entire being become only their shared pleasure.

Third was Will's own control. They charged into each other, until Lennox's ecstasy surged through Will. His self was lost, devoted to them and everything physical that joined them. Will came with Lennox; he collapsed onto him and his hard cock between them. He felt the gush of Lennox's final orgasm, shuddered at the feeling soaking into his skin.

"Yours," Lennox said when he could speak again. He rubbed his nose against Will's and stretched his legs.

"Yours, too."

Karen sent Oyster downstairs with a dozen tennis balls to wake them that afternoon. He barked and stumbled, knocking over Will's baseball bag and then his desk chair. One tennis ball hit the wall and bounced onto them.

"Woof! Arrrooo!"

"Ugh, shut *up*, seafood dog."

Oyster hopped on top of them and slobbered all over the blankets in search of the tennis ball. The other eleven balls rolled all over the room.

"She did that on purpose."

"Yeah, I did. I want you both upstairs in ten minutes. No excuses!"

Will's door shut. He rolled off Lennox's chest; dried cum stuck to them. They cleaned off in the bathroom and dressed, Will in a sweatshirt and jeans, Lennox in the clothes he'd worn yesterday. Karen was in the living room with a plate of cookies on the coffee table and two glasses of milk waiting.

"Sit."

They sat. Lennox snatched up several cookies, but Will watched Karen. Were they in trouble? What in the world could they have possibly done in a few hours?

Karen yanked the cookies out of Lennox's hands.

"Hey!"

"You get cookies when you tell me details."

Will stared at her in horror. The last thing he ever wanted was to explain the ins and outs of his sex life to Karen.

"Well, first we took our clothes off. Then we put condoms on. Safety first, right? And then Will—"

Karen smacked Lennox on the head. He winced, but grinned at Will, unhurt.

"I meant, where did Ben go, and what present did he get me?"

Oh, right. Will had forgotten that. "They went to brunch."

"Bullshit."

Lennox gaped at her. "Did you just say—"

"Yes, I did. And if you tell me, you can have this entire plate of cookies."

Lennox looked tempted, but Will hadn't mentioned his dad's scheme; they'd been busy with themselves all morning.

"You'll find out on Christmas."

"If he bought me *another* ride-on lawn mower, he's a dead man."

Lennox dived for the milk and cookies and took off into the kitchen with them, Oyster at his heels. Will stayed, eyeing Karen's sour look.

"It's not gardening stuff. Or anything at Home Depot."

Karen gave him a wary look. "You helped him pick it out?"

"Yeah, months ago. Don't bother Lennox, he doesn't know, okay?"

Karen still frowned, but she agreed, then turned the conversation spotlight onto him. "So when did Lennox get here?"

"Last night. *Late* last night. He snuck in through my window."

"You two are okay then? Talked everything out?"

"Well, no."

"Will..."

"We were *busy* while the house was empty."

Karen rolled her eyes. "Well, go talk. I need a shower. Then maybe we can hang the Christmas lights. We missed everything, what with your dad's health scare last year."

She went into the master bedroom. Will followed the ferocious sounds of Lennox eating and found him sitting on the counter, his face smeared with chocolate and icing and a fresh milk mustache.

"Pig."

Lennox handed him a gingerbread man as Oyster whined to go out. Skidding on the icy deck, they followed Oyster into the chilly afternoon. Will sat on the steps.

"We still need to talk."

Lennox sat, too. "Where do you want to start?"

Will swallowed his resolve. "I, I should go first, I think. It's my fault we're in this mess."

"No, it's not," Lennox said. "You were lonely and scared and miserable. I'm not mad at you for wanting me in New York with you. I mean, I was, but I get it. I miss being together every day too."

"It was selfish."

"Yeah, so?"

Will frowned. "I can't be selfish with you. We're in a serious relationship. We're an *us*."

"We're a Will and a Lennox, too." Lennox brushed Will's hair off his forehead. "And you're allowed to be selfish, Will. We both are. You'll never get anything you want if you aren't a little selfish."

"I'm not very good at that."

Lennox sighed. "I know. I wouldn't be at Berklee if you were. You always put everyone else first, sometimes in the most ridiculous ways. But what about *you*?"

"What about me? *Ouch*, don't pinch me!"

Lennox pinched him again though, hard on his neck. Will glared at him.

"You do the same. With your sister *and* with me."

"Lucy's different. I didn't have a choice. If I hadn't taken care of her, nobody would have." Lennox's gaze dropped, but he continued, "You're important to me, Will. And you should be to yourself too. Enough to put yourself first and figure out what you want with your life."

"I thought I did have it figured out," Will snapped. "My dreams aren't supposed to happen, I guess. They're all meant for that stupid box."

"That's not true. You just have to take some time to think about yourself. Stop worrying about me. Hell, about us. We're fine, right? Even if we're not in the same city or state, I still want what we have."

Will shivered in the cold. Oyster raced over, a long stick in his mouth. Lennox accepted it and lofted it into a snowy drift by the pool. A great cloud of ice and snow bloomed into the air, followed by Oyster, yipping and bouncing.

"I do, too. You're the one thing I'm really sure of these days."

"I can't be your everything though. You should be your entire life, not me."

Even as Lennox kissed his neck, Will faltered. Somewhere inside him a muffled explosion had gone off. Everyone had always told him something different. His life should be about school, about friends, or baseball, or a million other day-to-day interests, hobbies, or commitments. He should devote himself to some*thing* and some*one*, but never himself. Not even his parents had mentioned that.

"Shit, I'm going to sounds like Dr. Austin, but who are you? That's what he keeps asking me. Guess we both need to answer it."

Will chuckled. "But that's easy. I'm Will Osborne. I'm a son and a stepson. I'm your boyfriend. I'm Oyster's doggy dad."

Lennox considered him. "That's who you are to other people. Who are you to yourself? Without me or your family or anyone else."

He hesitated, and for Lennox that seemed to be enough.

"It's okay. I don't have an answer for that either. That's part of growing up, I guess."

"But we're adults now. We *are* grown up."

"Are we?"

* * *

THEIR CONVERSATION LEFT WILL WITH more questions than answers. He was glad to have the surety of Lennox's love again: the confidence that they were in this together, whatever *this* was. Will didn't get that, but he didn't pry either. Lennox opened up in his own time. For now, Lennox was right. He needed to focus on himself.

Ben and Karen offered a hundred suggestions around the television on Christmas Eve, everything from taking up knitting to getting his pilot's license. Some options were practical, like going to a different college in the fall. Others were absurd and reminded him of Lennox's crazy dreams from his first day in New York.

"You could become a professional merman."

Will stared at Karen. "I don't think that's a real thing."

"It totally is! I saw it on the news."

"What about one of those YouTube stars?"

"Dad, I don't have anything to say."

Ben and Karen continued to toss out options, but at the other end of the sectional couch, Aunt Mia kept quiet. She hadn't said much since Lennox left that morning. Will tried to catch her eye for the third time, but she stared right through him to the Christmas tree.

"These are all fun ideas," Aunt Mia said. "But none of them seem very you."

"I'm not really merman material."

Karen chuckled. "I was kidding. Mostly. All we're saying is that the sky's the limit. Well, the moon really. You could be an astronaut. A painter. *Anything*. Just because you achieved one dream and it didn't work out, doesn't mean that's it."

Will's mind drifted to the box under his bed. Most of those dreams had been silly ones, just blips on the radar, all except one, but baseball wasn't an option. That dream, much like New York, had been the most real, but it fell apart.

"You should come back to Pittsburgh with me," Aunt Mia said. "Try a smaller city. Get a chance to explore and see a bit of the world before taking whatever your next step is."

Ben nodded. "It'll do you good to be away from here."

"Right, because being in New York did so much good for me."

"Don't be a smartass. If you don't leave, you'll be stuck here, year after year, saying soon or next month. Twenty years later you'll have gone nowhere. That's what people do, Will. They come here and they don't leave. They settle for a piece of what they want, but never figure out what else they need. I don't want that to happen to you."

"I'm not sure going to Pittsburgh will help."

Ben shrugged. "Maybe not. But it's something new. Maybe you'll find a school there you like. Meet some new friends, locals. Find a new hobby. Live a little, have an adventure."

All three of them watched him, and Will found himself agreeing. He couldn't stay here. Not because Ben and Karen would throw him out, but for his own sanity. Boston wasn't much of an option either. He couldn't ask Lennox and Troy to share their dorm room, and even, if he did, what would he do while they were out and about all day in class or at campus events?

"When do we leave?"

..ıl twenty-one

CHRISTMAS EVE IN RICHMOND WAS a tense affair. Cameron's sickness—still unnamed and a topic Lennox's grandfather refused to discuss—was making itself known. As Lucy dumped out her stocking that evening, bright candies and a new soccer net and several lip gloss bottles rolled out on the living room rug. Cameron sat in his old leather chair; his skin was the color of cold oatmeal. All afternoon he'd been coughing violently.

"Lennox, can you open this?" Lucy shoved the soccer net box into his hands. She had a chocolate bar already unwrapped.

Cameron shifted in his chair. "Lucy, you're going to spoil your dinner."

She shoved an entire wedge into her mouth and choked on it.

"Don't be a brat," Lennox told her. He tore the top off the box and worked the hard-plastic cradle apart. "No more until after dinner."

"Why not? It's Christmas Eve."

"Yeah, and that doesn't mean you get to make yourself sick on chocolate." Lennox held his hand out for the chocolate bar, and, after one firm stamp of her foot, Lucy handed it over. "Go check on the lasagna."

Lucy stomped away into the kitchen. Cameron heaved up another coughing fit; his handful of tissues covered his mouth. Lennox went over to him.

"You were fine the other day." Lennox patted him once on the back, then stopped because it was too weird. He handed his grandfather his glass of water when his coughing subsided. "How bad is it?"

"Just a little cough."

"Yeah, and a little cancer?"

"Lennox, we've talked about this."

Lennox flared up at his words, an echo of Lucy. "No, we haven't. You won't tell me anything about it, or what your doctors say, and you *still* haven't told Lucy. She needs to know."

"She needs you." Cameron stood up and went to the kitchen.

Lennox glared after him. Everything was always left up to him. He'd have to tell Lucy and somehow explain without any real details.

Dinner was quiet and tense. Lucy was still mad at him about the chocolate bar, he was mad at their grandfather, and Cameron sat in stiff silence in denial of everything. Lennox went to his room—the guest room—after dinner and shut himself in. The walls around him were bare except for an ornate mirror in his grandmother's style and a solitary portrait of a wrinkled old white man. His eyes gave Lennox the creeps, as if someone's real eyes were peering through them. Only his backpack and a scattered pile of clothes were his. He plugged his phone in to charge and opened his laptop. Troy immediately pinged him on Skype, then called when Lennox said he was free.

"Hey, Troy."

"Happy Christmas!"

"Yeah, you too."

Two women waved from behind Troy, one older and the other their age. Troy glanced over his shoulder, and Lennox spotted a well-lit, beautiful kitchen.

"Mom and Anna say hi."

The women waved, then disappeared when Troy scooped up his laptop and left the room.

"That's your sister?"

"Cousin. They're visiting from California. Almost didn't make it because of the snow. Wyoming and all the fun weather I don't miss."

A door shut, and Lennox saw a bed and a chest of drawers. Troy sat and grinned at him.

"So, how's Richmond? Your grandparents aren't being shits?"

"Uh, well, Grandfather's being a pain, but," Lennox shrugged, "my grandmother died last month. That's part of the reason he invited me."

Troy watched him. "You okay? I mean, you don't seem too, well..."

"She hated me, so it's fine. I'm not sure he liked her too much either, to be honest." Lennox sat back on his bed. "My sister's great. Just mad I won't let her eat everything in her stocking tonight."

They talked for a while, catching up on their daily lives and new music they'd discovered. Troy seemed content to stay with his family, but Lennox itched to return to the frigid cold of Boston, to the snowy avenues and streets, to an entire campus that made his heart beat like a symphony.

They said their goodbyes, and Lennox checked his short Skype list. Nobody else was on. He shut his laptop off and climbed under his blankets. His phone rang a few minutes later—it was Otto.

"What's up?"

"Hey, asshole. How come you aren't in town?"

Lennox rolled onto his back and gazed up at the dark ceiling. "Visiting my sister."

Otto huffed and, in the background, Lennox heard Abe's voice squealing about some new robotics kit.

"You're with that asshole? Your grandfather's a dick."

"Well, he's dying now," Lennox said. "Figured I'd see Lucy and help get all of that worked out."

Otto swore. "So what? You're playing dad again then, is that it? That's a shitty deal, man, even if you like your sister."

"Just because you want to spoon your brother's eyes out—"

"Hey, one of us has gotta keep a level head." Otto's voice dropped. "So really? You're her new guardian?"

Lennox explained the discovery of his maternal grandparents and their agreement to care for Lucy once Cameron was no longer fit. Otto, for once, seemed thoughtful.

"Huh, I mean, that's better than you, but your dad never contacted them? He just cut them out of your lives?"

Lennox bit his lip. He'd done his best not to think about what his dad had done to their family since they'd met their maternal grandparents. Otto was right, though. James McAvoy had packed up and run—from his own family and his dead wife's.

"We're going over there tomorrow. Will's supposed to join us sometime in the afternoon." He frowned before adding, "*He's* coming, too. I'm hoping they'll tell Lucy then, or at least figure all of this out, but I'm sure he'll be an ass to them. It's kind of his thing."

"You come by it honestly, then."

"Shut up."

Otto chuckled and Abe continued to holler in the background.

"So where the fuck have you been? Last I heard you were holing up in Minnesota."

For a long time, Otto was quiet. Silences and thoughtfulness were unlike the friend Lennox recalled. Otto had always been a fierce person, loud and without fear of the consequences of his words.

"I just got back last month. It's different up there. They live on a reservation, you know? Don't have access to stuff like we do, even out in the country. I learned a lot. Not about making those stupid dreamcatchers Abe's painting the walls with, but... important stuff. About, like, our history. We're warriors. Most of my family's been in the military."

"But your mom doesn't want you to join?"

Otto was quiet again. Lennox waited.

"I always ignored all of this stuff. My heritage or whatever you want to call it. It wasn't cool to be interested in it, not with those jerks at school. I didn't want to have anything to do with my father, either. He left us, you know? And all of this—being Ojibwe and learning what that means, it was like if I did that, then I'd forgiven him." Otto cleared his throat. "Mom sent me there on purpose. She wanted me to understand our legacy before I decided."

"I guess that makes sense," Lennox said. "Throwing you out into the cold of Minnesota would get through your damn head better than words."

Otto didn't snap at him like he once would have. Instead he sighed over the line. "I'm still not joining, but... the people up there, the kids especially, they need help. There's drugs everywhere, and suicides, too. Maybe I can do something to help. I don't know. Be a different kind of warrior."

"Yeah, I get that. You going to be in town for a while?"

* * *

LENNOX, LUCY, AND CAMERON ARRIVED at Josephine and Henry's house around midday. The street outside was lined with cars. The driveway was full, too. Lucy chattered as Lennox circled the block. Cameron grumbled about the crowded street.

"Crowded neighborhood they've picked. We never have problems like this on *our* street."

"You've got a driveway the size of a baseball field. Look, there's a space."

Lennox parallel parked between a pair of pickup trucks. Lucy raced to their grandparents' house, but Lennox lingered. Cameron refused his help, but Lennox hovered anyway. He wasn't sure why he cared so much about him. This man had rarely cared for him. Yet he felt guilty whenever he looked at his grandfather.

"That's it?"

Cameron eyed the split-level home in distaste. Lennox shrugged. Every home on this block seemed small in comparison to his grandfather's colonial. His home was as close to a mansion as possible in Richmond.

"Come on. Lucy's already inside."

The door was open, and Henry greeted them, wearing a candy cane bowtie around his neck, suspenders with jingling bells, and a bright red Santa hat. He pulled Lennox into a warm hug.

"Merry Christmas!"

"Uh, yeah, right." Lennox cleared his throat and waved a hand at Cameron. "This is—"

"Cameron McAvoy, good to see you after all these years!"

Henry hugged him, too, and pulled Lennox into the crowded house. He glanced back at Cameron's stunned face before he was overwhelmed by people. Lucy was already being passed around, excited to meet every member of the horde filling the room.

"Lennox?" Nana Josephine appeared, batting her way through the crowd of adults and children and teenagers with her cane. "Oh, honey, it's all right."

"What? I'm fine."

She patted his face and led him to his first set of people. Lennox couldn't keep anyone's names straight after the fifth person. Arnold, Jasmine, Diego, David, Latoya, Keisha, Maggie, Lula, on and on the names went. Lennox shook hands and tried to avoid kisses from relatives he didn't recall. In the kitchen with Josephine, he managed to take a breath.

"You okay?"

"Fine."

She wacked him with her cane. "Don't lie to a blind woman."

Lennox grumbled. "Who *are* all of those people?"

He peered into the crowded living room. Lucy was the life of the party, telling her favorite story from her daycare days, complete with lifting her leg into the air. Cameron was nowhere to be seen.

"Arnold's our youngest. Keisha's his wife. Damon, Cheria, and Latoya are theirs. They're all in high school now."

Lennox continued to stare into the room, trying to place those names with the blur of faces. He couldn't.

"Jasmine's our oldest. Two years older than your mom. Lula and her finally married a few years ago. They've had kids for ages, though. Diego's their oldest, and that's his fiancé, Cassie. Alejandra, Mateo, Emilia, and Rose are theirs, too."

"That's way too many kids."

"Hush now. I've no doubt you and Lucy would be more than a pair if... if things had gone different."

Nana sniffed and turned away from him to dab at her eyes.

"Oh, Christmas gets to me. It's never been the same without her." She faced him again and did her best to smile. "But we have you two back now. That's all I could have asked for. It's all I've prayed for ever since your dad left with you and Lucy."

"I miss her, too."

In all these years, Lennox couldn't recall ever saying that to anyone. Not to Lucy or Cameron or any of his recent friends. Not even to Will.

"I'm sure you barely remember her."

"Fragments. Feelings more than anything specific. I remember her smile. And sitting with her at the piano in the afternoons. Mostly, just how good the world seemed with her there."

"I'll give you some pictures," Josephine said. "You and Lucy. It's important to remember her, especially for you."

She let him go back into the living room at his own pace. It was quieter when he returned, and for the most part everyone left him alone. Henry and Cameron were absent, but besides a few questions about Lennox's school, the focus was on the smallest kids, who were playing with their new toys.

After an hour, Lennox snuck outside to the front steps. Will's truck passed once, and then stopped. Lennox jogged out to him and hopped in without a word.

"Uh, hi. I was actually looking to park."

Lennox dragged Will's face right over the gear shift and kissed him until his head swam.

"Wow, okay. I guess we can circle the block."

Will turned left at the corner and drove down the next street over. Lennox clenched his hand on the gear shift. They found a place to park two streets away, but Lennox couldn't bring himself to let go of Will's hand.

"What's wrong?"

"I'm fine."

"Lennox, I know when you're bullshitting me. What's wrong? Did something happen?"

Lennox shook his head. He couldn't explain how overwhelmed he was by this unknown family that had materialized in his life. Part of him wished he'd never known. Everything was simpler when there were only a few of them.

"Len, hey." Will brushed his curls off his forehead and kissed his cheek. "It's just me."

"I don't like big families."

"Why not?"

"I just can't— They've all got names and *faces* and I don't know any of them. My mom had siblings! How did I forget that? I just assumed since nobody ever visited after..." He took several deep breaths. Will squeezed his hand.

"It's okay. That's a lot to adjust to, but you'll get to know them and remember everyone's name. I'm sure they'll be patient with you."

"But they're my *family*. I should already know who they are. And they've just... they've been here. Right here, this whole time, Will. If my dad hadn't moved us away, we could have lived here with them. Everything could have been so fucking different."

"Yeah, but it's not."

Lennox nodded.

Will reached around behind their seats. "I brought your present."

"You didn't have to get me something," Lennox said, his face burning. "I didn't get *anyone* anything. I suck at gift shopping."

Will set a guitar on his lap. Lennox sucked in a harsh breath. It was his old guitar, a little more polished, with a few extra chips on the edges. He ran his hands over it and plucked at a few strings. They sang to him out of tune.

"I would have tuned it, but I'm still as tone deaf as ever."

"How did you— Where did you find this? After those dicks vandalized my room I didn't think I'd ever see this again."

Will touched his cheek and swiped away the tears Lennox hadn't felt fall.

"I found it at the thrift store. Dad helped me buy it. I guess they pawned it."

Lennox ran his fingers over the frets; his mother's voice swept into his thoughts. *"Now don't get upset when your hands are still too small for this. This is a* real *guitar, Lennox. Happy Christmas."*

"Thank you." Lennox leaned over and kissed Will deeply. "You're the best. All I got you was a prostate wand."

"I expect a full test run of it tonight then."

"Deal."

"Come on. We'll go in; I'll get to meet them. Then we can go back to my house. Okay?"

They returned to the house, and Nana was on him again, whacking him on both shins with her cane.

"Don't you run off like that! You *say* something next time, you hear me?"

Despite her blindness, she had no problem tugging him into the house by his ear. She paused when she heard the door click shut behind Will.

"Who's that?"

Lennox pulled himself free and knocked her arm away when she moved to grab him again.

"Hi, I'm Will. Lennox's boyfriend."

"Lennox has a boyfriend?"

One of his cousins twisted around on the couch. He thought that one was Mateo.

"Is he cute? Where's he at?"

Nana Josephine beamed and embraced Will before passing him around the room the way she had with Lennox. Will was gracious and kind to everyone. He greeted Lennox's youngest cousins, a pair of twins around five, with a wide grin. Lennox watched him in wonder as he interacted with his family. Why couldn't he do that?

Will drew him in to a space on the couch. The afternoon was easier after that, with Will's arm around his back and his hand on his thigh. Lennox relaxed. He talked with Diego and his fiancé, Cassie, and Alejandra. They were the closest to him in age, Diego and Cassie at twenty-four and Alejandra in her final year of college at William and Mary. To his surprise, they had quite a bit in common.

"So you're majoring in piano?" Diego asked.

"Yeah, at Berklee."

"Well, who in our family doesn't play piano?" Alejandra said, handing out pieces of fudge from the tin making its rounds. "Pop had all of us around the piano when we were little. You and your mom always played when you were here for Christmas. Auntie Lyra was always the best."

"I think Lennox could give her a run for her money," Will said.

Lennox went quiet. There were so many memories he lacked, so many these people had of him and his mother and his family that had been scattered to dust for him. Cameron had taken up residence in the kitchen since Will's arrival, but he reappeared, clearly ready to leave.

"Lucy, Lennox, it's time we head back."

"Can't we stay a bit longer? Please!"

Cameron would hear nothing of it. Everyone else stood up, too, stretching and yawning as they checked the time on their phones.

"It's time we got back too," Lula said. "We've got a three-hour drive back to Silver Spring."

Everyone said their goodbyes, and Lennox found himself pulled into a dozen different pairs of arms. Coats were passed around and pulled on, presents were gathered up, and Henry forced tins of fudge and cookies into every pair of hands. Lennox ended up with two.

Lennox's aunts and uncle left first, clearing the driveway. Only Cameron, Lucy, Lennox, and Will lingered. Lucy still refused to leave, even as Lennox helped her into her coat.

"Can't I sleep over, Nana? Just for tonight?"

"That's up to your grandfather, sugar. You're always welcome here."

Cameron frowned at her pleading look. "Not tonight, Lucy. We have some things to talk about at home."

Henry and Josephine paused in their cleaning of the living room. Lennox didn't say anything. Lucy only rolled her eyes and hugged and kissed Nana and Pop goodbye. She went outside, dragging Will with her.

"You're telling her tonight?" Henry's concern only seemed to grate on Cameron.

"Yes, best not to keep putting it off now that we've settled everything. I'll get the legal documents drawn up after the New Year and get them to you."

They nodded. Nana Josephine looked as though she wanted to say more, but she stayed silent. Cameron said his goodbyes and followed Lucy outside.

Henry hugged Lennox first. "Take care of them, you hear? And yourself, too. Call us while you're at school."

"I will."

Nana Josephine squeezed him tight; her cane's handle dug into his back. "Don't be a stranger. Oh, I love you so much." She kissed his cheek and her scent filled his nose: soft vanilla with something clean that was distinctly her. "I know he's never been the kindest or the best, but he's only got a little time left. Try to find your peace with him, okay?"

Outside he was greeted by Will and Lucy spinning around while Cameron waited impatiently.

"Hurry up now. We need to get home."

Will grabbed his hand as a reminder.

"Actually, Will invited me over to his place for the evening."

"Lennox, no arguments. I told you we have things to discuss tonight."

He glanced at Will's sad expression, at the sternness of Cameron's gaze, but it was Lucy's bright smile that broke his resolve. Tonight, the comfortable world around her would crumble a bit more. He had to be there for her.

"Rain check for another day?"

Will sealed their agreement with a kiss. "Good luck."

..ıl twenty-two

BASEBALL HAD NOT BEEN PART of Will's plan. Aaron arrived at dawn and knocked on his window until Will joined him in the backyard. He'd gotten a new glove for Christmas and, after giving it a night in the oven, Aaron was ready to test it out. They tossed balls for a while to break it in, then worked Aaron through all of his pitches.

By midday, Ben called them in to eat. Platters of leftovers covered the kitchen table, along with Aunt Mia's strawberry waffles. They ate a little of everything, stuffing themselves full.

"God, food is so good." Aaron burped and added a fourth waffle to his plate.

"Right? All Lennox ever wants to eat is tacos, but *waffles*. Breakfast is the best."

They clinked forks and dove into the last of the waffles together. Aaron finished first. He sat back, groaned, and patted his stomach.

"I'm going to regret this come March."

"You've still got spring training to work it off."

Aaron shook his head. "No, I mean for tryouts. Minor league tryouts. In Charlottesville at the beginning of April."

Will perked up. Baseball was a dream that was over, no matter how much he'd wanted it as a kid, but the idea of trying out stirred up that same old longing.

"Really? That's a big step."

"It's worth a shot. Coach says, worst case I get some good experience and advice. Puts my name out there too."

"I'm sure you'll do great."

"Better if I had you to catch for me."

"Aaron, I'm not—"

"I know," Aaron said, holding his hands up. "I'm just saying. You'd be so good at it. I'm sure they'd take you. I don't get why you don't go for it."

"I just... It's not for me."

"Yeah, but *why?*"

Will didn't say anything. He'd never told Aaron the real reason he'd veered away from dreams of being a professional baseball player. After he'd come out in middle school, he'd tucked that dream into the same box as the rest.

"You don't have to tell me, but we used to talk about it all the time when we were little. Ha, you wanted to be a shortstop until you tried catching. You were going to be the next Derek Jeter, remember?"

"Of course I do."

Aaron finished his cup of orange juice, still watching him. "Come on, man. It'll be our secret, whatever it is. We've been best friends since we were kids. Why'd you never go for it? I mean, you're good enough."

"You remember back in middle school, when we first got on the varsity team?"

"Yeah, that was right after our second time in the Little League World Series. We never shut up about baseball."

"And you remember what else happened that year?"

Aaron frowned. "Uh, a lot of boring classes. Natasha moved to town. I dated that awful Veronica girl. She tried to cut my ear off when I broke up with her. Still have the scar."

"I came out." Will scraped leftover syrup around on his plate. "I told you and my parents that I was gay, because I had the *worst* crush on Lucas."

"The red-head from Little League? Man, I'd forgotten all about him." Aaron chuckled. "But so what? Yeah, you came out. You're gay. So what?"

"I stopped *because* I'm gay, Aaron. You know how half those guys reacted when they found out. If it hadn't been for you, they'd never have let me in the locker room. Gay guys aren't athletes, not professional ones."

"Says who? You could be."

Will shook his head and refused to answer when Aaron pressed him for more. They cleaned up their dishes, and Will walked Aaron out.

"I'll see you around. Roxanne was saying something about a movie or dinner before we all go back."

"Count me in. I'll ask Lennox."

Aaron got into his car and rolled the window down. "If you weren't gay, would you have gone for it?"

Will didn't answer. If things were different—if he were different—the decision he'd made as a kid would be the same one now. At thirteen he'd picked his sexuality over every dream. Denying who he was seemed more foolish than giving up on baseball.

"You can be both, man. André is, and he's not as good as you."

Will shook his head once more. "See you."

* * *

Two days passed before Lennox was able to visit. Lucy was devastated. She hardly understood how their grandfather being sick meant she had to leave almost all of her life behind. That weekend, Lennox arrived early in the morning, with a box of doughnuts and a warm smile. He carried a certain light in his eyes now, one that hadn't been lit before Berklee.

Aunt Mia snatched up the box of doughnuts. Will kissed Lennox and helped him out of his leather jacket.

"How is she?"

"She's at a friend's house for a sleepover. I think it'll do her some good." Lennox shrugged as they sat down on the couch. "I think she understands most of it, but she wants to stay with him. He's already told her no. My mom's parents are going to take her once her school year's finished unless he gets too bad before then."

"She'll be happy with them. So will you."

"I still haven't said I'm staying with them. It's weird."

"Well, you're always welcome here," Karen said as she entered the room. "I'm off to work. You two have fun. Mia, make sure they don't spend all day downstairs."

"Operation cockblock, reporting for duty."

"You know, you're really not making me want to come stay with you."

Aunt Mia handed him a doughnut.

Will and Lennox went downstairs and piled onto the bed with Oyster. For a while they held each other, hands brushing over sweatshirts and fingertips meeting in a pyramid above Will's heart. Delicate moments were what Will craved the most in Lennox's absence: hushed conversations, comfort in their closeness.

"When do you leave for Pittsburgh?"

"Monday. Aunt Mia only got a week off to visit."

"It'll be good. You can explore, see some baseball games once the season starts. Have you looked into any new schools?"

"No. I guess I should."

Lennox kissed his neck and rested his head on Will's shoulder.

"You go back soon?"

"Couple weeks."

Will swallowed. Being apart so much made his insides feel hollow. Lennox was happy at Berklee—the happiest Will had ever seen him. Not being a part of that still hurt, but Lennox was right. He had to strike out on his own until he found something just as good for himself.

"Any idea what you want to study or do yet?"

Aaron's face immediately popped into his head, talking about baseball and tryouts and the not-so-glamorous life on the road playing baseball until his body ached.

"Do you think I'm a good baseball player?"

Lennox lifted his head to meet his eyes. "Yeah. I mean, I'm no judge of what's great baseball or anything, but Otto's always said you're awesome. And I don't think Aaron would lie about that scout who was interested last year."

"Right." Will stared at the ceiling decorated with strands of lights he'd hung years ago to prepare for New York City. That dream was over too.

"Will, you can't give up on everything."

"I'm not."

"Well, are you thinking about trying baseball? You love it more than you love me."

Will gaped at him. "I do *not.*"

"Then you've loved it longer than me. Fair?"

"I guess," Will said. "But I can't try baseball again. Even if I want to."

"Do you want to?"

"I can't."

"That not a real answer."

Lennox sat up and stretched. Oyster climbed right into his lap and curled up.

"Look, there's nothing wrong with going back to an old dream and realizing you still want it. Or that you're ready for it now," Lennox said. "I mean, I never imagined Berklee at all. Not even before my mom died. But I loved playing, wanted to do it for the rest of my life. I'm doing that now."

"I doubt I'd make it."

"So did I when I applied to Berklee. It doesn't hurt to try, Will."

Lennox rubbed Oyster's belly and convinced him to roll over onto Will's legs. "Okay if I use your shower? I hate the one at my grandfather's house. It's like walking into a room lined with squirt guns."

Will paced his room while Lennox shut himself in the bathroom. Oyster whined from the bed. He stopped to examine his bookshelves:

the dozens of novels he'd read as a kid and had rarely touched since, the baseball knick-knacks, the old binder of baseball cards, photographs of New York's skyline and others from Little League with his young smiling face.

His whole life was still in this room. Every bit of who he was stared out at him from the shelves to the box tucked under his bed. Will sat on his floor and slid his old box of dreams out.

Oyster hung his head over the bed and licked his cheek.

"What do you think, boy?"

"Arrr-aarrr-wooo!"

"Yeah, I know the feeling."

As Oyster chattered at him and rolled around on his back, Will popped the box open and carefully pulled everything out: dorky notes from middle school, his old yo-yos still twisted into a mass of string and plastic, his Power Rangers, and everything from Little League. Nothing of New York was in this box yet, and maybe... Maybe it didn't have to be here. His most cherished dreams and memories deserved better than a weakening cardboard box.

"Going to be a yo-yo enthusiast again?" Lennox sat next to him, his back against the bed. Oyster gave him a loving kiss. "Ugh, now I have to brush your dog germs out of my mouth!"

Oyster yipped, hopped to his feet, and leapt around the room. He took off upstairs with a proud wag to his tail.

"Ass."

"You want to help me take this stuff out? I think it's been in this box long enough." Will told Lennox. "Well, maybe the old notes can get trashed."

Lennox unfolded one and laughed. "Did you *really* draw penises all over this?"

The paper was an old history worksheet. Aaron's narrow writing lined the top and edges.

"What can I say? I've always been a fan."

THAT NIGHT, WILL PACKED FOR Pittsburgh. Lennox helped where he could, but for the most part he watched and kept Oyster out of Will's suitcase. They sat in the backyard afterward, while Oyster sniffed around the trees, enjoying the soft breeze and the warming temperatures. All the snow had melted, leaving squelchy mud and wilting brown grass.

"You ever feel like our lives are a revolving door onto your back porch?"

Will smiled and leaned into Lennox. "It's a good spot. When do you think we'll be back again?"

Lennox kissed his hair. "I don't know. Maybe summer?"

Will yawned as he relaxed into Lennox's side. His stomach was knotted from the suitcase pile he'd set at the foot of his stairs. He didn't know what Pittsburgh would bring him. So far he hadn't done any research on things to do or see. He was going all in the way Lennox had. No plans, no expectations, and he'd see where he landed when that tug of happiness lit him up inside.

"I never said sorry for when I threw juvie in your face," Will said.

"It's fine. I never apologized for turning you down."

"You were right to turn me down."

"Not how I did." Lennox shrugged until Will lifted his head. "We need to work on our arguing, I think."

Will frowned. "I don't know if that's something you can work on."

"I'm sure we could. Like, that whole not going to bed mad thing. Or us not throwing our worst memories at each other to hurt."

"Like juvie."

"And your dad's heart attack. The things that will always hurt without us making it worse."

"Okay. We can try that. I don't want to hurt you if I can help it."

Lennox kissed him; his lips were salty and sure. Will breathed him in, took comfort in Lennox's warmth and strength. When had that changed? Some part of their relationship seemed to have shifted. For so long, Will had been the solid foundation that had gotten both of them through last year. Now Lennox stood on his own and had found happiness without being dependent on him.

As they broke apart, it hit Will how fine Lennox was without him, how he stayed with Will by choice and not out of desperation or necessity. He wasn't built around Lennox's dependence on him. Their relationship was more than that.

* * *

AUNT MIA WAS READY TO go when the first strands of sunlight lit the sky. Will tossed his backpack into the back of Aunt Mia's car on top of an old air mattress. Mist seemed to crystallize before him as the sun glinted through it. The mountains were pale with frost; the grass was limp and damp under his sneakers. Oyster hovered around his knees.

"It's okay, boy. I'll be back before you know it."

Ben stood on the porch with Karen and Aunt Mia still trying to push money into her hand.

"Ben, it's fine. I'm more than set to cover Will staying for a while. Don't worry about it."

Still, Ben stuffed a wad of money into Will's hand when he hugged him goodbye. "Take care of yourself. I know New York didn't work out, but you'll find your way. Don't rush yourself. Go at your own pace, okay?"

"Thanks, Dad. I will. I promise I'll call a lot too."

Ben squeezed him tight, then passed him on to Karen's embrace. She hugged him tighter than Ben. When she pulled back, she hesitated to speak. Will watched her expression shift from worry to sadness. They'd hardly spoken since he'd returned for Thanksgiving. If he was honest, they hadn't really spoken as they used to since last spring.

"Pittsburgh will be better," Karen said. "I'll come visit or pick you up if you change your mind."

"I'll call you tonight," Will said. "I promise."

"Call when you get there. I love you."

Will bent to hug Oyster. "Miss you already, boy. My bed's all yours."

Oyster whined as Will climbed into Aunt Mia's car. They drove off into the dawn light; Oyster's miserable howling faded behind them. Aunt Mia punched him on the shoulder. She offered him the open box of cereal on her lap.

"Chex?"

"I'm good."

Will gazed out the window as they drove through town, past his dad's shop and the signs for the hospital. Eastern High was quiet. All the shops lining the main road were closed. Only the laundromat was open. Will eyed the motel and saw the pickup truck he'd once dreaded.

Aunt Mia slowed as they drove past. "Is that where Lennox used to live?"

He nodded. His throat felt as if it had ripped open. Nothing in Leon had changed, not his high school, not the shops, not even the inhabitants of the motel. Only Lennox had escaped. Of course, he hadn't spent his entire life here, either.

"Bet he doesn't miss that," Aunt Mia said. She took the last turn toward the highway and pulled into the McDonald's. "You want anything?"

Will shook his head. Aunt Mia ate more than an elephant. She ordered two meals for herself and a third for him. He ate it, munching on his sandwich and hash browns as they merged onto the highway. They drove for hours before the sun rose above the trees. Will watched the landscape as they followed the mountains north into West Virginia, and giggled at the brief stretch of Maryland.

"This is always my favorite part of the drive," Aunt Mia said. She laughed as they sped across the mile-high bridge that was all that counted as Maryland. "And Pennsylvania now."

"I don't get why they didn't just add this part of Maryland to another state," Will said, eyeing the river far below. "It seems kind of silly."

"I think they used the river to set up the boundary."

Will nodded as they passed back onto land and a welcome sign for Pennsylvania appeared.

"You ready to call this place home for a while?"

"I guess."

Aunt Mia nudged him with her elbow as if she was chicken dancing in her seat. "Come on. Have some enthusiasm!"

Will tried to smile, but his chest seemed to close up. He missed Lennox, his parents, Oyster.

Aunt Mia passed him the box of cereal. "Look, we'll get there, get unpacked. You can call your boy. I'll call Victoria and see if she wants to do dinner with us. There's this great Italian place not far from my apartment."

Will pulled out his phone. He was trying to be brave about another city, but thoughts of New York kept drifting back. What if he failed all over again?

"Will, it's okay to be scared."

He shook his head. "I shouldn't be."

"Doesn't mean you aren't. Just take a deep breath and try. And if you fail, do the same thing tomorrow. Wake up, take a deep breath, and *try*. Eventually, you'll find something that works. I promise."

"Okay."

"So is that a yes to dinner or not?"

Will breathed deep and nodded.

...ıl twenty-three

LENNOX STUFFED THE LAST OF his clothes into his ratty backpack. In the morning, he'd return to Boston. Ava and Sadia had texted him to make plans for the afternoon. Troy wanted to get everyone together for dinner, and Lucy and Kelly were vying for his time too. His sister sat on his bed, a firm pout on her lips, as she watched him check the guest room for the last of his belongings.

"Do you really have to leave?"

"Yeah, my classes start Monday."

"Can't you do your classes from home or something?"

Lennox pulled one of his socks from under the bed. "It doesn't work like that."

Lucy fell back on his bed. "But all the commercials talk about getting degrees from home."

"Not for music schools like mine. Come on, cheer up. You get to visit Pop and Nana next weekend. You've got school again too."

"Ugh, school is stupid. All everyone talks about is *dating*."

"Well, soccer starts before you know it. I'll try to come see you play. My semester ends before your classes."

"Really?"

"Yup. I'll do my very best to come watch you play."

"Bu you're *sure* you have to leave?"

"Yes."

"Is it because of your nightmares? Do you not have them at school?"

Lennox tensed. His nightmares had returned since Christmas, blasting into his usual dreams with a fierceness he found difficult to ignore. Every night, he seemed to revisit the juvenile detention center. Sometimes, he dreamed of the motel too.

"What makes you think I'm having nightmares?"

Lucy pinched his stomach. "I have ears, you know. Ones that work. I can hear you sometimes, through the wall." She raised her legs over her head and tapped her toes against the wall behind them.

"No, I, I still have nightmares at school."

"Why? What are they about? I'm sure I could help get rid of them."

Lennox shook his head. "They're memories, Lucy. You can't really get rid of them."

"Oh."

They stretched out on the bed, heads and shoulders together. Lucy raised her feet and kicked at his shin.

"You've got a lot of growing to do if you want to be taller than me."

She stretched her legs as far as they would go, and when she couldn't reach his ankles, she pushed herself down the bed until her toes passed his.

"Hey, no cheating!"

"You're still growing, so you're cheating, too."

He tickled her, just to get a few giggles, and then settled down. His eyes followed the slow circling of the ceiling fan. If only they could see each other all the time... But it was better for her this way. Lucy needed stability.

Lucy flicked his nose. "Can I ask you something?"

"You just did."

"Can I ask you *several* somethings?"

Lennox nodded.

"What's sex like?"

If he'd been drinking something, he would have spat it all over her face. "Huh?"

Lucy sat up on her feet. "Sex," she repeated, her cheeks darkening. "You and Will do it, don't you?"

"Uh, well, yeah. We do. Where's this coming from?"

Lucy shrugged. "Some people at school have been talking about doing it with the people they're dating."

Lennox stared. "You guys are, like, eleven."

"Almost twelve! We're basically grown up."

Lucy tilted her chin to look down her nose at him.

Lennox sat up and rubbed his face. "Um, okay. Didn't Grandfather or Grandmother talk to you about this?"

She shook her head. Now that he'd given her a response, she only seemed eager to hear more. "Is it true? That you put your," Lucy paused and waved a hand over the front of her jeans. "That you put your *junk* inside someone else's *junk*?"

"Oh, my god, this is not what I wanted to do today."

Lucy punched his arm. "Don't make me feel stupid. I don't have anyone else to ask about this kind of stuff. Do you put your *junk*—"

Lennox pressed his palm to her mouth. Lucy glared at him and tried to bite his hand.

"Okay, we're doing this then." Lennox stared at his sister, his lanky, little weed of a sister. He didn't have a clue how to start. "Sex can be a lot of things, Lucy."

"But you do it with your—"

"If you talk about my junk one more time, I'm telling you nothing."

"*Fine.* But what's it like? What do you *do*?"

"Lots of things. Sex is physical. It's emotional too. Having sex with someone—someone you really care about—it changes you."

Lucy scrunched up her nose. "That's not what everyone at school says."

"Well, whose word are you going to take? Mine or a bunch of sixth graders who haven't had sex yet?"

"Good point."

Lennox explained some of the mechanics to Lucy at her insistence: about how two bodies could join together, how to be safe when doing so, how different bodies connected in different ways. She nodded along for a while before bombarding him with horrifying questions again.

"But how do you *get* an erection? Do you have one all the time? How does that work?"

His face burning, Lennox explained that too. She was bursting with questions when he finished. Lennox answered what he could, trying his hardest not to reference his own sex life, but Lucy made that impossible.

"So you should only do it with someone you love? It's only good that way? Cause Jackie and Nate totally *don't* love each other, but Nate swears they did it."

Lennox sighed. "It's *best* with someone you love, Lucy. Nothing compares to when I'm with Will."

"So you've done it with people you don't love? Was it the erection kind or the mouth kind?"

Lennox rubbed his temples. He was going to be explaining the mechanics of sex over and over again for a long time. Still, Lucy's eyes were pleading. She needed to know this information, not just for her curiosity, but for her safety. He never wanted her to have the experiences he had; didn't want her sexual life to start like a rockfall.

"I have. Before I met Will. It feels good, Lucy. That's why so many people do it with people they don't love. And there's nothing wrong with that as long as you and whoever you're with consent to what you're doing. If anyone isn't sure, then that means no."

"But it's better with Will?"

"A thousand times better. We trust *and* love each other," Lennox said. "Sex is best when you have that."

Lucy nodded and lay down beside him again. She watched the ceiling for a long time.

"Does it hurt at all? It sounds kind of messy."

"Oh, it's definitely messy. And it can hurt, if you don't do it right too."

She sat up, still looking thoughtful. He'd have to start doing research when he got back to Berklee, maybe ask some of his friends, too. Sex for his body would undoubtedly be different from Lucy's experiences. He wasn't sure if she'd learned about puberty yet. Or if she menstruated.

Lennox eyed her, but saw no obvious signs. "Has Grandfather talked to you about puberty yet?"

Lucy made a face and shook her head. "No, we watched a creepy video in school for that!"

"So you know about periods?"

"Mostly. Wait, is that messy, *too*?"

LENNOX DEVOTED HIS LAST AFTERNOON to Lucy's questions. They researched information online about periods and the puberty she would experience, then took a trip to the store to buy her pads. Lennox called his friend Lucy once they got there and begged her for help.

"I never thought I'd be explaining this to you."

"Please, I don't think my grandfather is going to be any help and I want to make sure she's set if I'm not here."

"Okay, no tampons. She's going to be confused enough when she first starts without adding *that* into the equation. Get the pads with wings if she wears regular panties."

"Wings?"

Lucy hopped right over to the shelves and dragged her finger along the packages.

"This one's got wings! So does this one! They look *funny*."

"Does it matter which one?"

"I always liked the Velcro wings, they stayed put better for me. Don't get stuck on any hair. Get ones for different flows, too."

"Right. Didn't think about that, thanks. You're a goddess. I owe you tacos and a dozen doughnuts and whatever else you want."

"I'm holding you to that." Lucy hung up.

Lennox scanned the dozen packages his sister had thrown into the cart. "She said the Velcro ones work best. Get ones that are light and heavy, too."

Lucy flipped through everything in the cart and shoved the non-Velcro ones back onto the shelf. She held up the three remaining.

"These ones?"

"Yeah. That should last a while once you start." Lennox added in his head. Sixty would last a long time, right?

They returned home. Lucy went straight to her room to stick a few precautionary pads in her backpack for school. Lennox shut himself in the guest room and called Will.

"You're never going to believe how I spent my day."

Will laughed through his entire story, from the sex talk to the purchases.

"I mean, that's good though, that you're teaching her. I'll ask Aunt Mia and Karen for any words of wisdom. I can't imagine it's easy to get used to bleeding like that."

"She was pretty excited to buy them, but I'm sure she'll hate using them soon enough. How was your day?"

"Took a tour of the city now that the weather's warmer. Aunt Mia and her girlfriend are taking me to their gym tonight."

"You made any friends yet?"

"No," For once Will didn't seem sad about it. "I found a local LGBT center that has group meetings. I'm probably going to try that. See what sort of baseball things they have in the area for spring. Who knows, right? I've got all the time in the world."

Lennox smiled. "Yeah, you do."

* * *

BOSTON'S STREETS WERE LINED WITH walls of snow when Lennox returned. Classes started immediately, and Lennox felt himself coming to life again. Ava was in three of his classes. Sadia was in his ensemble. His world re-formed within days. His meals were full of his friends' laughter, his walks around campus were filled with waves and greetings from people he'd met the previous semester. Troy insisted on the pair of them playing a jazz set at a local coffee shop for Valentine's Day.

"It's going to be so cool. You on piano; me on saxophone. We even get *paid*."

Lennox agreed, much to his own surprise. Something about Berklee freed the parts of himself still tethered to Virginia's uncertainty.

Thursday afternoon, Lennox made his way to his first private instruction of the semester with Dr. Austin. They hadn't selected anything to play via their emails during break, only settled on a time.

"So, how was your break? You look much happier."

Lennox hesitated at the cheerful smile directed at him. Even now, nobody at Berklee understood his past. He'd told Troy a piece of it, but that didn't count as a full portrait of his life or who he was now.

"Saw my boyfriend, some family, friends."

"Good, good. So, today's lesson," Dr. Austin said with a clap of his hands. "I told you we'd return to my old question in the spring, so, any new thoughts. Who are you? Who've you been? Who do you want to be?"

Lennox stayed quiet. Better thoughts than last time ran through his head and chased each other back and forth through a kind of maze.

"I'm still not sure about who I am right now," Lennox said. "I kind of know who I want to be. Maybe. I can tell you who I've been."

Dr. Austin waved for Lennox to continue.

For half an hour, Lennox spoke. He took his time detailing his childhood, his unexpected venture into parenthood for his sister, about being locked up, and then being released. Dr. Austin listened to everything that had happened until the day Lennox had set foot on campus.

"Thank you for sharing that with me, Lennox." Dr. Austin patted Lennox's shoulder. "You okay?"

Lennox nodded. His throat was tight, and he'd skipped some parts, but Dr. Austin's gaze hadn't changed. He saw no pity or worry, no discomfort at the reality he'd set between them. Dr. Austin only nodded once more.

"All right, time for some sight reading." Dr. Austin dropped a new piece of sheet music in front of him. "Let's get to it."

* * *

LENNOX WOKE EARLY FRIDAY MORNING with sweat on his face and a bright light shining in his eyes. Someone was shouting. It took a few seconds to realize it was him.

"Dude, wake *up.*" Troy shook him. Lennox swallowed and choked. "Are you okay?"

Lennox rubbed his aching throat. Outside their window, fat snowflakes were falling.

"I, I'm fine."

Troy frowned and gave him a small shove. "That's bullshit, but whatever. I'm going back to bed."

Lennox shivered and wrapped himself up tight in his blankets. He'd been back in the juvenile detention center: that same first night again, the same one that always haunted him worse than the rest of his time there.

"Troy?"

Troy's bed creaked and his phone light flickered on.

"I'm sorry. I can't stop the dreams."

"I know that. I just wish you were quieter about them." Troy sat up. "Have you ever thought about, like, talking to someone about them?"

Lennox snorted. "What? Like some shitty psychologist or something? I don't need a therapist."

"Everyone needs a therapist," Troy said. When Lennox didn't answer, he continued, "Look, I can get you an appointment. I work as an aid in the counseling office, even have my own appointments with Dr. Jennings. There's no shame in it. It does me a lot of good with managing my workload and everything."

Lennox shrugged, then rolled his head until his neck cracked. "I don't need a shrink."

"Well, then duct tape your mouth shut when you go to bed. You're my friend, but I'm sick of getting woken up by you screaming, man."

Troy went back to bed, but Lennox walked down the hall to the empty study room. He dragged his blanket behind him like a cape and wrapped himself up in it. Will picked up after the fourth ring.

"Hello?"

"Hey, sorry. I shouldn't have woken you. I, I'll call back tomorrow."

Will's voice shouted at him to stop as he pulled the phone away from his ear.

"Sorry. Are you sure this is fine? It's like three in the morning."

Will yawned. "Two my time. What's wrong? You sound like you're losing your voice."

"Bad dreams." Lennox took a deep breath, teetered on the edge of cracking this solitary secret open as he never had before. "Nothing I can't handle. I'll let you go back to sleep. Night."

He hung up. Lennox pulled his knees up to his chest and rested his forehead on his kneecaps. At some point, Will would start asking. He couldn't bear the thought. His phone rang, lighting up with Will's smiling face.

"Hello?"

"You hung up."

"Yeah, I know."

Will sighed over the line. "Lennox, you can talk to me about anything. *Anything.*"

"There's nothing to talk about."

"That's not true." Will clicked his tongue and sniffled. "It's about juvie, isn't it? Your nightmares."

Lennox nodded, then made an agreeable noise when he realized Will couldn't see him.

"I've never pushed you to talk about what happened in there," Will said. "I don't ever want to force you to talk about things you aren't ready to discuss, but if you're having nightmares about it, may you *should* talk about it."

"It's really not a big deal," Lennox told him. "I mean, a lot of stupid and awful crap happened in there. It's not like I was raped or anything."

He shivered and paced in front of the window. The streets were painted a fluffy, bright white; the sky was clouded dark gray. Will was quiet.

"I'll let you get back to bed," Lennox said. "It's not fair to keep you up all night too."

"Do you want to know what I think happened that you won't talk about?" When Lennox didn't respond, Will continued. "You once told me that blowjobs make people like you. The very idea seemed ridiculous to me, you know? And I think you get that now, but that was true for you in juvie. I'm sure there were a lot of blowjobs, forced or otherwise, and you can't wrap your head around what all of it means or how much it hurt you."

Lennox flinched and pulled the phone away from his ear.

"Lennox?"

"I'm fine. Goodnight, Will." He hung up again, before Will could answer. Every word Will had spoken sliced through him like a hot knife. A flash of that first night ran through his mind: brought to an empty cell by one of the gangs, forced to his knees; forced to make a decision his sixteen-year-old brain hadn't fully understood.

Lennox crept back to his room, changed out of his pajamas, and left for a practice room. He wasn't going back to sleep. Haunted sleep was no use to anyone.

..ıl twenty-four

WILL'S THIRD TRIP TO AUNT MIA'S gym left him with a bruised butt. The streets of Pittsburgh were sheeted with ice; a drizzle fell around him, not truly rain or snow. He rubbed his ass as he tried to climb to his feet and slipped again; his hip hit the ground.

"Whoa, careful. You okay?" A muscular in basketball shorts and a tank top slid toward him. He steadied himself and reached out a hand for Will. "Here, grab on."

"Thanks."

Together, they managed to get to their feet and find their balances. Moving as if he had ice skates hooked to his feet, Will slid to the gym's door. The man beside him did the same.

"Dangerous place to be tonight," Will said.

"Right? I'm glad I'm only across the street."

They made it inside and scanned their gym tags. Will followed the man into the locker room and stuffed his jacket and keys into a free locker. Back on the main gym floor, Will glanced around. Only two other people were there, both jogging on treadmills. The man from the street stopped beside him and stretched his arms above his head.

"I'm Max."

"Will. Thanks again."

"Sure, man. Listen, you doing any lifting tonight? We could spot each other."

Will agreed. They focused on chest for the night, and Will learned quickly that Max had an incredible knowledge of both the body's muscle structure and lifting techniques. He'd learned a bit during his baseball training in high school, but his coach had focused more on baseball than muscle training.

"Right, make sure you don't move your lower body at all. Try to only use your arms or you might strain something."

Will lifted, heaved a huge breath, and repeated for his final rep. Max caught the bar and hooked it onto the rungs.

"Awesome. You play a sport? You look pretty fit."

"No," Will said as they switched places. "Well, just baseball in high school."

Max eyed him. "Guess those workouts are pretty tough too. I play football at the University of Pittsburgh. What school are you at?"

Will shook his head; his heart thudded faster in a way that had nothing to do with his workout. Talking about school had become difficult ever since he'd left NYU. He'd been in Pittsburgh for three weeks now—no friends and no new plans. Aunt Mia and Victoria had made a point of including him and dragging him out to all their favorite spots. Will enjoyed their cheer and company. They knew all the great restaurants, the best obscure theaters to see rerun movies, and the greenest parks to stroll through. Yet, he couldn't stand being a tagalong for their dates. They weren't much for staying up all night the way he was, either.

"No school. I'm visiting my aunt for a while. Checking out the city." Will swallowed. "I was going to school in New York, but it wasn't for me."

"New York? No way, man. I could never do that. All right, add twenty-five more on that side."

Will added the weight and then spotted Max through his reps. They made their way all around the gym, ending with a few yoga poses after a twenty-minute jog on the treadmill. Max seemed impressed with how well he kept up.

"Half my teammates call it quits halfway through that workout.

Will sat on his mat, winded. Tomorrow, he was going to ache so much he'd be lucky if he got out of bed. Max sat, too, and wiped his forehead with his arm.

"We should do this again. What days do you usually go?"

"Whenever. Evenings mostly, when it's quieter," Will said.

"Yeah, evenings are my favorite. I hate the crowds. Tomorrow night?"

"Yeah, sure."

They wiped down their mats, grabbed their things from the locker room, and walked out onto the icy street. Max cackled as they slid across the street again.

"I used to love winter back in Virginia," Will said as he stumbled along. "I might hate it now."

"This one's me." Max toppled against his apartment building's door and clutched the door handle. "How far are you from here?"

"About five blocks."

Max pushed the door open and fell flat on his face. Will helped him up.

"You can stay here, if you want. I've got some extra blankets, a couch."

Will hesitated. Max seemed kind enough, but the last six months had made him wary of strangers. "Think I'll risk it."

"Well, here. Give me your number and text me that you made it back without a concussion."

They traded numbers, and Will left, skating clumsily along while cars skidded on the road. He managed to make it back to Aunt Mia's apartment without incident.

Aunt Mia lived on the ninth floor of a towering apartment complex in the heart of downtown Pittsburgh. Will's stomach churned at the thought of the price tag, but the one-bedroom was a decent size for a single person. The living room was furnished with splashes of every color Will could name—purple, green, orange, red, amber—and the kitchen was well-lit with a small island. He crept to the back corner of the living room, behind the wood paneled divider. Aunt Mia had been using the cubby space as an office, but right now it served as Will's bedroom. They'd blown up an air mattress and piled all the free blankets in the apartment onto it.

Will tossed his sweaty clothes into his empty suitcase and pulled on his pajama pants. He was just stuffing himself into a hoodie when the bedroom door opened. Aunt Mia appeared with her blue-eyed tabby cat curled up on her shoulder.

"Howdy, little nephew."

Aunt Mia dug a packet of popcorn out of the cabinet and tossed it into the microwave. She put her cat on a bar stool. "Who's my good boy, Sapphie? It's you. Yes, it is. You hungry?"

Sapphie meowed and placed his paws on the counter.

"I can't believe you feed him at the counter."

"Don't you listen to him. Will's a meanie." Aunt Mia set a dish of tuna in front of Sapphie. "So how was the gym?"

"Good." Will took a seat next to Sapphie, who was scarfing down his dinner with his bright blue eyes on Will. "I met someone."

"Oh, yeah?"

"His name's Max. New workout buddy maybe."

"Better than working out with us old ladies?"

"You aren't old."

"Hmm, tell that to my knees." She sat on the couch. "Movie night?"

"Sure."

* * *

WILL TEXTED MAX A LOT over the next week. They met at the gym each night, blasting through different workouts until they'd focused on every muscle group on Max's list. On Friday, Will met him once more for some cardio, and was surprised by the bag Max dragged into the locker room.

"You have a dead body in there or something?"

Max stuffed it into a tall locker and chuckled. "Nope, going out with some friends afterward. Actually, you want to go with us? We're going to Rocky Horror. It starts at midnight."

"Rocky Horror?"

Max grinned. "Don't tell me you've never done Rocky Horror."

Will shook his head. He'd seen the movie once, several years ago when he'd found it in a bargain bin at the thrift store, but this sounded like something else entirely.

"Holy shit, you've got to go. It is the *greatest* thing in the world."

"Isn't it just watching the movie?"

Max grinned wider. "You are *so* going with us tonight. We haven't had a virgin in our group in *years*."

"I'm not a virgin."

They picked a pair of free treadmills and started at a steady walk.

"You are for Rocky Horror," Max said, then he went on to explain. "They have a stage and people who dress up as the characters and act out their parts. Everyone shouts things at certain parts, and they give us props. It's a lot of fun. They have a Virgin Ritual, too, for people who haven't done it before."

"What kind of ritual?"

"Depends on the night. It's fun, I promise. They only pick a few people, so you might not have to do anything." Max turned his treadmill up to a slow jog. "You in?"

Will turned his machine up too. Rocky Horror sounded like an experience, one that Lennox would enjoy if he was here. The Virgin Ritual seemed less appealing. He scanned the people at the gym: ordinary, sweaty people. He'd come to Pittsburgh to have fun, to learn about himself, to decide on a possible future other than New York.

So far all he'd done was go to the gym, sit in his bed with Aunt Mia's cat, and talk to his old friends and Lennox on Skype.

"What time does it start?"

Pittsburgh's subway dropped Will and Max a few blocks from the theater. Will, unfamiliar with this part of the city, eyed the buildings nervously. He was lost already, relying on Max to get him back home. Max had changed at the gym and now he strutted along in massive heels, fishnets, and a corset. He'd even added makeup to his face. An envious rush filled Will at the sight of him. Ever since he'd seen drag costumes in that shop in New York, Will had longed to try it.

"So, we're going to meet some of my friends, okay? They caught the train behind us. And my girlfriend, too."

"Girlfriend?"

"Jada, yeah."

"Oh, cool."

Max struck a pose and blew him a kiss. "Let me guess, you thought I was gay?"

Will shrugged. "A little. I mean, I am so..."

"I'm bisexual. No worries. Oh, they're here!"

A small group of people came out of the subway. Like Max, they were all dressed in outfits that included fishnets and drag. Max did a round of introductions.

"This is Jada." A tall black woman waved at Will. "August," a stocky man in black lingerie, "and Imani."

Imani smiled at him. "Nice to meet you...?"

"Will Osborne."

Her grin reminded him of Lennox's toothy smile with one crooked bottom tooth. Her eyes were dark brown instead of hazel; her skin was darker too. Before Will could blink, she'd grabbed the back of his head and used red lipstick to draw something on his forehead.

"What are you—"

"Welcome, virgin. I'm marking you myself."

Imani kissed his cheek as the group laughed and patted Will on the back.

"So, you've at least seen the movie, right?"

Will nodded at Jada. "Yeah, I own it. Found it at a thrift store."

"A *thrift* store? How dare someone!"

Everyone laughed again, including Will. Max's friends were nice, so far. He told them about his small-town life when prompted, about his dad's shop, and growing up far from the city.

"Yeah, I did, too," August said as they queued to get tickets. "Central Pennsylvania. My family took a trip to Virginia once, for Luray Caverns and, uh, some road through the mountains."

"Skyline Drive?"

"Yeah, that's it."

"My parents live right by one of the entrances."

Will passed his ticket money to Max. He tried not to rub the lipstick on his forehead despite how gross it felt. The ticket booth worker smiled at him.

"I see someone's already marked!"

Will nodded.

"Don't look so worried, honey. You came on an easy night."

Max handed out their tickets. He gave Will his as the others rushed inside. "You ready?"

"Uh, kind of."

Max squeezed his shoulder. "Relax, have fun. You're going to love this."

Will followed him inside; his hands squeezed air. Lennox would enjoy this, too. He wished, as he always seemed to these days, that Lennox was at his side; that he missed him less. Lennox had his own life now, though. He deserved that. Somehow, he had to figure out his own, on his own. Will took a seat beside Max, showing off his walk, and watched the show begin.

"—AND THEN THEY HAD ALL of us play this game. I forget what they called it, but they asked each of us if we knew what weird sex acts meant. So like, I got Strawberry Shortcake—"

"Isn't that where you come on someone's face and then punch them?"

Will giggled as he lay on his air mattress bed in Aunt Mia's dark living room. Sapphie was curled up in his armpit, purring. He stroked his fur and watched the city lights flicker over the ceiling. Giddiness crashed over him in waves. The entire evening had been a blast—the Virgin Ritual, the shouting, the props, the dancing, even eating at a late-night diner afterward. For the first time since he'd left home in August, Will had truly had an enjoyable time without Lennox.

"Sorry, that's not funny, but yeah. That one. I didn't know it, so they called me a dumbass, but people who got theirs right were smartasses. Then for the last person." Will paused to chuckle. "She was asked, 'What's a Charleston Chew?' and she tried to make something up like everyone else was, and the guy was like 'Wrong! That's a candy bar, dumbass!'"

Lennox laughed with him then, before yawning. Will pulled his phone away from his ear to check the time. Almost four in the morning.

"I should let you go. It's super late."

Lennox yawned again. "No, it's fine. We're in the middle of a blizzard. Ended up napping all day. We made cakes in mugs with the microwave because the dining halls are closed. It's whiteout conditions. They're talking forty inches."

"Wish you were here," Will said. "I can't give you forty inches, but definitely a solid seven."

Sapphie stretched beside him. Lennox laughed, and Will, despite his euphoria, realized how ridiculous he sounded.

"Really? You think you're only seven?"

"Rough estimate. And we aren't measuring." Will smiled so wide his view of the ceiling became a thin line. "Better than my usual stammering?"

"Yes, not as good as you in action, my novice flirt." Something beeped on Lennox's side. "I'm glad you had fun tonight. I miss hearing you like this."

"You mean happy?"

"Sort of. Happy without needing me, I guess."

"We're going back next weekend. I might dress up. Hey, you should go with us when you visit. When are you coming down?"

"I'm not sure, between the weather and everything I've got going on. Troy and I are playing at that coffee shop again. They liked us so much they wanted us back for Valentine's Day."

"That's fine. We wouldn't have much room here anyway. I'll come see you in a few weeks, if the weather's good."

"Awesome."

They said their goodnights, and Will tucked his phone under the desk where his charger was. Sapphie rolled onto his back and meowed.

"Well, you're no Oyster," Will told him, still grinning, "but you're a good snuggler, Sapphie."

Sapphie blinked slowly at him and continued to purr. Aunt Mia's bedroom door opened down the hall as the first rays of dawn light lit the living room windows.

"Will, did you steal my cat again?"

...ıl twenty-five

Blizzards buried Boston for the rest of January and all of February. Lennox and Ava thrilled at the tunnels the locals dug to reach everything. Unlike Virginia, the world didn't shut down in the continuous snow. They lost a few days of classes, but Boston plowed right on, heaps of snow be damned. He missed Will visiting, but their six weeks apart zoomed by. Concert season had begun. Lennox spent half his weeknights attending or practicing or helping someone prepare for a performance. He devoted every free minute to an activity that pulled his mind away from the nightmares still waking him in the middle of the night.

"You might as well double major," Ava told him one afternoon in their library study room. She was reading his list of everything he had to do that weekend. The list was a nice habit he'd had Will help him with over Skype the last few weeks. "I mean, you're a comp major and you're taking *two* private instructions!"

Lennox tugged his page-long list back. Spread out on a sheet of paper, it did look like way too much, but almost all of it was fun for him: practice for piano and guitar; finish reading for his literature class; finish papers for solfege, arranging, conducting; finish his composition assignment; meet with his ensemble and then Troy to practice for performances.

"I want to get back into guitar before I forget. Maybe harp next semester. Do you think harp is difficult? Besides, I probably will double major. I tested out of half the music core classes, so I might as well add something else, right?"

Ava rolled her eyes. "Since when are you such a stellar academic?"

"It's not like this is a chore or something."

"Well, yeah, it's wonderful, but you're piling a shitload on at once. If you took any more credits, you'd need special permission."

Lennox twisted away from her grabbing hands. She'd spent half the afternoon trying to play with his hair instead of working on their reading assignment. "Maybe next semester. Come on, let's finish this."

"Right, our charming lit class."

"What could be more fun than reading dystopian novels while nor'easters bury us alive?"

"Eating a dozen doughnuts."

"Or a dozen tacos."

"Skydiving."

"Surfing."

They spent the rest of their afternoon study session listing everything that was more fun than their current reading assignment, each one getting more ridiculous.

"Astrological navigation."

"Butt plugs."

Ava snickered. "You *would* say that. Come on, let's finish this so you can sob over everything else on this crazy list."

Lennox finished reading the last few pages of their assignment out loud. Ava spun around in her chair, half listening. They chattered through the discussion questions for their next class before packing up. Sadia, in a flowing turquoise hijab, met them for dinner.

"What time's our ensemble practice again?"

Lennox tugged his phone out of his pocket to check. Will had helped him with that, too. They'd Skyped almost every day during the last six weeks, and Will, always with a sharp eye on Lennox's facial expressions, had recognized the stress of his spring schedule. With eight classes, three of them upper-level, Lennox had dived right in. Will's ideas to keep him organized had been a great help.

"Seven. Guess we'll head over after this."

Ava left them after dinner, walking through a different carved-out snow path toward her dorm. Lennox led the way in the other direction with Sadia at his side.

"Think you'll finally get to see Will this weekend?"

"Maybe. Roads are mostly clear. I think he's got plans, though." Lennox wobbled on a patch of ice. "Ugh, I'll be glad when we get to the 'everything is flooding' part of spring."

"It isn't as pretty as this," Sadia said. "Fall semester is definitely my favorite."

"So, question, you're a double major, aren't you?"

"Performance and Music Education. Are you thinking of adding something?"

"Maybe Performance. Or Songwriting. I really like composing, but I want to *play*, too, and learn more about lyrical structure. We've been playing at that coffee shop a lot and it's... I don't know. Is soothing weird? Helps me sleep better."

Sadia nodded. "Troy said you've been having nightmares."

"Fucking Troy," Lennox said. "His mouth is, like, a gaping asshole."

"He'd appreciate that comparison." Sadia held the door open for him at the music hall. "Double majoring is tough, but it's worth it. I'm doing what I love, so I have no problem working my ass off for it."

"Yeah, that's how I see it. What about triple majoring? Would that be nuts?"

"Yes. I don't think they'll allow it."

Lennox nodded. "Sounds like a challenge."

"Lennox, don't kill yourself before you're even a sophomore."

* * *

"Okay, you know the drill. What have you decided on for the fall?"

"I want to triple major."

Dr. Austin stared at him. Lennox raised his chin, and tried not to grimace when he caught sight of himself in the window. His sister did the same thing when she wanted to be more grown up. At least he had a fuzzy chin to make him look older.

"Which majors are you considering?"

Lennox startled. "Uh, well, I want to change composition to jazz composition, then add songwriting and performance."

Dr. Austin scribbled a note, then pressed the tips of his fingers together. "How about you start with a double major first?"

"I want to do all three."

"Let's start with two," Dr. Austin said, "and if you're still insistent next semester, we'll consider it. You'd need the department's approval for three."

"Songwriting and jazz composition then."

He'd just sneak all the performance requirements into his schedule until it became silly to *not* add it. Dr. Austin gave him printouts for each major, then reviewed his list of fall classes with him. Lennox went back to his dorm expecting Troy to be practicing, but their room was empty. He finished a few more assignments for solfege and his tonal harmony class before going to bed.

Lennox feel asleep quickly, but, as always these days, his dreams were haunted by old, dark memories. He woke to his own shouting, drenched in a cold sweat. Lennox squinted around the room, at the dim shapes of the wardrobes, instrument cases, his old guitar tilted against his desk. Nothing was out of place. Nobody else was here. Still, he fumbled for his phone and shined its light around the room to be sure. At least he hadn't fallen out of bed this time.

"Look at this pretty new mouth, you like sucking dick, pretty boy?"

Lennox startled, twisted around as the winter wind rattled his window. Nobody. Just him and old ghosts. He almost called Will before he checked the time. He couldn't call Will at four in the morning. Troy must have stayed over with a friend. He curled himself into a ball of blankets and stared at the bright white of the snow falling and the brightness of the rooftops across the road, then pulled up a game on his phone.

Distractions, that was all he needed. If he piled up enough distractions, all these old memories would vanish as they had last year. All he needed was more important things on his mind—not fights or forceful agreements or desperate choices to protect himself from worse.

"You look like hell," Troy told him the next morning. He'd come back while Lennox had been showering to keep himself awake. "More nightmares?"

Lennox shrugged and went back to brushing his teeth.

"Are you sure you don't want to talk about it?"

"It's nothing." Lennox spat toothpaste foam in the sink.

"Dude, I get it, whatever this is about isn't something you want to deal with, but—"

"It's nothing. I'm *fine.*"

Troy slung his backpack over his shoulder. "If you want to lie to me, fine, but don't lie to yourself. Piling real life on isn't going to make whatever this is go away. Talk to someone. Hell, talk to Will if you aren't already. Do something. You're going to have to deal with it eventually."

He left. Lennox finished brushing his teeth and walked to class. Troy didn't get it. Nobody got this. Telling the truth wouldn't change it.

All week, Lennox kept himself from sleeping more than a few hours at a time. He guzzled soda and took hot showers to perk himself up. He even went on a brisk, freezing jog one morning with Sadia and Troy. No amount of extra work or activities or exhaustion helped. By Friday afternoon, Lennox's thoughts were hazy. Will's bus arrived just after the evening rush hour.

"Lennox! Over here!"

Will crashed into him; his arms enveloped Lennox in the first real warmth he'd had all winter. He pressed his face into Will's neck and breathed in the vanilla and strawberry, the unmistakable scent of the boy he'd stood beside as he built this new world. Will felt fuller in his arms, firmer in his body, and, when he pulled back, his smile made Lennox's heart thud with its brilliance.

"I missed you." Will kissed him, just a fleeting peck. "You look exhausted."

"Long week," Lennox said. "How's Pittsburgh?"

"It's great. I mean, I've got friends and I've started going to some of the museums. Pittsburgh's easier than New York was. Feels more like home."

"Are you going to try a school there then?"

Will frowned as they walked back to campus. It was one question Lennox had let slide while Will tried out a new city, a new life.

"No. I mean, it's nice, but I don't want to stay there. I needed these last few months, no rules or schedules or anything to set my life around."

"So what now?"

"I've been redoing my application to Sarah Lawrence, but I don't know. I guess I'll give it another try. Aaron keeps pestering me about baseball tryouts too."

"Well, you certainly look like you've bulked up since Christmas." Lennox squeezed Will's bicep, then his shoulder. "Doesn't hurt to try?"

"It scares me. Like, if I fail this, too, then there's just nothing for me."

"You'll find something, even if it's not baseball."

Lennox led them into his building and up the stairs to his empty room. Troy was downtown, playing a show with one of his bands. Will sprawled out on his bed, and Lennox climbed onto his lap, straddling his hips.

"You're about to rip out of this shirt." Lennox popped the top button and smiled at how the next one popped open, too. "Whoops."

Will chuckled as Lennox undid the rest of the buttons. Lennox ran his hands over Will's chest, his stomach. His abs were firmer, still not defined, but exquisite and warm under his palms.

"You've got a six pack."

"Do not."

"Sure you do. Bet I can prove it." Lennox kissed his chest, then his stomach. Will giggled beneath him.

"Oh, yeah? How are you going to do that?"

Lennox continued to run his hands over Will's chest, the smooth skin, the pricks of hair near his nipples.

"Like... *this!*"

Will squawked with the first wiggling tickle of Lennox's fingers. His abs did appear then; his stomach clenched tight as Lennox tickled his sides.

"Okay, okay! You win!"

Lennox pinned Will's hands to the bed, pressing his ass down against Will's hips.

"You going to help me undress, too, or what?"

Will heaved in a deep breath after Lennox stopped tickling him. "You look way too tried for sex right now."

"Well, that's why you and your abs are going to do all the work."

Lennox didn't get a response. Will sat up and eased Lennox off his lap. He was still smiling, but some of the light in his eyes had faded.

"Maybe later, tomorrow. I'm pretty tired from that bus ride. Let's have a nap first."

As Will settled down, Lennox tried to think up an excuse to not join him: a practice session, a class to study for, even a need for a shower, but they all fell flat in his head. Every one of those could wait. If he went to bed with Will's arms tight around him, his warmth easing him to sleep, he'd have one of his nightmares.

"Come on, I need my snuggly boyfriend."

Lennox settled in his arms, stiff as a board. Will pulled the blankets over them and shifted around to get comfortable. "What's up? You're being weird."

"Just sore from jogging the other day."

"Since when do you jog?"

"Troy made me."

Will kissed his cheek and shut his eyes. Lennox tried not to get comfortable when Will fell asleep. He twisted his left arm into an awkward angle that made his hand numb and pinched his face with the other. However, Will's warmth and soft snores were contagious. Lennox tried to fight, but his eyelids drooped, no matter how much he pinched himself. Before he could stop himself, Lennox fell asleep.

..ıl twenty-six

WILL WOKE WITH A START as someone kneed him in the stomach. He rolled away from Lennox's flailing and sat up.

"Lennox, wake up." Lennox continued to twist around; his body jerked as if he was trying to free himself from something. Will shook him, but it made no difference. His face was contorted in fear, anguish. Sweat covered Lennox's face and neck.

"Lennox... Lennox! Wake up!" He grabbed Lennox's arm and Lennox swung at him. Will jerked backward; Lennox's knuckles landed on his chest.

"Ouch! Lennox, hey, it's me. It's Will!"

Lennox blinked and sat up. Will leaned away, half out of bed, rubbing his chest where Lennox had punched him.

"Will?"

"Yeah, it's me. You were having a nightmare. Are you okay?"

"I'm fine," Lennox said, his voice croaking. "It's nothing."

"Didn't sound like nothing. What's going on? You're crying."

Lennox wiped his eyes and shook his head. "Just sweating."

"From your eyes?"

Will got out of bed and turned the lights on. He stood by the bed watching Lennox carefully—every tremble, every sniffle. Lennox refused to make eye contact. Will sat down beside him again. He suspected what this was about, the same missing history of Lennox's past that he'd never really explained; the same nightmares from January.

"You can tell me anything," Will said. He found Lennox's hand in his twisted blankets. "I'm here for you."

"I know that. There's nothing to tell."

"Lennox..."

"Just drop it, Will." Lennox pulled his hand away. He curled his knees into his chest and seemed to be focusing on his breathing. Will curled up behind him and wrapped an arm around his chest.

"It's about juvie, isn't it?"

Minutes passed before Lennox spoke. His voice was so quiet, Will almost didn't hear him. "I told you they pierced my tongue in there, right?"

Will nodded and kissed Lennox's neck. Lennox shivered.

"You did. First night, I think you said."

"I chose that."

"That's not true," Will said, his voice hard. "They forced you to do it."

"They gave me options and I, I fought them instead of— Forget it. It's done. It doesn't matter."

Lennox crawled over him and got out of bed. He went right to his sink and began rinsing his face, then brushing his teeth. Will followed, stood behind Lennox and watched every shift of Lennox's reflection in the mirror. His face was ashen; his cheeks and chin were covered in facial hair. He looked sick with huge dark bags under his eyes.

"You look terrible."

Lennox only shrugged. "Too many classes this semester."

"And nightmares every night?"

Lennox didn't answer.

"Why haven't you told me about this?"

"About what? There's nothing to tell." Lennox glared at him in the mirror.

"You've got a lot to tell. Look, I know enough to know that whatever happened in there, you didn't want to do it, okay? Whatever happened wasn't your fault."

"I made my choices, Will. Just drop it."

"No, you survived. Please, just tell me. Talking about it will help."

"Help what?" Lennox slammed his toothbrush on the sink. "Talking doesn't change what happened. It doesn't make it better or make it go away either."

"No, but it can help you learn how to deal with it."

Will moved forward, eased his hands onto Lennox's thin shoulders. He squeezed at the tense muscles, massaging until Lennox relaxed.

"Look, I've made my own guesses about what happened in there, no point in lying about that. Yeah, I want to know, because I want to help you. But maybe you're right. Maybe talking to me isn't what's going to help."

Lennox shook his head, even as Will hugged him tight and kissed his cheek.

"Talk to someone about this, please. You've been having such an amazing time here," Will said. "I don't want to see that end for you."

Lennox shivered against him, and Will did his best not to crumble. Had Lennox felt this same helplessness months ago, when he'd been in New York?

"Please. Do what's best for you. That's exactly what you asked me to do last year, remember? And I didn't listen. Don't keep punishing yourself like this."

"Okay."

* * *

A SHARP PAIN FILLED WILL'S chest when he boarded his bus back to Pittsburgh Sunday afternoon. Lennox had agreed to seek out a therapist on campus, but Will didn't trust that he'd follow through. Nothing seemed to scare Lennox more than his year in a juvenile detention center. He only mentioned that same night over and over, the first one, when he'd had his tongue pierced. Everything was vague hints, snatches of what Will had assumed was the truth.

"So I let them stick this shitty thing in my tongue. Suck a few dicks when I needed to. Blowjobs make—"

"Everything better?"

"Make people like you."

Will swallowed. Every thought that branched off from that conversation made him queasy. Lennox had always insisted life in there had been about blowjobs. A warped understanding of sex had been his biggest takeaway, but he'd never gone into detail.

Aunt Mia was asleep on the couch when Will got back to her apartment. Sapphie leapt up to greet him, tangling himself around Will's ankles and meowing. He scooped him up and carried him to his bed corner. As Sapphie curled up on his lap, Will called home.

"You make it back finally?"

"Yeah, Dad. How's Oyster?"

"Miserable. Your bed's covered in his fur. How's the, uh, Rocky Terror? Still having fun with that?"

Will laughed; some of the weight in his chest eased. "Rocky Horror, Dad. It's fun. I might dress up this time when Lennox is here. I don't know. Pittsburgh's nice, but I miss home too."

"You're always going to miss home," Ben said. "Less and less, but I still think about when I was little. It creeps up on you if you think about it for too long."

"I might come back in a few weeks. Aaron's been talking about those baseball tryouts."

"Are you trying out, too? Put that birthday present I got you to good use."

"Dad..."

"What? You're good at baseball. Used to dress up as a major league player when they had career days at school. Why not give it a shot? Might give you some new ideas."

"I can't, Dad. I gave that dream up a long time ago."

Ben sighed. Will scratched Sapphie's head as Aunt Mia grunted on the couch.

"All these years, you've never really said why. I thought, I don't know, maybe you'd been pretending to love baseball for me. Trying to hide you were gay, you know? But I knew, even then. Your mom was convinced by the time you were three."

"Why would I pretend that?"

"I've read books," Ben said, laughing at him. Will flushed at the sound. "Yeah, I know you think I don't read a damn thing. Look, I read lots of books after your mom died. Was trying to figure out how to be the best dad for you without her. How to help you feel safe being gay. A lot of those guys, they spent half their lives pretending to be people they weren't. Hunting, playing football, being the meanest, most macho guys you've ever seen. You didn't do that, did you?"

"No way. I love baseball, Dad. It was all I ever dreamed about back then. Dreams change, that's all. I came out, and that... that was that."

Ben didn't say anything, but his silence was worse. Will was sick of this conversation. So what if he'd given up on baseball? Whether or not he was good enough didn't matter. No professional athlete he'd ever read about or seen was anything but straight. He'd gone through every sport imaginable and searched for one mention, but he'd found nothing. A career in baseball wasn't possible for him.

"Dad, do you think athletes can be gay?"

Ben snorted. "I raised you, didn't I?"

"I know that. I mean, like, professional ones. I've never heard of any."

"Huh, you know, I think you're right. I never thought about it before." Ben's voice grew fainter. "Hey, Karen, you know of any athletes who are gay?"

"Dad, it's fine. Honestly, I'd rather be honest about myself than play baseball."

"Is that what— Did you give up because of that?"

Will hurried to backtrack, but it made no difference, his dad had heard the truth.

"No, Dad, that's not—"

"No, no way. No kid of mine is going to let who they are stand in their way." Ben huffed and ranted and for a while, Will let him. Karen ended up taking the phone away from him.

"You still there, Will?"

"Yeah."

In the background, Ben continued to rant about how he'd failed as a parent, about how Will should never have given up on his dreams just because of his sexuality.

"I'll calm him down later," Karen said. "Ben... Ben! Go, you're fine. Will's fine. You're a great father. Go take your shower. Go!"

His dad's voice faded.

"Why's he think you not being in the majors means he's a failed parent?"

Will swallowed. "We were talking about baseball, how I wanted to play professionally."

"And you gave up on that because you're gay."

"I didn't say that."

"You don't have to say it, Will. I figured that out a long time ago."

Karen had known him so well, so quickly, when he was a kid. She been every idea he'd dreamed up for a mother: kind, encouraging, caring, and always willing to listen.

"First time I spent the day with you, baseball was all you talked about. It was your entire life. Then you came out, and baseball was still there, but it was like you muffled it, caged it."

"Nobody's a gay, professional baseball player."

"Not yet," Karen said. "Why can't you be the first?"

"I—well, I mean, it's an idea, but—"

"But what?"

"What if they won't accept me? Or if, I don't know, they don't pick me because I'm gay. Or the fans, if I made it that far, what if—"

"Are you going to live your live running all over the place avoiding 'what ifs'? Will, you are a fantastic baseball player. Your coaches have always raved about your skills. Those scouts last year were interested, too. The only thing stopping you is fear."

Will sucked in a deep breath. For one brief day in middle school, to a skinny thirteen-year-old, the idea of being such a hero had been exhilarating. He'd spent that entire afternoon running around his bedroom pretending he was all of his favorite, legendary players—Jackie Robinson, Cal Ripken, Jr., Derek Jeter, Hank Aaron. All the hope and excitement had lasted until he'd gotten to school the next morning, when his classmates had found out. They'd teased, they prodded, they'd whispered everywhere he went. By the afternoon, the other boys on the baseball team had barred him from the locker room.

"Will, whatever you decide, we're your parents. We'll support you through anything and everything. But don't let fear of homophobes stop you from doing what you love. Value your happiness more than what they think."

"Right," Will said. "I think I could do that."

"That's one of the main things I want for you," Karen said. "You're our son. You're *my* son. We want you to be happy, but we want you to be brave and fierce and wonderful, too. So if baseball gives you all of that, then go for it."

His insides bubbled. Baseball, what a wild dream that had been at six and ten and thirteen! Not unachievable, but unlikely. Aaron had always believed in him, though. One of his teammates in college was gay. Nobody on that team had seemed to care. He might not make it, but the chance was worth it.

"I'll be back in a few weeks," Will said. "Aaron said tryouts are being held there for the minor leagues."

"We'll see you then."

* * *

WILL SPENT HIS FINAL WEEKEND before leaving welcoming Lennox to Pittsburgh. He arrived Thursday evening, still tired looking, but happier. Lennox sank into his arms the moment they arrived at Aunt Mia's apartment.

"I've missed you."

"How've you been sleeping?"

"A little better." Lennox took a lap around the main room. He hadn't spoken of his nightmares or whether he'd set up an appointment with an on-campus therapist. Will had refrained from asking. As always, Lennox needed to make these choices on his own, just as he did.

"And did the counseling center have any openings?"

"Does your aunt eat anything besides cereal?" Lennox peered into the pantry. Every shelf had at least two boxes of cereal. The top one held nothing else.

"She knows what she likes," Will said. Then he waited. He had his own news to share, and then shopping to do with Lennox before they went to Rocky Horror tomorrow night.

Lennox glanced at him and cleared his throat.

"Next week. Thursday, before my piano instruction."

"That's good."

Lennox shrugged. "I guess."

"It's okay if it scares you," Will told him.

Lennox cleared his throat. "What about you? You said you have big news. Did you turn in your Sarah Lawrence application?"

"No." Will shook his head and joined Sapphie, who was luxuriating on the couch. "Hey, Sapphie."

Lennox snickered. "Did Mia really name her cat Sapphic?"

"What? His name's Sapphire. Sapphie for short."

"Sure, that's what she wants you to think." Lennox sat on his other side and dropped his backpack on the floor. "So, big news?"

"I'm going to try out for the minor leagues next weekend."

Lennox's grin surprised him. "Yeah? That's great. You'll be awesome."

Will nodded. "I mean, I'm pretty good, but I'm out of practice, too."

"You've been training, though. With Max at the gym. That should help."

"It's a long shot," Will said. Some of the reality of his decision sunk in then. "I'm going to try it. See what they say and then go from there. They have camps and stuff, too, that you can train for. I could try a college team, too."

"I think you'll make it through their tryouts. Before you know it, you'll be a pro star."

Will shook his head. "I doubt that, but it's a start. Now, come on, let's figure out how we're both fitting on this air mattress."

..ıll twenty-seven

PITTSBURGH WAS NOTHING LIKE NEW York City. Lennox didn't like it half as much as Boston. The weather was kinder than the blizzards he'd experienced all winter, but Pittsburgh was only a city, a city that carried none of his heart or his dreams, a picture with too many filters and nothing raw. However, Will seemed at peace on these streets and comfortable with this environment that was the same landscape as New York, but without any of the same pressure or soul. Every step he took as he showed Lennox around was different from last semester. A spring was in Will's steps; the fear and uncertainty were gone. So was the weight of all Will's expectations. He smiled as he led Lennox into a shop: Sparkle Queen.

"Max showed me this place. He's started performing once a month at this drag queen show for amateurs. I want to dress up for Rocky Horror tomorrow night. Oh, we both could!"

"Uh, let's start with you." Lennox eyed the outfits on display. "Don't know that drag's my thing."

Will scurried around the shop, pulling different outfits out and holding them up. Lennox, having no idea what Rocky Horror was, stared at each.

"Which do think works better? This? Or this?"

Lennox cleared his throat. "Uh, both?"

Will rolled his eyes. "Fine. I'll try it all on. I'm going for sexy, okay?"

"You're already sexy."

But Will wasn't listening. He got an employee to open the fitting room and shut himself inside. Lennox leaned against the wall outside. As Will fumbled in the dressing room, Lennox scanned a shelf of books and movies. Each cover showed a drag queen, with sharp, colorful makeup and sequined gowns. He flipped through a few books while he waited.

"Lennox? Is, uh, anyone else out there?"

"Just me and some book queens."

Lennox set the book down and turned back to the dressing room door. His mouth fell open. Will stood inside the dressing room, shirtless in skimpy panties and fishnet leggings. He tugged at the waistband and stumbled in the bright purple heels he was wearing. Lennox swallowed; his head spun as his stomach began to burn. Will's cock was undeniably prominent in those tiny panties. They were so small he'd had to angle himself along his hip, and even then, the waistband was held away from his stomach by his cock's girth.

"I look stupid, don't I?"

Will bit his lip and twisted his arms. He grabbed his shirt, then gasped. Lennox pressed him into the wall of mirrors, and kicked the door shut with his boot.

"You are so hot."

Lennox groaned as he traced his hands over Will's thighs, over the soft fabric of his fishnets to the silky red panties that didn't contain him.

"Really?"

Will's hands fumbled against the wall as Lennox dropped to his knees. He stared up at Will, doing his best not to pant at the lust coursing through him. Lennox ran a finger over the swell of Will's cock.

"You should wear this all the time."

Will blushed; an adorable smile formed on his lips.

"I mean, they're kind of small."

"They're perfect. Just like my mouth and your dick."

Will snorted, his hand catching Lennox's fingers as they moved to free his cock.

"We can't do that in *here*."

"Sure we can. Only be a minute. You know how long you last when I deep throat."

Lennox didn't wait for another answer, he eased Will's cock out of his panties and stroked him. Will was already half-hard; after a few firm strokes Lennox took him into his mouth. He groaned as his jaw loosened, as the weight of Will's cock pressed down on his tongue. Will whimpered above him and slid down the wall to the bench.

"Fuck, you're way too good at this."

Lennox pulled his mouth off and laughed. "You love my blowjobs."

"Yeah, I do."

He took Will back into his mouth, hollowed his cheeks and sucked. Will shivered and moaned. Lennox bobbed his head, taking Will deeper, feeling the head of his cock hit the back of his throat. He breathed deep through his nose, relaxed his jaw, and sank all the way down. Thick and heavy, Will's cock slid into his throat. As Will jerked under him, Lennox shut his eyes, breathed, and felt the heat of his own cock hard in his jeans.

"Lennox, I'm—shit, I'm going to—"

He swallowed around Will; his eyes watered as he inhaled through his nose. Will was too deep for him to taste his cum, but Lennox felt it in his throat. Lennox gagged for breath, and Will eased his head back until their eyes met. The sight of Will's hazy, green eyes made Lennox's stomach churn. Will kissed him, gentle and sweet, but Lennox's entire body suddenly wanted to revolt from everything intimate, from the swollen feeling of Will's cock still deep in his throat. Will wiped the tears from Lennox's eyes, but more replaced them.

"Are you okay? Did I hurt you or—"

"I'm fine." Lennox wiped the saliva off his chin and stood up. "I'll wait outside for you to change."

He left before Will could say another word. Lennox ran all the way to the street corner before he managed to stop himself. A blowjob had never made him feel so wonderful and then so terrible, not with Will. He wiped his tears on his shirt and waited.

Will, tiny shopping bag in hand, found him five minutes later.

"Lennox?"

"What's next then? You said you wanted to show me a park."

He started for the crosswalk, but Will didn't move. Will waited for him to walk back. Every step was weighed down as if his wretched memories were all pouring into his legs. Lennox stopped in front of Will.

"Come on."

"We need to talk about that. I mean, I loved it until..."

Lennox shook himself and stepped into Will's arms. "Memories. Same as my dreams."

"You've got that appointment this coming week," Will said. He rubbed his hands over Lennox's arms to warm him up. "That'll help. I'm sure it will."

"I hope you're right."

* * *

ROCKY HORROR WAS AN ADVENTURE Lennox had never thought to want. Will didn't wear the red panties from the dressing room, but he did wear a tight pair of shorts that he'd bought, along with his fishnets, and a corset Max let him borrow. Lennox declined to wear any lingerie. The night had still been fun: watching Will stumble along as Max taught him to strut down the road, the movie on a big screen with stage actors joining in. Even the Virgin Ritual he'd been subjected to had been fun. Will had cheered himself hoarse when Lennox won his group's contest to fake the best orgasms.

"Your real ones still sound better," Will had whispered when Lennox, the crowned Virgin King, had retaken his seat.

Their weekend together in Pittsburgh was short. Lennox's dreams still plagued him, but Will's presence helped ease the haunted feeling that had started to follow him. No place granted him freedom from them: not Boston or Pittsburgh, not Richmond or Leon or Charlottesville. His nightmares followed because they weren't a place or a person. They were a tangled-up feeling that never left him.

Lennox went back to Boston on Sunday, heavy with dread. His first therapy appointment was only days away. He tried to distract himself with work, with classes, but he couldn't get his mind away from it. Ava kept pinching him during lit class, pointing her pen at his notes. Every time he looked down, he'd trailed off in the middle of a thought that always ended with the same words: *Therapy Thursday.*

His grandfather had always raved about the absurdity of psychological studies. Cameron had insisted only lunatics needed therapists and that those people hardly needed help unless that meant a strait jacket.

"You're losing it," Ava insisted, after class ended Wednesday. "If you're that scared of it, then don't bother."

"I'm not scared. Even if I was, running away doesn't fix anything."

Ava swayed her head from side to side. "Just stop obsessing over it. I don't have any notes from you to compare with now."

She waved as she jogged away to her next class. Lennox, however, went to the subway and to Lucy's apartment. His classes were over for the day, and they'd decided to meet for the afternoon. Lucy was dressed in a charming sundress and leggings. He'd never seen her looking so put-together and cute.

"Look at you," Lennox said after she'd hugged him. "Is Kelly turning you into a sunflower or what?"

Lucy curtsied, then dragged him into the kitchen. She had a full spread of vegetables on the counter as well as a crockpot. Together, they chopped and sliced and tossed everything in the pot. Lucy added some broth and chicken and left it to stew.

"How was Pittsburgh?"

"Fine. Will's good. He goes back to Virginia tomorrow."

Lucy nodded as they curled up on the couch and flipped on the television. "You ready for your appointment tomorrow?"

Lennox stared at her. "How do you know about that?"

"Will asked me to keep an eye on you. He's worried."

"He's good at that. I'm fine."

Lucy pinched his nose. "You keep saying that, but it doesn't make it true. He's right to worry. You're holding everything together, but you're exhausting yourself. I'm glad you're going tomorrow. You need this."

"Right, cause I'm insane. Got to send all of us crazies to the mental wards."

"You are not. You need to talk to someone about what you've been through. Someone who's not involved in it or as close to you as Will or me or Troy."

When Lennox didn't answer, Lucy sat up. "You *are* going tomorrow, right?"

"I told Will I was."

"But do you want to?"

Lennox looked away. He had no answer for that. Nightmares had been a constant in his life since his childhood, but never as persistent as these. They'd been fleeting wisps of smoke back then. So much of his daily life had plagued him worse than any nightmare could. Getting rid of them now was a wondrous idea. As a kid, it had always been enough to distract himself with his sister's care, with school, with making sure they both ate, then later with using all of his willpower and wit to survive his sham of a life.

"I want the nightmares to stop," Lennox said. "I want to fucking sleep like I did last year with Will, you know? That was the calmest I've ever been. Nothing's working. They just keep coming back, night after night and I can't— Talking about them won't make them stop."

"You don't know that. Nothing else has worked for you. Why not at least try this?"

Lennox shrugged. "How's Kelly? I haven't seen her since Thanksgiving."

"She's getting ready for a... trip? Tour? I forget what they call it, like a retreat to do ocean current stuff. Somewhere up near Canada. Going to have the place all to myself for a few weeks."

"Sounds impressive."

"Yeah, she loves it. They're putting in a request to transfer to somewhere on the west coast in a few years. They want to keep her on. Did I tell you I got an interview at the local social work office? As an intern, but still. It's something while I finish my bachelor's."

"Really? That's awesome!"

"Right? So I've got interview questions in mind. Could you run through these with me?"

* * *

THURSDAY AFTERNOON ARRIVED TOO SOON. His arranging class sped by like an asteroid. One minute he was taking notes, the next he was walking to lunch, and then in a blink standing outside the administration building in the dull spring sunlight. The counseling office on the third floor was brightly lit and smelled of fresh cinnamon rolls. Lennox checked in with the receptionist and only had to wait a few minutes.

"Lennox? Hi, I'm Dr. Jennings."

He shook her hand and followed her into an office. The room was cozy with a plush desk chair and a squishy green couch. Lennox stood in the open space between as Dr. Jennings shut the door.

"Have a seat wherever you're comfortable."

She took the desk chair and Lennox, his legs stiff, sat in the middle of the couch. It sank beneath him as if a hundred asses had sat there before. Lennox tried not to snort at the thought.

"Okay, Lennox, how are you doing?"

They chatted. Lennox did his best to answer all of her simple questions, about his classes, his friends, his roommate. Everything seemed to avoid the obvious reason he was here, but Dr. Jennings didn't know about his nightmares. She didn't know his life before college either.

Dr. Jennings scribbled something on her notepad when Lennox mentioned who his roommate was. "Troy's a wonderful young man. I've been seeing him for a few years. He's talked about you a bit."

"Yeah, he likes to talk."

She wrote another note.

"Do you really have to get to know me with a fucking notebook?"

Dr. Jennings eyes had never left him, but her hand paused. She set the notebook on the table beside her. "No, you're right. So, tell me, Lennox, what's brought you here? You don't seem stressed about school. No friend problems that you've mentioned."

"They thought I should see you."

"They?"

"Troy. And Will."

"Is Will another friend?"

"He's my boyfriend."

"And why did they think coming here was a good idea for you?"

"I— It's nothing. I just did it to get them off my back. That's all."

"They sound like they care a lot about you."

Lennox shrugged and crossed his arms. "Yeah, I mean, I love Will. He loves me. Troy's been a good friend. He's just sick of me waking h—"

He clamped his jaw shut, but Dr. Jennings seemed to have worked out how that sentence ended—that or Troy had expressed his concerns.

"Because of the nightmares?"

"Troy tell you that?"

"And if he did?"

Her words were a challenge. Lennox faltered as he met her gaze. She seemed to be changing tactics, and Lennox could figure out why. Dr. Jennings was trained for this. She could figure him out as she had so many others: the best ways to talk to him, to get him to let his guard down, to convince him to share the real reason he was here instead of at lunch.

"He's got a gaping asshole for a mouth then."

Dr. Jennings chuckled. "Have you told him that?"

"Few times. He just laughs."

She nodded, and they both went quiet. Lennox twisted around in his seat, considered taking his jacket off because it was getting warm, but decided against it. He didn't want her thinking he was getting too comfortable.

"So your nightmares, do you want to tell me about them?"

Lennox stared at the notebook on her table.

"Okay, tell me about Will then. Have long have you been dating?"

"Long enough that I deepthroated him in a dressing room last week."

She only nodded. "So you two have a healthy sexual relationship?"

"Uh, yeah, I guess. We use condoms and it's good. All of that."

"And Will, is he your first sexual partner?"

Lennox swallowed. "First one I've liked."

Seriousness came over Dr. Jennings face then. She looked as though she wanted to grab her notepad, but she didn't. "And what didn't you like about the others?"

"Weren't my taste," Lennox said, trying not sneer. "Small dicks, you know."

Dr. Jennings stayed quiet, watching him.

"This is stupid. Talking isn't going to get rid of nightmares. What happened happened."

"What did happen, Lennox?"

Her voice was gentle, but it set Lennox on edge. Will did that to him. That same kind concern, the wish not to pry, but to know. To somehow think that hearing the truth meant he could share it.

"It doesn't matter. It's over."

"Over enough to give you nightmares? That doesn't sound over to me. Does it to you?"

Lennox snapped as he stood up. "Look, I sucked some dicks to get by, all right? It's not like they raped me or whatever the fuck everyone else is thinking. I agreed to it. I made that choice."

Dr. Jennings' desk timer chimed with the end of their session. Lennox tried to make for the door, but her gaze rooted him to the spot. She was concerned, but not judging, not unkind or horrified.

"Okay, Lennox. How do you define rape? Agreeing to an act, under coercion, doesn't make it consensual."

"I agreed," Lennox repeated. He couldn't bring himself to look at her. "That's enough."

"Did you agree because you wanted to or because you had to?"

"Whatever, okay? Can I go?"

Dr. Jennings turned to her desk and wrote a note. She handed it to Lennox. A date for the following week and the same time was jotted down.

"You want to see me again?"

"I think there's a lot you need to talk about," Dr. Jennings said. "At your own pace, too. But I do think talking through what you've experienced will help. You've been ignoring a lot of what's happened to you, and that will give you nightmares if you don't deal with it. We can talk about whatever you want when you visit here. Classes, friends, family, boyfriend problems. Whatever's on your mind, okay? I'll see you next week."

..ıl twenty-eight

WILL AND AARON ARRIVED AT the tryouts location early. Aaron was bouncing all over the parking lot, full of jitters and energy. As they signed in, Will was sure he was going to vomit on the man at the table. He gave all the information they needed, then slapped his tryout sticker onto his jersey. Aaron did the same beside him.

"I hate waiting."

"That's what you get for being a pitcher."

When the tryouts started, Will and Aaron were separated. Will went with the main group, decked out in his full catcher pads. They ran through basic drills first, then a few more-complicated exercises. They all took the field; players separated to their main positions. Will waited by the backstop with the four other catchers. They rotated, each covering several other infield groups on grounders and fielding. Part of his job as a catcher meant controlling the infield, telling people how to play various people, how to position themselves under different circumstances.

At noon, everyone took a break. Will found Aaron at the car. They dug their sandwiches out of the cooler they'd packed and sat on the truck.

"I'm third up after lunch," Aaron said. He was trembling. "God, I hate waiting. All they had us do was some warm-ups while you guys did fielding work."

Will nodded. "I've got the first round behind the plate. I'm not sure how many pitchers that's going to cover. How many of you guys are there?"

"Too many." Aaron choked on a chunk of chicken in his sandwich. "Ugh, this was a bad idea. I don't have the guts to get through all of this."

"You're going to be fine. We both will. So what if we don't make it? You've got next year and all of college still. Baseball's… Let's just focus on today and then forget it for a while."

After they ate, all the men trying out returned to the field. Will eyed the lines of players: strong, broad shoulders, some looked as if they could break him in half. Aaron and he weren't the smallest or the youngest, but compared to the other catchers, Will felt like a baby in a onesie.

He took his place when called, working the first few pitchers through the rotations they told him they were throwing. Nothing got by him, but several of the batters got some decent hits off the second pitcher. Aaron was up next, and Will was relieved when he wasn't called away.

Will met him halfway between home plate and the pitcher's mound.

"Just like we've always done, okay? Back home at Eastern."

Aaron nodded. "Right, right. I— Fuck, I'm going to fuck this up."

Will shook his head. "No way. This moment is all yours."

Aaron laughed. Will dropped the ball in his glove and smacked his butt.

"Come on, Sandyman. Let's do this."

He returned to the catcher's box, and let Aaron work through his warm-ups and then his real pitches. Behind him, he heard the clicks of the radar guns the officials were using. He let Aaron toss two more before waving a batter up. That seemed to be the real test: How well could Aaron fool them after they'd watched him throw?

The man dug into the batter's box and took a swing at the first curve ball Will called for. Of the ten pitches he saw, he only connected on three, and two of those went foul. The second batter missed them all.

A coach called Will and Aaron off. They dropped onto the benches behind the chain-link fence for some water. Several other players joined them.

"A lefty catcher?" A tall, thin man sat down in front of them. "I'm surprised you don't pitch."

Will shrugged. "My Little League coaches tried to make me, but I hated it. Kept hitting batters. I'm Will. This is Aaron."

"Evan."

"Blackwell, you're up!"

"That's me." Evan left for the field. Will and Aaron watched him bat, then take shortstop. He was a great fielder, better than any of the people Will had seen on his old teams.

"He plays for Tech," Aaron told him. "Nice guy. Hits a lot of homeruns."

Will gazed around at the group. Maybe fifty people had showed up to try out. Most were a little older than him; others were in their thirties. A few looked high-school-aged. He couldn't see how he stood a chance with the talent he saw. Everyone was strong, balanced, had great accuracy and aim.

"Will Osborne, up to bat!"

Aaron shoved him toward the field.

Will felt clumsy with all of their eyes on him. He tried not to look at the officials recording pitch speeds behind the dugout. The coaches' eyes were harder to avoid. The man behind home plate gave him an appraising look as he checked Will's name off.

"You're the lefty catcher, right?"

"Yes, sir."

The coach wrote something, then asked how he batted.

"Left, but I'm okay at switch, too."

"Ten on each side then." He hollered instructions to the catcher and pitcher as Will dug in righty first. As a kid he'd always been told to bat on the right side, despite his own comfort and his left-handedness. He took a deep breath and focused. The first two pitches were a blur. Even with a little practice since he'd returned to Virginia, his batter's eye was off. He popped two foul balls, hit a third grounder, and then popped up on the final pitch.

"Okay, Osborne, switch."

Will crossed the plate and dug his cleats into the fresh dirt. This side was always cleaner. Fewer feet ripped up the dirt. He got to dig his feet into his own comfortable space instead of trying to find that in someone else's.

Again, he let the first two pitches go by. His eye was sharper on this side, but he needed to see a pitch, needed to get the movement and the speed to adjust himself. On the third, he swung, the bat vibrating from the hard contact. The ball sailed down the third base foul line, landing in the grass just fair. Will let out a breath. He still had it.

Will did better on the left: another double down the line, two singles into the outfield, and a few grounders. He made contact with every swing, ending with a third double along the first base line. He ran on that one as instructed, easily getting into second with a stand-up double.

Everyone switched on the field, and Will returned to home plate to collect his bat. The coach there was still writing on his clipboard, but he stopped Will on his way off the field.

"Very level swing you've got, Osborne."

"Oh, thanks. I'm not as good on the right side."

"Matters more that you're good on your dominant side," the coach told him. He squinted at Will. "You a local high schooler?"

Will's hopes sunk. They thought he was still a kid, a young, high school kid without the talent and dedication.

"No, I graduated last year."

"Playing for a local college now?"

Will shook his head as the rest of the coaches joined them. He waved Will off and he returned to Aaron's spot on the benches. His insides shriveled. No matter what Aaron and Lennox and his parents said, he wasn't good enough. He'd given it his all, but it wasn't enough.

Aaron sat beside him, looking as dejected as he felt. They stayed for the final thoughts of the coaches and to listen to what they could expect. Some of them would receive letters if they weren't chosen, others would get calls in the coming weeks from interested minor league teams. A few may even get calls from major league clubs.

Aaron led the way back to the car. They didn't talk for the drive back to Aaron's campus. They grunted goodbyes. Will pulled over at a Burger King just off the highway. He'd done it. He'd tried. Yet they'd assumed, based on what they'd seen, that he was only a high schooler. He smacked his steering wheel and then rest his forehead on it.

Ever since that conversation with his dad and Karen, he'd opened himself back up to wanting baseball, to dreaming of the fresh cut grass smell, the stains on his pants, the heavy feel of a wooden bat in his hands. Every moment had been leading him toward this as a kid, but he'd given up. Instead of dreaming big, he'd given up on himself.

Will went back home and spent an evening in his parents' empty and quiet house. Oyster nuzzled into him, but he longed for Lennox's strong embrace. Lennox was in Boston, playing at a concert on campus with the promise to call when he was finished.

He sat up on his bed, knocking Oyster off him.

"Aaarrooo!"

"Sorry, boy." He scratched Oyster's side. "I'm going to be okay. So what if I wasn't good enough? I'll try again. Or see what Sarah Lawrence says. I'm not going to fall apart again, okay?"

Oyster licked his hand and panted at him.

Will chuckled. "You're the worst conversationalist ever."

WILL SPOKE TO LENNOX THE next morning. His concert had gone over well, and Troy had already lined up another coffee shop gig for them at the end of the month. All in all, Lennox was booked solid.

"I don't know how you do all of that," Will told him. "It'd drive me nuts."

"It's not so bad. I'm sure finals week will be a disaster, but we aren't doing any gigs then. How was your tryout?"

Will grimaced. "I don't know. I think I did okay, but they didn't seem too impressed."

"Well, I think you did great, just for giving it a shot," Lennox said. A few piano chords chimed on his end. "When do you find out?"

"Probably May. They said a few weeks for most of the outcomes." Will settled down at his desk chair in his room. "I just started to let myself really want it again, you know? And now... I don't know. I hope Aaron gets something positive out of it. He's never given up like I did."

"He never had to wonder if being gay would hold him back either."

"Yeah, I guess." Will clicked through the open tabs on his laptop, some for schools he'd begun to look into, others for road trip ideas for the summer. "What do you think about taking a road trip this summer? Just the two of us?"

"Sounds like fun. Do I get to blow you while you drive?"

"We'll see. I'm thinking Louisiana. Like New Orleans. Maybe head out to the Grand Canyon or something, too."

"I'm game. Well, once Lucy's settled with Nana and Pop. She's supposed to move in with them at the end of June."

"Right, I forgot. How's your grandfather doing?"

"Honestly? I'm not sure. He won't say anything and Lucy's not very good at explaining it. Guess I'll see after my finals."

"Last week of April, right?"

"I'm done on May second. Figure I'll take the train to Richmond, see them first, then come see you. We can check out some of the schools in Virginia you've started looking at too. Otto wants to look at a few of them."

"I thought he never wanted to go to school again after high school."

Piano keys rung over the phone line. "He changed his mind. He wants to do, like, social work or education. Something so he can help kids up in Minnesota. Hey, when we road trip, could we hit up Wyoming and visit Troy?"

"Oh, we could go to Yellowstone! That'd be so much fun. I'll look and see what we could do."

"Cool."

Lennox hummed along to the piano notes he was playing, and Will smiled.

"You seem happier," Will said. "How's your therapy been going? You told me the first one was stupid, but..."

"Still think it is. All of it. She's nice though, Dr. Jennings. She keeps wanting to talk about sexual assault and how to define consent and rape and all of that, but mostly we talk about what's going on with me now."

"Has it helped your nightmares?"

"A little. I'm sleeping better most nights. I don't know. It's like she wants me to admit to all of these things that happened in juvie. But they didn't. I mean, I was there, I should know."

"And what did happen?" Will held his breath before plowing on. "Besides the tongue piercing, you've never said."

If Will hadn't hear Lennox breathing, he would have thought he'd hung up. For several minutes, Lennox didn't speak, but when he did his voice was croaky.

"I don't know. I just always... it wasn't a big deal. I never tried to make it into one. I was just a stupid-ass kid, didn't know what I was doing. I gave a lot of blowjobs. If I sucked them off, they protected me with their gang. The other guys didn't try to beat the shit out of me. They didn't either. Most of the kids in there were in one gang or another. I, I had to do something to not be a target."

"Lennox, that's terrible."

"It was just life. That's all."

"Did... did you offer that? Or did they... did they make you?"

Lennox went quiet again. He played a few piano chords over the line. "They gave me a choice. They always gave me a choice. Do whatever it was they wanted or..."

"Or what?"

"Have the shit beat out of me. Or something worse." Lennox's end of the phone became garbled. "Can we talk about something else?"

Will agreed, more because of the distress in Lennox's voice than anything else. Dr. Jennings would ease all of that out of him. He hoped she would. They had the next three years to talk and get Lennox to explain everything he'd endured, the sacrifices he'd made first for his sister and then to protect himself, to admit to what was already clear to Will.

Lennox had only ever made the choice to survive.

..ıl twenty-nine

THE END OF LENNOX'S SECOND semester approached in a whirlwind of concerts, exams, and performances. Every day he seemed to be practicing for something or with someone new. His ensemble class was to record a performance as their final. One that, if approved, would be on Berklee's website in the weeks or months to come so that incoming students could see what the school was all about. Dr. Austin kept him just as busy with several pieces each week on top of his main one for the solo pianist concert at the end of April.

However, Dr. Austin surprised him with more news the week before the annual concert: a request from the staff and academics board that was asked of every student who'd received his scholarship.

"A video?"

"Every year, they try to get as many scholarship recipients together as possible and have each of you do a video about your first year. Usually short. Playing your instrument, talking a bit about your experiences. The opportunities you're getting."

Lennox agreed, albeit reluctantly. He didn't know how much he had to offer for that, but if it was part of the scholarship keeping him here, then he would try. Dr. Austin then had him play his final piece for the semester. He critiqued a few areas before shutting the piano.

"All right, I'm ending playing early today. I'll see you for your final next week. It'll be that same piece, as well as some sight reading, and my age-old question: Who are you?"

"Oh," Lennox said, his heart sinking. "Right. I should have an answer by then."

If Dr. Austin recognized his lie, he didn't call Lennox on it. Lennox left for a quick dinner and then walked to the counseling office for his therapy appointment. He'd moved his slot to a later time a few weeks ago. Dr. Jennings' sessions always left him drained, and going to his piano instruction afterward had been a terrible experience.

Dr. Jennings welcomed him into her office as she always did, a wide smile and a cheerful deposition. He'd asked her once, during their third session, how she managed to act so happy all the time. She'd written a long note and then asked him a lot of questions about his own emotional experiences.

Today, she seemed as chipper as usual. Lennox sat on the couch and waited.

"Anything new or interesting to report?"

Lennox shrugged. "Uh, just performances coming up. Will's still waiting to hear about his baseball tryout. He thinks he didn't get in."

"What do you think?"

"I think he did. He's good. Like, really good, and I know next to nothing about baseball. I can't even remember what the team here is."

Dr. Jennings chuckled. "Well, I hope he hears soon. He seems to really love baseball."

"He does and..." Lennox hesitated. His mind ran back through their conversations since Will's tryout. They always seemed to come back to him, back to juvie and the progress of his persistent nightmares, to his therapy sessions where he did his best to avoid discussing them. "I miss him. I haven't seen him since he left Pittsburgh. He keeps asking me about my nightmares."

"Are you still having them?"

Lennox nodded. His entire body always seemed to stiffen at the mention of them. "Not as bad as they were, but they're still there. He wants to know what happened in juvie."

"It's natural that he'd want to know. Will cares about you. He wants to help you deal with those memories and that old pain."

"It doesn't matter."

"I think you know that isn't true," Dr. Jennings said. "You're still having nightmares, so it matters to you." She scribbled a few notes before setting her pen down. "Do you remember what I asked you at the end of our first session?"

Lennox flinched. He could still hear her words perfectly, but he resisted. "Something about consent and, like, assault or something."

"I asked how you defined rape and consent. Then I asked if you'd agreed to the experiences you've had by choice or force. I'm going to ask you that again now, okay?"

His first instinct was to bolt from the room. But Lennox stayed in his seat on the couch and kept his eyes on his lap. Will's worried face kept flickering through his mind along with the euphoria of their encounter in that dressing room and the way he'd crumbled from it.

"Rape is, like, sex. Like, penetrative, but against someone's will." Lennox crossed his arms and added, before he could stop himself, "I just did blowjobs."

"Okay, and aren't blowjobs, by their nature, a form of penetration?"

"I—well, I guess."

"Okay, how about consent?"

"Something you agree to do it."

Dr. Jennings gave a brief nod and tucked her pen behind her ear. "Yes and no. Let's do a bit of situational work. Say you and Will are together in a few weeks. You're excited to see each other and you both are very excited to have sex. You do. Is that consent?"

Lennox snorted. "Duh."

Dr. Jennings nodded again. "Second situation. The next morning, Will wakes up and you make out. No asking if it's okay or if you agree, you both are happy to do so without saying it. Is that consent?"

"I—well, yeah. Sort of? I, I'm not sure."

"Third situation. You tell Will you want him, so you two begin to move into something more sexual, but then you hesitate. You're uncomfortable even though you say yes to continuing. Is that consent?"

"Well, no. Maybe? I mean, we'd stop. You know, talk and see what's wrong and then maybe we'd have sex after that."

"Will doesn't want to stop though. He gives you an ultimatum. Either you two have sex or he'll break up with you. You agree to have sex. Is that consent?"

Dr. Jennings waited for him. Lennox turned each scenario over in his mind. His brain was buzzing with the beginning of a throbbing headache. Will would never do that to him, he was certain, but he'd known that place before.

"Do you understand what I'm trying to explain?"

"I think so." Lennox frowned. "That consent can be complicated and it can change while you're doing something? That it's important to make sure you're both on the same page when you have sex."

"Yes, that's very true. Can you say that's true about your experiences while you were in juvie?"

Lennox hesitated. The words to agree and shove that time aside stuck to the back of his throat. His eyes burned as he stared at his knees.

"No. I, I mean, I agreed, but... not like with Will."

Dr. Jennings squeezed his knee. "What happened to you was not your fault. You didn't choose it any more than you could have chosen your mother's death. I'm not going to say you were raped or assaulted or anything else, Lennox. That's your decision. How you define those experiences are up to you, but know that any consent you gave was forced. That's not true consent. It's okay to grapple with what happened. If you can't admit that to me yet, that's okay too. But I want you to admit it to yourself right now. Both what happened and the *fact* that you didn't choose it."

A chasm cracked open inside of him. Himself with Will and this cherished world at Berklee on one side, his terrified fifteen-year-old self with the prick of a pocket knife against his neck on the other. He clutched his elbows tight, and his knees blurred because of his tears. Both pieces of him tumbled into that abyss, right into his heart, solidifying in one messy mass.

"I didn't want it," Lennox said. "I just did what I had to so I survived."

* * *

LENNOX SLEPT BETTER THAT WEEK, even though his nightmares persisted. He still fell back into that juvenile detention cell, still felt himself being dragged along with the too-high blindfold. But then the blindfold was swept off. There he was, his older self, staring at him, a hand extended to help him up.

He spent his last two weeks studying with Ava, joking with Troy at all hours of the night while they worked, and then practicing with Sadia for their ensemble performance. Lennox made it through his finals in one piece, arriving at his last final for his private instruction better rested than he'd been since December. Dr. Austin greeted him at the door and shut them into the room. The piano was open and waiting.

"Okay, wow me with your brilliance."

Lennox swept his way through each piece, every task Dr. Austin set in front of him. His chest soared with the crescendos and fluttered at the mezzo pianos. Every measure left him with an extra kick of exuberance. He smiled when he finished, and Dr. Austin sat quietly jotting notes.

"Fantastic as always. Okay, just the final part. My still unanswered question: Who are you?"

"I'm a survivor," Lennox said. "I'm a musician, too. Those are what I've always done. I'm fucked up too. I'm a lot of crazy things and a lot of different things to other people, but I'm always going to be me. No matter what happens. I'm always going to be Lennox."

Dr. Austin smiled. "I'm glad to hear it. And who do you want to be?"

"I don't know yet. I want to always be a musician. Maybe you can help me figure out how to do that?"

"I think I can manage that. We'll make a lesson plan of it for next semester."

"Bring it on."

* * *

LENNOX RETURNED TO RICHMOND AT the start of May. Lucy was dimmer when he hugged her. Cameron had driven them to the train to meet him, but he insisted on Lennox driving back. The brick colonial was the same was ever: clean, well-maintained, the picture of a perfect home that hid all the wrongness inside. Cameron retreated to his room. Lennox watched him climb the stairs, one painful step at a time.

"Come on," Lucy said. She grabbed his hand and pulled him into the living room. "Do you get to stay the whole summer?"

"Yeah, I'll be around. How's Grandfather been doing?"

Lucy didn't meet his eyes. "He says he's fine, but he's lying. Is he really going to die?"

Lennox sat with her on the couch. She looked older. She wasn't taller, but her face was a little thinner, more mature. Her voice, too, had deepened, no longer the squeaky lilt of a child, but the voice of someone growing into a young adult.

"Yeah, he is. Some day we will too. That's how life works. You live for a while and then you're gone."

Lucy wiped her eyes and traced her fingers over her knees, crisscrossing from one to the other. Her legs were smooth, a stark difference from the last time he'd seen her.

"Did you shave your legs?"

She laughed. "I'm twelve now. All the other girls are doing it too. Do you think I need a training bra yet?" She grabbed the back of her shirt and pulled it flat over her chest. "See? I've got little ones now."

Lennox chuckled. "God, why are you growing up already? Yeah, we'll take you to buy some this weekend."

Lucy hugged him and raced off to the backyard. For a while, Lennox watched her dribbling her soccer ball. The sun had started to sink when Cameron appeared; the windows reflected like gems. A tank of oxygen with him, he sat in a chair beside Lennox.

"When did you get that?"

"Last month," Cameron said. His voice was weak. "I know we've all agreed Lucy's going to your mother's parents once her school year's done, but..."

Cameron coughed then, a deep rattling sound that made Lennox flinch. He understood then. The struggle, the lethargy, the rapidness of everything that had happened since he'd left for Boston in January.

"I'll stay here with her. Make sure she gets to school and her practices," Lennox said. "Don't worry about her. Do what you have to do."

Cameron shuddered with his next cough. For several minutes, he couldn't stop. Lennox squeezed his shoulder. The guilt was still there, but a part of him breathed better knowing this was almost over.

"You're a good kid, Lennox. Always have been. If I could go back—"

"Don't. What happened is done, okay? Just focus on what you've got left. Be there for Lucy. You can't change what happened with us, and I don't want you to either. Give Lucy your best. I don't need it."

Lennox stood up. "I'm going to go see Will tonight, okay? Before you go to the hospital."

"Go. Enjoy yourself. We'll get everything sorted out this weekend."

WILL WAS RACING AROUND THE backyard when Lennox arrived. He followed the sounds of Oyster's howls and barks to the fence line and spotted the pair of them chasing each other around. Lennox hopped the fence and took a seat on the porch, waiting. It took a while for Will to notice him in the dark.

"Lennox?"

"You finally going to say hi then?"

Will jogged to him, leaving Oyster to shake his stick around and fling it into the pool. He leapt in after it with a huge splash. Karen appeared at the window.

"Will, what did I tell you about letting him in the pool tonight? He takes forever to dry."

"Sorry!"

Lennox greeted Will with a kiss and a long hug. They sat on the porch together, basking in the warm breeze while Oyster paddled around the pool. Will leaned back on his hands and tilted his head skyward.

"I can't go back to the city," Will said. "I miss this view too much. Do you think you'll stay in Boston after school?"

"No idea. I like it there, but I miss the stars too."

"And me?"

Lennox laughed as Will kissed his cheek. "Yeah, and you, too. Have you heard anything yet?"

Will wilted and breathed deep. "No. Aaron hasn't either. I don't think we're going to get contracts. Maybe next year."

"You're going to try again?"

"Definitely. I love to play. They've got some adult leagues in Charlottesville. I've started playing on the weekends. It's not as competitive as I'm used to, but it's nice to be on the field again."

"I'm glad you are."

"Will? Will, you've got a phone call!"

Ben pushed the sliding glass door open. He waved the house phone at him. Will and Lennox exchanged a confused glance before Will took the phone from him.

"Hello? Yes, this is Will."

Lennox went to corral Oyster out of the pool and returned several minutes later. Will seemed to be frozen, even when Oyster leapt at him, soaking his shirt and shorts.

"Who was it? Will?"

"Um, it was— Oyster, down!"

Oyster whined at them, retreated through the still-open sliding glass door, and dripped water all over the floor. Lennox took the house phone from Will's hand. Will wrapped his arms around his chest and squatted. He rested his head on his knees. Lennox knelt next to him.

"Will, what's wrong?"

"Nothing. No, it wasn't bad. I just—holy shit."

"What?"

"That was one of the clubs. They offered me a spot on their AA roster."

"Holy shit. Will, that's great."

Will fell back on his butt with a huge grin on his face. Then he met Lennox's eyes and some of the light in his gaze dimmed.

"It was one of the Diamondbacks' minor league teams."

"I have no idea who or what or where that is."

Will swallowed. "Arizona."

Lennox nodded, his throat tight. "It's great either way. I can't wait to go see you play."

"But, it's so far from Boston, from here."

Lennox took Will by the face and kissed him deep until he relaxed. When he pulled away, Will was crying despite his smile.

"Will, it's okay."

"I know, but we're going to be so far away."

"Yeah, for a few months. But the rest of the year, during the summer I'm free. I can come out to visit. When you've got your off-season you can come visit me at school."

Will nodded. "We'll make it work."

"We always do."

THE END

..ıll about the author

ZANE RILEY IS A TRANSGENDER writer who wrote his first work of fan fiction in the fourth grade. He is a recent transplant to Vancouver, Washington where he spends his time watching long-distance baseball games, hiking, and exploring the musical depths of the internet. His novels *Go Your Own Way* and *With or Without You* were published by Interlude Press in 2015 and 2016.

One **story**
can change **everything.**

@interlude**press**

Twitter | Facebook | Instagram | Pinterest

*For a reader's guide to **When It's Time** and book club prompts,*
please visit interludepress.com.

interlude ✦✦ press™

you may also like...

Go Your Own Way by Zane Riley
Go Your Own Way Book One

Will Osborne plans to a quiet senior year, hoping that college would help him close the door on years of harassment. But transfer student Lennox McAvoy changes all of that—he's crude, flirtatious, and the most insufferable, beautiful person Will's ever met. From his ankle monitor to his dull smile, Lennox seems irredeemable. But Will soon discovers that there is more to Lennox than meets the eye.

ISBN (print) 978-1-941530-34-4 | ISBN (eBook) 978-1-941530-38-2

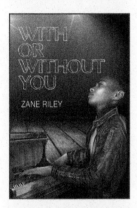

With or Without You by Zane Riley
Go Your Own Way Book Two

In the sequel to Go Your Own Way, Lennox and Will are challenged by their new relationship and by Will's disapproving father. When a violent incident forces Lennox to give up his independence, he must come to terms with his past just as Will is grappling with his future. As Will's college plans become reality, will Lennox have the courage to go after the opportunities he doesn't think he deserves?

ISBN (print) 978-1-941530-76-4 | ISBN (eBook) 978-1-941530-77-1

What It Takes by Jude Sierra

Milo met Andrew moments after moving to Cape Cod—launching a lifelong friendship of deep bonds, secret forts and plans for the future. When Milo goes home for his father's funeral, he and Andrew finally act on their attraction—but doubtful of his worth, Milo severs ties. They meet again years later, and their long-held feelings will not be denied. Will they have what it takes to find lasting love?

ISBN (print) 978-1-941530-59-7 | ISBN (eBook) 978-1-941530-60-3